"Ha

J.T.'s voice, low and subdued behind her, was oddly reassuring considering he was the reason for her misfortune. "I doubt there's any electricity, but I'll try the light—wait—no, nothing. There should be a flashlight up on the shelf, just give me a—"

The door slammed closed, plunging them into darkness.

Lyddie yelped. J.T. cursed.

"Don't move," he said.

"I won't."

"Let me get the door open again." He moved slowly behind her. Something warm—a hand, probably—grazed the small of her back. And all of a sudden, it wasn't nervousness that was making Lyddie's heart do double-time in her chest.

For the first time in four years, she was alone in the dark with a man. And now all she could think about was Zoë's voice, laughing on the phone, telling her to jump him.

Oh. Dear. God.

Four years of zero interest in anything sexual ended in the space of a breath. Every erogenous zone roared back to sudden, urgent, demanding life.

Dear Reader,

This is the book that almost didn't happen.

I first conceived and wrote this story about a decade ago. The thought of creating a romance between a hero's widow and the town's legendary bad boy was one that I couldn't ignore. I wrote a synopsis and three chapters and sent them to an editor who had requested them at a conference. While waiting for a reply, I entered the book in some contests and finished the first draft. By the time that draft was finished the book had been rejected by the editor, had bombed in contests and had landed on my top ten list of experiences I never wanted to revisit.

Years went by. I sold a book to the Harlequin Superromance line. In talking about future books with my awesome editor, Piya, I remembered this story. I pulled it out, girded my loins and started to read. Imagine my surprise when I discovered that the story wasn't nearly as bad as I remembered. In fact, parts of it really gripped me. By the time I got to the end of that rough draft, I could see it for what it was—a story with a lot of flaws but a whole lot of potential. All it needed was some insight from a fabulous editor and a second chance.

I dove back into it. This time, guided by Piya, it was a joy to revisit the story. J.T. and Lyddie forgave me for the years I neglected them and welcomed me back into their world. I am delighted to share their story with you, and hope you will visit me at www.krisfletcher.com to learn more about them and future stories from Comeback Cove.

Yours,

Kris Fletcher

KRIS
FLETCHER

—

Now You See Me

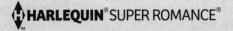

Recycling programs
for this product may
not exist in your area.

ISBN-13: 978-0-373-60810-2

NOW YOU SEE ME

For questions and comments about the quality of this book,
please contact us at CustomerService@Harlequin.com.

Printed in U.S.A.

TM www.Harlequin.com

ABOUT THE AUTHOR

Kris Fletcher has never owned a coffee shop or burned down an historic attraction, but there are times—such as that moment halfway through climbing the Eiffel Tower—when she gives serious consideration to one of them. She'll leave it to you to decide which. A four-time Golden Heart finalist, Kris grew up in southern Ontario, went to school in Nova Scotia, married a man from Maine and now lives in central New York. She shares her very messy home with her husband, an ever-changing number of their kids and the occasional grand-hamster. Her greatest hope is that dust bunnies never develop intelligence.

Books by Kris Fletcher

HARLEQUIN SUPERROMANCE

1845—A BETTER FATHER

Other titles by this author available in ebook format.

Dedicated to all those who call me Mom:
the Fraulein, the Geek, the Maestro, the Mensch,
Her Royal Highness and the Tsarina.
You have introduced me to new worlds,
challenged my sanity and filled my heart.
Good trade.

Acknowledgments

Many thanks are due to the usual suspects, who are all unusual in the very best ways.

The Purples—Gayle Callen, Christine Wenger, Molly Compton Herwood and Carol Pontello Lombardo—who continue to be my lifeline to sanity in a world filled with kids, deadlines and those school activities that always seem to expand to three times as much time as I projected.

Renee Kloecker, World's Best Hostess, who so generously allows the Purples to take over her country home during our retreats. And Elisa Koniezcko, who so generously answers our many many medical questions (and keeps us howling with laughter) when she joins us on retreat.

The folks at Priceline for cheap hotels—so essential during deadlines. And my husband, Larry, for making sure there is still a parent in the house when I announce I must disappear for a weekend or twelve.

Jessica Faust, Uber-Agent, for making me believe I could do this.

Piya Campana, Editor Extraordinaire, for the fresh eyes, the amazing insights and the smilies. And especially for catching my mistakes before they get sent to the world.

And, as always, to the writers of *Galaxy Quest,* who gave me the ultimate words to write by: Never give up. Never surrender!

CHAPTER ONE

THERE WAS NOTHING LIKE walking into the town he'd almost killed twenty-five years earlier to make a man feel there was a bull's-eye painted on his back.

For the fifth time in as many minutes, J. T. Delaney forced himself to stop checking over his shoulder. He wasn't in danger—at least, not of the physical kind. Comeback Cove, Ontario, was a small tourist town on the St. Lawrence Seaway. *Quiet* was the word most often used to describe it, especially at dinnertime on an early June weeknight. He'd passed all of three people since he set off down Main Street toward the river.

But three people was enough. Especially when they were all old-timers who reached protectively toward their wallets the moment they recognized him. That hurt. He might have been the terror of the town when he was a teen, but he'd never picked pockets.

Taking the heat for things he'd done, he could handle. Taking the heat for things he hadn't done was not gonna happen.

His steps slowed as he walked past the hardware store. Other than a new coat of paint and fresh awnings, it looked the same as it had back when he used to buy supplies for his adolescent pranks. Same story two doors down, in the drugstore where he'd shop-lifted his first pack of condoms. Now, with the wisdom of forty-two years behind him, he knew what a damned fool chance that had been. But he still could empathize with the testosterone-driven youth who would rather risk being hauled in front of the police than pay for rubbers under the eagle eye of a pharmacist who'd known him since birth.

Ah, memories.

Seeing the stores and walking the still-familiar route to the river made him keenly aware of the fact only a fool would forget: small towns don't change. Not the buildings, not the faces, not the sentiments. The only thing different, it seemed, was him.

For as he'd learned the hard way over the years, the last thing most people wanted was change. Especially when it came to changing their minds.

At last he reached the corner of Main Street and River Road and the sight that had drawn him downtown on his first night back: the St. Lawrence River. It lay straight ahead, peaceful on this cool evening, calling him from the other side of the parking lot that connected Patty's Pizza Express and River Joe's coffee shop.

Gravel crunched beneath his feet as he hurried across the lot. Technically, this land—and the pizza place and coffee shop, and a few other buildings around town—was now his, bequeathed to him by the father who had died last year. But he hadn't come to play landlord. Not yet. Tomorrow he would begin the task that had brought him back to town—selling off the buildings and helping his mother move to Tucson with him.

Tonight, though, was his. He increased his pace as he rounded the corner of River Joe's. Tonight, it was him and the river—

And a woman. There was a woman sitting in his spot.

J.T. stopped so fast that he had to grab the weathered cedar shakes of the coffee shop to steady himself. Talk about your reality checks. The alcove formed by the corner of the shop and fronted by the river was private, true, but come on. Had he really thought no one else would claim it in twenty-five years?

Okay. So every so often, some things *did* change.

He started to backtrack, but the woman raised her hand as if to wave. Since it was the first friendly overture he'd received all day, he stepped forward, stopping again when he realized she hadn't been gesturing to him after all. She was talking on her phone and had no idea he was even there.

He should leave before she noticed him. Even in Comeback Cove, a lone woman would be startled by the sight of a strange man hovering nearby. But she seemed intent on her conversation, so he allowed himself a moment to place her.

She wasn't a tourist. Not only was it too early in the season for weekday visitors, but she also didn't have the air of someone who'd come to see the sights. No, this woman, with her reddish-blond hair pulled back and sneakers lying beside her bare feet, seemed to belong here.

That intrigued him. She appeared to be about his age, and the town was small enough that he used to know everyone within three grade levels. He studied her more closely, mentally ticking off vivid blue eye shadow, a shaggy hairstyle and higher breasts—all the features that had characterized the girls when he was in high school. Still no clue.

It was possible that she had moved here since he left. But who in their right mind would do that?

She said something and burst into laughter. Even if he'd wanted to leave, that sound alone would have stopped him. Her laugh was like the river—light at first, rippling, then dropping into something full and liquid, with just a hint of mystery.

Whoever was on the receiving end of that laugh was one lucky bastard.

Her "Bye, hon" skipped toward him like a stone across the water. She shoved the phone into a pocket of those pants women loved but men hated—the kind that ended halfway between knee and ankle, revealing enough skin to entice while hiding all the good parts beneath loose beige cotton.

She stood and stretched her arms over her head, fabric pulling tight, and he saw that the good parts were very good indeed.

She slipped into her shoes and scooted around the far side of the building. Intrigued, he waited a couple of seconds before following.

He wasn't trying to catch her. She was undoubtedly married, and even if she wasn't, he was only here for the summer. Less, if he could get everything done in time. But he was curious, and this was a lot more fun than waiting for someone to shove that knife in his back.

She followed the walkway that hugged the side of the coffee shop and turned onto River Road, waving to someone he couldn't see yet. He held back, watching. She took a slow step down the main sidewalk, calling a welcome. In a moment she was joined by a group of elderly women he recognized as friends of his mother. In his day they had ruled the town. They greeted her warmly, drawing her into light embraces that undoubtedly reeked of too much perfume.

This was getting stranger by the minute. Comeback Cove was one of those towns where you were considered an outsider until your family had been around for at least two generations. Yet this woman had been accepted.

Who the hell was she?

J.T. waited until the group had moved on, his quarry firmly surrounded by print dresses and blue hair. For a moment he considered heading back to his now-empty bench by the river. He was a desert dweller now, but he could never go near water without remembering the river.

He'd go back in a minute. After he tailed his mystery woman.

He turned in the direction she'd gone. There she was—straight ahead on the other side of the road, mounting the steps of Town Hall while the older women gazed up at her and waved farewell. It was like watching the queen ascending the stairs.

He took two steps before old instincts kicked in. Town Hall also housed the police station. Given the reception he'd gotten, they probably still had his face on a homemade Wanted poster in the lobby.

Comeback Cove wasn't that big. He would find out who she was soon enough. In the meantime, there was a river calling. When he inhaled he could smell it, fresh and still familiar. Maybe he would even kick off his sandals and stick his feet in the water.

But when he began to retrace his steps, he knew he was screwed. For there on the sidewalk was one of the many reasons he had stayed away all these years.

He swore under his breath, then gave in to the inevitable.

"Hello, Jillian."

She came to an abrupt halt, glanced at Town Hall and looked back at him. J.T. had detected more warmth from planets at the farthest reaches of the solar system.

"So it's true," she said. "You're back."

It wasn't an open-armed welcome, but at least she spoke to him.

"How are you?" J.T. nodded toward her blue power suit, the briefcase, the heels. "You're looking very official for a summer night."

"I am official," she snapped. "I'm the mayor."

"That's right." He remembered his mother mentioning it. "Congratulations—I think."

She glared. "What does that mean?"

He shrugged. "I'm just surprised to see you here. Weren't you the one who always bragged about having more ambition than the rest of the town put together?"

Jillian scanned the sidewalk, no doubt ensuring he hadn't insulted any potential voters, then ran a critical eye over his travel-rumpled Hawaiian shirt and baggy shorts. "Enough small talk. Why are you here, J.T.?"

"My parole officer finally let me leave the country."

"Don't be cute. How long are you staying?"

He considered telling her that it was none of her business, but reminded himself that some things weren't worth the fight.

"Just for the summer."

"You're sure you're not here to stay?"

"What, move back? Hell, no!"

She narrowed the big blue eyes that she used to bat so effectively back in high school. "You don't have to be that emphatic. This can be a pretty good place, you know." She paused, then added with lethal softness, "That is, when you're not here stirring up trouble."

So that was how it was going to be. He hadn't been imagining that bull's-eye on his back. It was as real as the fact that in the eyes of this town, he would never be anything other than the juvenile delinquent who burned down the prime tourist attraction all those years ago.

Okay. They had every right to hate what he'd been. He'd caused a lot of hurt to a lot of folks, and if some of them couldn't forget that, well, neither could he. Half the reason he lived in the desert now was because nothing there—not a tree, not a river, not even a flower in the grass—was the same as the ones found in this lush green village. No reminders. Knowing what he'd done still hurt that much.

But he also knew that there was a hell of a lot more to the story than most folks wanted to hear.

"What trouble? I've been back a couple of hours, done nothing more than walk down the damned street and you're already judging me?"

"Some things never change," Jillian said. "Some

people never change. There's a reason we called you J.T. You were Just Trouble back then, and from the looks of you, I'd say you're still Just Trouble."

Further proof that change was the one force designed to generate the most opposition from the greatest number of people.

"You know, Jillian, it's been a long time. I screwed up. I admit it. But that was a frickin' lifetime ago. We're adults now. How about we make the summer a lot more pleasant for both of us and call a truce?"

She took a step back as if in disbelief, then fixed him with the same glare that he had required years of effort to forget. "Here are the rules. Lie low this summer. Do nothing to destroy my town. And be gone by Labour Day."

Something about this wasn't sitting right. Hell, nobody had given him a warm-and-fuzzy homecoming, but Jillian's reaction seemed extreme. There was only one reason he could think of for her to be this defensive. Luckily for her, it was a memory he was more than happy to leave buried.

Jillian squared her shoulders, checked the time on the clock outside Town Hall and shifted her briefcase to her other hand. "I have to go," she said. "But I'm warning you, J.T. Don't mess with my town."

He faked a salute. "Ma'am, yes, ma'am."

"You haven't changed at all, have you?"

Before he could come up with an answer, she walked a wide circle around him and vanished from his sight. He let his grin slip as the sound of her heels faded away.

He didn't want to upset Jillian. Not really. For one thing, he had enough bad Comeback Cove karma already. For another, it probably wasn't smart to annoy the mayor when he was trying to sell off a bunch of properties, many of them needing planning-board approval.

On the other hand, if he were going to walk around with a target on his back, he might as well have some fun with it.

LYDDIE BREWSTER SCURRIED into the Brewster Memorial conference room in Town Hall and slid into one of the last empty chairs gathered around the polished maple table.

"Thank God this is the last time this committee has to meet," Lyddie said to the older woman on her right. Beneath the table, she eased her shoes off and wiggled her toes. Some days were harder on the feet than others. "Please tell me I'm late enough that the meeting is over and I can go home."

"Sorry, kid. Her Worship hasn't made an appearance yet." Nadine Krupnick was not only Lyddie's assistant at her coffee shop, River Joe's, she was also both friend and secret keeper to half the town. More important, she was the only one who could get away with calling Mayor Jillian McFarlane "Your Worship" to her face. "What made you late, anyway?"

"Sara called. She wanted to tell me every detail of her day."

"I thought she wasn't speaking to you."

"I'm her favorite mom again since I said she could go to my sister's for the summer." Lyddie raised a hand in anticipation of Nadine's protest. "I know, I know. She's only fourteen, Vancouver is too far away, yada yada yada. But there's not much for someone her age to do here all summer, and Zoë can use the help. It'll be good for Sara to take on some responsibility."

"No need to sound so defensive. I think it's a great idea."

"You do?" Lyddie reached into the paper bag Nadine pushed toward her and pulled out one of the muffins left from that day's baking. Lemon poppy—her favorite. She peeled back the paper before helping herself to a healthy bite. Tart lemon and crunchy seeds combined to give her the most sensual treat she'd known in ages. "Everyone else thinks I'm crazy."

"Let me guess. By 'everyone,' you mean your mother-in-law."

Lyddie stayed silent, not ready to let Nadine know she'd hit the nail on the head. Nor did she want to get into a discussion of why Ruth Brewster was afraid to let any of her family slip beyond the town line. Lyddie understood her mother-in-law's sentiments. She couldn't deny that there were times late at night when she, too, feared that Sara would never want to return to a quiet little tourist town after two months in Vancouver.

But in the light of day, things seemed far more optimistic. This was home now, and had been for four years. Sara was old enough to remember their old life, but still, this was her reality. Of course she would come home.

"Speaking of getting away, I booked my own flight last night." Nadine must have understood that Lyddie was ready to talk about something other than family. "As soon as Labour Day is over, I'm out of here. Las Vegas, here I come."

"Planning to hit the jackpot and run away with an Elvis impersonator?"

"Hell, no. I'm holding out for a magician. I figure if they can saw a woman in half, maybe I'll find one who can slice off some wrinkles, shave off a few years then put me back together so I look like I'm thirty-two again."

Lyddie laughed. "Throw in a breast lift and I'm next in line."

"Like you need it. Wait until you hit your sixties and it takes a crane to get the girls off the floor."

Good thing there was a water pitcher on the table. Lyddie needed a drink, fast, after Nadine's comments left her choking on a poppy seed. When she had finished coughing and Nadine had delivered a final blow to her back, Lyddie shook her head.

"You might have twenty years on me according to the calendar, Nadine, but you still have the mouth of a teenager."

"Three decades slinging hash in the school cafeteria stomped the shrinking violet out of me real fast."

The door to the conference room flew open. Jillian marched in, heels snapping on the floor, two bright spots of color burning high on her cheeks.

"Uh-oh," Nadine whispered. Lyddie agreed.

Jillian set her briefcase on the floor, dropped into her chair and smacked a handful of papers against the table.

"Good evening, folks. Let's get moving."

And with that, the Discover Downtown meeting was launched. Jillian led them through the agenda at breakneck speed, slowing only when Tracy Potter, the local postmistress, tried to slip in unnoticed fifteen minutes late. Jillian glared at Tracy with such righteous indignation that it was all Lyddie could do to keep from bursting into laughter.

Honestly, the things she endured for this town...

By Lyddie's standards, it was a reasonably successful night. Jillian seemed too distracted to try to rope anyone into extra duties, and the rest of the committee members actually spoke up on their own a couple of times instead of waiting for Lyddie to speak first and then echoing her thoughts. The final report was given, and the meeting railroaded to a close. Lyddie, Tracy and Nadine walked together into the coolness of the night, chatting as they rambled toward Lyddie's van.

As soon as they were out of earshot of the other committee members, Nadine broached the subject that had kept Lyddie entertained throughout the meeting.

"What bug crawled up Jillian's arse and bit her tonight?"

"No idea," Lyddie said, but Tracy was practically dancing with excitement.

"You mean you haven't heard? You'll never guess who's back."

"Is Bill Shatner here again?" Nadine asked. "He owes me money."

Tracy laughed and pulled black curls back from the breeze. "Better. J. T. Delaney."

For only the second or third time in their years together, Lyddie had the immense pleasure of seeing Nadine struck silent. She hoped it wouldn't last long. Tracy was obviously dying to spill, and Nadine could weasel out any forgotten tidbits Tracy might forget. Lyddie needed to get home soon—there were three children waiting to dump a day's worth of living on her—but after years of hearing stories about the legendary bad boy of Comeback Cove, she was dying to know more. She leaned against her van and waited for Nadine to regain her powers of speech.

"J.T. is back?"

Tracy nodded. "Yes, ma'am. I saw him myself,

late this afternoon, driving Iris's little Honda up Main Street. At first I didn't think it was her car because it was in the middle of the road instead of the middle of the sidewalk. That woman really needs to stop driving, you know? Then I saw who it was and I almost went off the road myself. And I was walking!"

"How's he look?" Nadine leaned forward in her favorite you-can-tell-me-anything pose. Tracy grinned and fanned herself.

"Still?"

Tracy nodded. "Just like that picture in the year-book where he was voted *most likely to deflower a nun*."

Lyddie nudged a pointy bit of gravel away from her tired feet. "So what exactly did this guy do? I mean, I know he started that fire. But there was more than that, right?"

Nadine's words came slow. "He wasn't bad, really. Just a little wild. The long hair, the leather jacket… All those things that make a boy look suspicious."

"Don't forget when he reset all the clocks on the village square to different time zones. Or the time he stuffed the cannon in the square with dead fish, so when they set it off for Canada Day it rained fish guts on everyone."

Nadine's nose wrinkled. "He had his moments, I won't deny it. But I don't recall him ever hurting anyone."

Tracy snorted. "Except when he broke Ted Mc-Farlane's nose."

Nadine waved Tracy's words away. "That was Ted's fault, and you know it. Still, J.T. would have been okay if not for the fire."

This part, Lyddie knew. No one could live in Comeback Cove for long without hearing about the Big Burn, in which the town's primary draw of the time—a reconstructed historic village—was destroyed in a few blazing hours. The resulting drop in tourist business had left many on the edge of bankruptcy. It had taken years for Comeback Cove to recover.

"They never proved he started it, did they?" Lyddie asked.

"Not enough to press charges. But he was spotted running from the fire, then he took off that night and never came back. Except for his dad's funeral, of course."

Lyddie couldn't blame him for leaving. In a town where public opinion was king, J.T. wouldn't have needed anything as mundane as a trial. If he'd stayed, he would have lived a never-ending prison sentence every time he went out in public.

"Twenty-five years," Nadine said, staring at the river. "What finally brought him back?"

For the first time, Tracy looked uncomfortable. "It's getting late. I should head home."

Uh-oh. Lyddie was no expert on body language,

but even she knew that Tracy's averted eyes and sudden lunge for her purse were not good signs.

Nadine latched a bony hand on the would-be escapee's arm. "Tracy Potter, I have known you since before you were born. You can't con me. Tell us why J.T. is back."

"Well, nothing's certain yet—" translation: Tracy had heard something from two sources but had to receive definitive proof "—but word is he's home for Iris."

"She's okay, isn't she?" Lyddie asked. "I saw her yesterday and she looked fine. I know she was sick in the winter, but—"

Tracy shook her head. "No, nothing like that. Look, Lyddie, I know Iris is your landlady and all, so I hate to be the one to tell you. But what I heard is that he's here to finish up his father's estate."

Lyddie's gut did an unhealthy lurch. "What does that mean?"

Tracy sighed and sent a pleading look toward Nadine. It only made Lyddie's suspicions shoot higher.

"*Now,* Tracy."

"Iris is moving, Lyddie. Probably to Tucson with J.T., though nobody's sure about that. He's here to sell all the buildings his father owned." She jerked her head back toward River Joe's. "Including this one."

CHAPTER TWO

J.T. STOOD IN the cramped upstairs bathroom of his mother's home bright and early the next morning, carefully peeling the backing from the temporary tattoo he'd applied to his arm.

"There," he said to the lumpy mutt lying half in the bathroom, half in the hall. "It's not a heart that says *Mom,* but it should do the trick."

Charlie—the latest in a string of mongrels— yawned, obviously not impressed with the way the morning sun gleamed off the stylized maple leaf now adorning J.T.'s biceps. J.T. shrugged, wadded up the paper and tossed it toward the trash, congratulating himself when he hit it the first time. Courage bolstered, he turned to the mirror to see if he passed muster.

Good. He looked only half as idiotic as he felt.

He'd left his hair uncombed, both to increase the rumpled look and to hide the gray that had started taking hold. A day's worth of stubble paraded across his jaw. The bags under his eyes were a by-product of flying across time zones, but they added to the seedy appearance. An earring would have been a nice touch, but he had his limits.

Black biking shorts and an electric blue muscle shirt completed the mugger-in-training look. All he needed was a motorcycle. But he'd spent years learning caution and common sense since leaving town, and he wasn't about to abandon them completely. He'd settle for Rollerblades and hope they were enough to cause a stir.

Satisfied that he looked vaguely reminiscent of the delinquent teen he'd once been, he stepped over Charlie and crept down the stairs, hoping he could make his escape without his mother hearing. She would have to see him like this in time, but he didn't want to ruin her breakfast.

"J.T.?"

He should have known. The minute he walked into town, his luck turned tail and hopped the next flight out.

He nearly tripped over the damned stealthy dog and steeled himself for the worst.

Iris Delaney stood in the hall, thinner than she'd ever been in his life, snug in a white housecoat festooned with the flowers she'd been named for. She had a mug cradled in her hands and an expression of sheer horror on her face.

Wait for it....

She opened and closed her mouth. Raised one hand to her lips. Lowered it again.

At last she spoke.

"Make me a happy woman. Tell me you're going jogging and then you'll shower and get dressed for real."

"Sorry, Ma. What you see is what you get."

"Do I dare ask why?"

She could ask, but he wasn't sure he could explain. He knew that when he left town, he'd broken her heart. Her hurt was compounded when she realized that no matter what he did—graduating from university, getting his PhD, moving to Tucson to teach high school and the occasional university class— no one wanted to hear about it. She'd been deprived of both her son and her bragging rights. She didn't need to know that he'd already been tried and condemned on his first day back.

"Let's say I'm giving the people exactly what they want to see." He kissed the top of her head and swiped her mug with every intention of helping himself. One whiff of the contents made him hand it back, fast.

"What the he—heck is that?"

Iris rolled her eyes. "Please. You're leaving here dressed like a hoodlum but you won't say *hell* in front of your mother?"

"I figured you'd wash my mouth out with soap. What is it?"

"Astragalus tea. Strengthens immunity and enhances body energy and defenses."

So she was trying to build herself back up. Good.

"When was your last doctor's appointment?"

"About three weeks ago. Maybe longer." When he started to speak, she shushed him with a shake of her head. "Don't fuss. I'm fine now."

"You've said that before."

"Mothers don't like to worry their children." She stared into her tea. He tipped her chin up so he could look her straight in the eye.

"And children don't like being kept in the dark, Ma."

"I'm not hiding anything." She paused, before adding, "Not from you, I promise. Not anymore."

He could live with that. If Iris wanted to keep the rest of the town from knowing the truth about her ongoing fight with seasonal affective disorder, well, that was her right. As long as she didn't try to hide it from him. He never wanted to get another phone call like the one he'd received last winter—the call in which an artificially calm voice informed him that his mother had tried to kill herself.

But she was doing better now. She was gradually adjusting to life without his father. And it was summer, when the long light-filled days held her depression at bay. As long as he got her out of Comeback Cove before fall, she would be fine.

The trouble was that while Iris said she was ready to move, he had the feeling she was really hoping for some sort of reprieve. Something, perhaps, like convincing him to move back.

"So." He sniffed the tea again, turned up his nose. "Where can I get a cup of real coffee these days?"

"The same place you always could. River Joe's." She looked him up and down. "You know it's going to be crowded this time of day."

It was a gentle hint that he might want to change. Little did she know that there was no way he was going to reveal the depths of his changes to this town. He could handle them rejecting the kid he'd been. The man he'd become, though—that was off-limits.

Besides, it was fun to put on the old ways and tweak folks a bit. He kind of missed letting his inner daredevil have his day.

"River Joe's, huh?" A picture of the woman he'd spotted the previous evening flashed through his mind. Maybe the answer to her identity was closer than he'd expected.

He snagged his Rollerblades from beside the deacon's bench in the front hall, then sat down and wriggled the first foot in. Keeping his voice casual, he asked, "Who's running it these days?"

"Lydia Brewster."

"Who's she?"

"Buddy Brewster's daughter-in-law."

J.T. wound the laces around his hands, tugged

and looked up. "Glenn's wife? How did she end up with the shop?"

"Glenn's widow, yes. She moved here with her children after Glenn and Buddy died."

Memories raced through J.T.'s mind, outtakes from the one and only time Comeback Cove had gained national attention. There had been a tanker on the seaway—a common enough occurrence. But this tanker had been targeted by a nutcase with a statement to make and enough explosives to make sure he was heard. Buddy and Glenn had been out deer hunting when they stumbled across the man. They stopped him. But in the process they lost their own lives.

J.T. tied a quick bow and moved on to the next foot. "Must have been tough for her."

"It was. I'm sure it still is."

The slight catch in his mother's voice was proof that she understood Lydia Brewster's pain better than he ever would. He hunted for something to say that would keep them on even emotional ground. "What made her come here?"

"You say that like it's a life sentence."

"You mean it isn't?"

"Maybe when you're a child. But adults usually enjoy it."

Any minute now, she'd start a commercial on the joys of life in Comeback Cove. "Lydia Brewster?" he prompted.

Iris sighed. "Well, she and Ruth were both hurting, as you can imagine. Ruth was all alone in that big house, and Lydia's children were so small—the youngest was little more than a baby. She brought them here, and Ruth helped with the kids while Lyddie ran the store. It was good for both of them."

It made sense. But he still couldn't see how moving to the Cove could be in anyone's best interests.

"This is her home now," Iris continued, "and people are glad to have her. Losing Buddy and Glenn was terrible. It helps to have her and the children here, like a part of them is still with us. And Lyddie is so sweet and brave that everyone wants to help."

J.T. could only imagine. From what he remembered, if the nutcase had succeeded, the resulting explosion could have destroyed the town far more completely than he ever had. Lydia Brewster must be the next thing to a saint around here.

If she were indeed the woman he'd seen, it explained the ease with which she'd been accepted into town. Even the Cove couldn't keep a hero's widow at arm's length.

He gave the laces a tug vicious enough to risk snapping them. He hoped to hell that this Brewster woman either wanted to close the shop or had enough money tucked away to buy her building from him. Because even with skates on, he doubted he could outrun the wave of condemnation that would crash over him if he had to sell Lydia Brewster's business out from under her.

THE WEDNESDAY-MORNING RUSH was in full gear, leaving Lyddie little time to worry about Tracy's revelation of the night before. Good. If she let herself think too long about this, she could come up with a dozen possible outcomes, each one scarier than the last. She was all too aware that the worst-case scenario really could happen in a life.

She could lose her business. Have to start over in another location. Worst of all, she would have to say goodbye to another piece of her children's history— the shop their grandfather started, the place where their father carved his initials into the kitchen wall.

But all that had to wait. Right now she had to draw a hazelnut roast for Jillian.

"Leave it black, please," Jillian called, as though this were a new request. Every morning she ordered the same thing. Nadine and Lyddie were getting on in years, but even they could remember a medium hazelnut, no cream, no sugar.

On the other hand, Jillian hadn't attained the office of mayor—and every other title in town, from Little Miss Fall Festival on up—by leaving anything to chance. Maybe Lyddie should take a lesson from her. Jillian would never find herself breathless and foundering while her building was sold out from beneath her, that was for sure.

"How about a blueberry muffin, Your Worship?" Nadine was in fine form. "Mmm, look at that brown sugar streusel."

Jillian, queen of the Thighmaster, shuddered visibly. "No. Just coffee. No food."

On the other hand, there had to be a more positive role model than an anorexic power slut.

"I need music," Lyddie announced, and scooted around the counter to reach the long-outdated CD player. Usually she didn't start the tunes until the morning rush had cleared and conversation had dwindled. But today she needed all the distraction she could get.

She thumbed through the CDs and shook her head. Gregorian chants, harp music, the sounds of relaxation… None of those felt right. She needed in-your-face vocals that would give her a socially acceptable outlet for the frustration perking inside her. She needed—

"Oh, yeah."

Bonnie Raitt's greatest hits slid into place. In a moment, assertive guitar chords punctured the atmosphere, mingling with the warm smell of coffee and the casual ambience. It was almost enough to make her relax.

She boogied her way behind the counter where Nadine waited with her arms crossed and eyes rolling.

"Lydia, it's bad enough you make me work at this

hour. Force me to listen to that and I'll report you to the labor board."

"Stop. This is good. People like it."

"It has a beat, I'll give you that." Nadine scanned the room, pausing briefly at the opening door. "But I think you need to try something... Oh, my God."

"What?" Lyddie looked up, more worried by the sudden drop in Nadine's volume than her words. Then she realized that the entire room had gone suddenly, eerily still. If it hadn't been for Bonnie belting from the CD, asking if she was ready for the thing called love, there would have been dead silence.

"Nadine?"

A nod toward the door was the only answer.

Lyddie glanced in the direction indicated and saw that a man had entered the shop. Dark hair. Slightest hint of stubble on the chin. Electric blue T-shirt over black biker shorts. The most remarkable thing about him was the Rollerblades on his feet, and even Comeback Cove had progressed enough to handle those.

On closer inspection, this guy didn't need anything remarkable to stand out. He wasn't what she'd call drop-dead gorgeous, though he certainly was making the second look worth the effort. It was something about the way he held himself. The set of his shoulders, the slight quirk at the corner of his mouth, the calm and purposeful way he scanned the room sent a clear message that this was a man who knew exactly who and what he was, and nothing would change him.

So why did she get the feeling he was braced for attack?

"It's him," Nadine whispered. "J. T. Delaney."

Ooooooooh.

The quirk spread into a cocky grin. "Nice to see I still know how to make an entrance."

The room echoed with the sound of about a dozen throats being cleared.

His gaze settled on Lyddie. Something like recognition flashed in his eyes, confusing her. "Okay to wear these in here?" he called over the coughing and harrumphing.

"Uh…" Somewhere in her brain she understood he was referring to the skates. She wanted to toss off a casual reply, but something—anger?—had started curling low in her belly, interfering with her thought process.

It wasn't fair. She hadn't had time to think, no chance to determine her plan of attack. Why was he here already?

And why did he have to look so…interesting? Despite what Nadine and Tracy had said, Lyddie had expected a middle-aged version of his late father: sober and responsible, slightly balding, wearing sensible loafers and madras plaid shirts. *That* kind of man she could handle. What was she supposed to do with James Dean the Second?

His grin widened. "If you'd rather I didn't, could we pretend this is a drive-through?"

From the corner of her eye she saw a flash of red. *Oh, no.* Jillian was moving in for the kill.

"Well, well, well. So much for that line about being adults." Jillian crossed her arms and looked him up and down with—in Lyddie's opinion—a bit too much interest. If Ted heard about this, there would be hell to pay. "You're still as crazy as ever."

"Only when I'm here, Jelly."

Behind Lyddie, Nadine snickered back to life. *"Jelly?"*

Lyddie had much the same thought. She'd never met anyone who could put Her Worship in place with five little words. When the mayor clamped her lips together and hustled out the door, Lyddie had to remind herself that this was the potential bad guy in front of her.

But bad guy or not, she couldn't leave him standing in the doorway. She waved to let him know the blades were acceptable but couldn't keep from adding, "After all, it's your place, Mr. Delaney."

The soft whir of wheels across slate marked his progress. That and the swiveling of every head in the room. He moved slowly, as if making sure everyone had a chance to size him up.

"Morning, Mrs. Krupnick."

"Morning, J.T." Nadine spoke far more cautiously

than Lyddie would have expected. "What can I get for you?"

"A cup of French roast." There was a slight pause before he added, "Please."

Lyddie stifled a groan. Just what she needed. A landlord with a God's-greatest-gift complex.

She had to meet him eventually, so she straightened her shoulders and prayed that she would come off as an efficient businesswoman instead of the brain-dead twit she was currently channeling. Though how she was supposed to do that when he'd dropped in on her out of the blue like this…

"Hi." She thrust out a hand, well aware that it was more challenge than greeting. "Welcome to River Joe's. I'm Lydia Brewster."

"J. T. Delaney." He took her hand, palms meshing in a perfect fit. An unanticipated fog rolled through her brain. All she could think was that he sure didn't look like a landlord. Nor, to be honest, did he resemble her idea of a wild arsonist. She wasn't sure why. He certainly had the "wild" part down. Maybe it was his teeth. They seemed far too straight and white for someone with a juvenile past.

Nadine slid a full mug in his direction. He lifted it and inhaled like a drowning man who'd just found an oxygen tank.

"God, that smells good."

Okay, he appreciated good coffee. That was a plus. But looking at him made something bubble inside

Lyddie. She couldn't put a finger on it. She was irritated and intrigued and frustrated and fascinated, all at the same time, but none of those emotions seemed to capture exactly what she was feeling.

All that was certain was that she needed to know the truth—not through a rumor, but from him.

She gave him a moment to swallow before saying, as casually as possible, "I hear you're selling the building."

The room echoed with a dozen sudden inhalations.

J.T., however, showed no reaction other than a slight quirk of an eyebrow. "Word travels fast as ever, I see."

She nodded. Crossed her arms. Settled her hip against the corner of the counter so he'd know she was in no hurry.

A slow smile spread across his face. No surprise. It was the brief hint of some other emotion flashing in his eyes that made her pay attention. Was that guilt she spied?

But his next words laid to rest her brief hope that J. T. Delaney was having second thoughts.

"That's right." He spoke clearly, slowly. She had the impression he wanted to make sure everyone in the room caught every word. "I'm selling this and every other building my father owned. I want it done quickly and easily so I can leave at the end of summer. The sooner I can get back to Tucson, the better."

A chorus of whispers filled the room. Lyddie was glad for the solid wood against her hip. It compensated for the weakness in her knees.

He looked straight at her, but again the words were meant for the crowd. "This is prime waterfront property, Mrs. Brewster. I won't have any trouble selling." He fished in his pocket, tossed money on the counter. "I'll stop by at closing time to discuss the details."

He saluted her with his mug and took another long swallow before setting it on the counter with what looked like regret. Without another word, he skated out the door.

Silence filled the shop.

"Damn that boy." Nadine's words were soft but heartfelt.

"Ditto." It was the only word Lyddie could manage. Too many thoughts vied for attention in her head, pushing her toward panic mode. The rumors were true. Could she buy? Would she get a new landlord? Was her rent going to jump? Would she have to move? Would he—

"He never was any good at math." Nadine whisked the coins off the counter, shaking her head, and Lyddie finally clued in.

Not only had J. T. Delaney stolen her piece of

mind and upset her business for the morning, but he'd also shorted her on the price of the coffee.

WELL, THAT HAD definitely not been one of his finer moments.

J.T. sauntered down Main Street that afternoon on his way back to River Joe's, hoping no one could see that beneath the outer confidence, he was beating himself up. He kept a practiced, slightly patronizing smile in place as he observed the street, never once letting on that he was actually impressed with what he saw.

Last night he'd been so intent on searching out familiar landmarks that he hadn't noticed the changes. How was that for irony? He had locked up his perception of the town just the way the town had frozen its opinion of him.

But today, after cursing himself for the way he'd behaved in the coffee shop, he could see the bigger picture. The Cove was still no crowded tourist hotspot, but it had grown and even thrived over the years. He remembered a sad downtown in which there were three empty storefronts for every one business clinging to life. Now there wasn't an empty space to be seen. Pizza and doughnuts, T-shirts and antiques, even a natural food and vitamin shop—all seemed to be bustling between the standard grocery, post office and hardware store.

No wonder Lydia Brewster got that deer-in-the-headlights look when he said he was selling. There was no place for her to go.

The load of guilt on his shoulders got a little heavier—again—at the memory. She hadn't deserved to get drawn into his give-'em-what-they're-expecting joyride. She hadn't done anything to him, and he had no right to assume she would condemn him like the rest of the town. He couldn't let himself get ticked off at the way he'd been treated and then turn around and do the same thing to someone else.

Even at his worst, he'd never been heartless—yet he had a lousy feeling that he'd been exactly that this morning.

It hadn't helped that when he walked in and recognized her as his mystery woman, his first thought was of the way she'd looked when she stretched the night before—long and curvy and inviting. *That* had knocked his carefully prepared words flat out of his mind. By the time he realized what he was saying, he'd already messed up.

It was all he could do to keep a determined spring in his step as he pulled open the door to River Joe's, setting bells tinkling. He hoped to God he could get everything sold quickly. The kick he'd got from resurrecting his long-ago persona was fading fast.

"Hello?" He peered around the deserted dining room. No signs of life. Chairs were neatly upended on round tables, the counter was empty, lights dim.

If it hadn't been for the unlocked door he'd have thought she stood him up.

He was about to make tracks for the kitchen when that door flew open. Out marched Nadine Krupnick. He recognized the scowl on her face. He'd seen it enough times back in school, when she was the lunch lady and he was the idiot who'd just yelled, "Food fight!"

"Afternoon," he said cautiously, turning so she couldn't get between him and the exit.

"Afternoon? Ha. More like, high time someone talked straight to you, *Mister* Delaney."

The bitter twist to her words told him precisely where Nadine's loyalties rested. Before he could muster up an apology, Nadine was in his face, bobbing like a pissed-off bantam hen. The fact that he stood a good eight inches over her did nothing to dispel the feeling he'd just come between a mother bear and her cub.

"Listen here, J.T." She poked his chest. Hard. "Up until about nine o'clock this morning, I was ready and willing to give you the benefit of the doubt. Then I heard what you're doing. From your own lips, no less. And all I can say is, if you take this place away from that girl, then you might as well turn yourself in to the police right now, because you'll be killing her just the same as that nutcase killed her husband."

She finished her words with another jab that

barely avoided being a punch. It took all his effort to keep breathing in a seminormal manner.

"You been working out, Mrs. Krupnick? I don't remember you having such a mean right hook back in school."

"That's because you still had some brains back then. And a heart. Now it seems you've got a rock in your chest. And as for what's filling your head instead of brains, well—"

"Nadine."

Lydia leaned against the counter the way she had earlier that day, but this time she seemed almost relaxed. Even with her arms crossed tightly over her chest, she seemed more amused than worried. Maybe it was the smile tugging at her lips. He'd spied it this morning, briefly, before Nadine had obviously told her who he was. He hadn't realized how much he'd wanted to see her smile again.

Too bad it was currently directed at Nadine, not him. When she glanced in his direction she frosted over. Wariness replaced the amusement that had encompassed her just a second earlier.

I did that. His shoulders sagged.

"Kick him out, Lyddie. Don't talk to him until you call your lawyer."

But Lydia shook her head. "It's his building, Nadine. Besides, I'm certain Mr. Delaney and I can come to some reasonable agreement."

Nadine muttered something under her breath. He

wasn't positive, but he was pretty sure that back in school, if she'd ever caught him saying what he thought she'd just said, he would have been carving yet another notch in his favorite chair in the principal's office.

"Absolutely." He ducked his head, stepped back and opened the door with a show of politeness. Nadine flounced through the opening, looking from him to the river behind them so pointedly that he would have to be an idiot to miss her meaning.

He allowed himself one lungful of the coolness coming off the water before turning back. Lydia stood by the set of love seats that flanked a coffee table at the fireplace end of the room.

"No Rollerblades this afternoon?"

He glanced at his sandals. "This is a business meeting. I thought I'd go formal."

Something like amusement twitched at her lips before quickly fleeing.

"Shall we get started?" She gestured to one seat before sitting in the opposite one. She moved with a fluid grace that reminded him of the waves he'd spied on the water. But just like the water, he was pretty sure there was a lot more beneath the surface than she was going to show. At least to him.

He sat, well aware that he had some atoning to do. He hoped he could get through this meeting without turning back into the rebel without a clue.

"It's been a long time since I've been in this place,"

he said. "Even when I lived here, I usually wasn't allowed inside. My dad came here to hang out with his buddies. Your father-in-law was his best friend. Having me here would have cramped their style."

She nodded. "Your father never came back after... after I took over."

"Really?"

Another nod. "I'm sorry you lost him."

"And I'm sorry, too. For your loss, I mean."

This time she merely pursed her lips, as if he'd said something unexpected. It took him a moment to realize that expressions of sympathy might not go with the image he had presented that morning.

God, when he messed up, he did it big-time.

After a moment of silence, she spoke again. "I don't mean to be rude, Mr. Delaney, but my—"

"J.T."

"Fine. I'm Lydia, and my children will be here soon so I can drive them home from school, so could we please skip the getting-to-know-you stage and get down to business?" She leaned forward slightly. "I want to buy the building."

He tried to answer. He really did. But when she leaned in, he got a glimpse of something purple and lacy beneath her no-nonsense polo shirt, and boom, his neurons went into some kind of overactive shock. Which, as a scientist, he knew wasn't possible. But he also knew that science couldn't explain everything.

"Mr. Delaney? J.T.?"

"Uh…sorry, I…long day yesterday. I'm still foggy."

"Then let me say it again. I want to buy the building. How much are you asking?"

He wasn't seeing the Realtor for a couple of days, but he knew the assessed value of the building. He added a few thousand for good measure and named the resulting figure.

She blanched just a little.

"That's a bit more than I expected."

He reminded himself of the costs of moving his mother and establishing her in a new home in a country without subsidized medical care. "This is a good-sized building. It could probably be subdivided into two or three stores. Or it could stay as one large space, which I gather is what the other potential buyer plans to do with it."

A bit more color drained from her face. "Someone else wants it?"

In going through his mother's papers he'd found a letter from a Brockville snack maker asking about the possibility of buying the building to house a Comeback Cove spin-off of his establishment. J.T. didn't want to come off like a hard-ass, but she needed to know that he had to get the best possible price.

"There is other interest," he said slowly. "It would be a lot easier to sell to you, and I have no problem doing that. But I can't dismiss another buyer simply because you were here first." Then, because the way she was shrinking in on herself made him feel like he'd stepped on a robin's egg, he added, "I need to do what's best for my mother."

He wished he could tell her the truth, that he wasn't a heartless bastard, that he was only cutting as many ties as possible to make sure there was no reason for his mother to ever come back to this place of long, dangerous winters.

But Iris had gone to great and elaborate lengths during her hospitalization to convince the town that she was suffering from a very contagious flu. If he breathed so much as a hint that she was actually being treated for depression she would never forgive him. Worse, she might never leave town with him. She had already been dropping too-casual hints about how good life was in Comeback Cove and how the school could use an energetic science teacher. If he pissed her off, she would stay here with her friends, for another winter, and pretend she could ride out her illness on her own.

And he would lose her.

"Your mother. Of course. I understand." Lydia stood, smoothing the fabric of her khaki-colored pants, drawing his attention to nicely rounded hips. All thoughts of the building and the town and even his mother fluttered from his mind at the sight of long fingers sliding nervously down her thighs.

He shook his head. Four months of celibacy was obviously too long. If this were anyplace but the Cove he could try to amend that sad condition, but the mere thought of finding someone here was enough to bring a wry smile to his lips.

"My children will be here any minute." Her words pulled him back to attention. "I need to get ready for them."

"Right." He sprang to his feet, reached for her outstretched hand. Her shake was firm. His grasp lasted a fraction of a second too long. Well, to him it was too short. Who would have suspected that her palm would nestle so intimately against his? But from the slight frown and the speed with which she pulled back, he knew he'd overstayed his welcome.

"I don't want a bidding war, but I'm not giving up and moving out meekly, Mr. Delaney. I have too much invested here to let go just like that."

He nodded, certain that if he tried to say anything, he'd end up apologizing all over himself and practically giving her the building. "I understand. Why don't you take a day or two to consider your options and get back to me?"

Lydia's gaze darted around the room, lingering in the oddest places—a scarred section of the fireplace, a pane of glass in the window that didn't seem to match those surrounding it. He would have thought she was reassessing as she looked around, but the soft glow in her eyes told him he'd missed the boat.

"I'll be in touch as soon as possible," she said as she walked him to the door. He nodded and reached past her for the handle. For a moment they brushed against each other. He was close enough to breathe in the scents of coffee and vanilla that clung to her, near enough to hear the small breath that escaped from her lips when he touched her. He was filled with a crazy yearning to forget the door and reach for her instead.

It was impossible, of course. She might not have judged and dismissed him like the rest of the populace, but a hero's widow and the town bad boy—reformed or not—wasn't what anyone would call a likely pairing.

The best thing he could do was hope that from now on, she would wear shirts that wouldn't get him thinking.

CHAPTER THREE

WHERE WAS SHE going to get the money?

Lydia gave the wheelbarrow a vicious push as it caught on a root hidden in the grass of her front yard. Officially, she was toting the embers from the evening's barbecue out front to dump on the giant maple stump in the middle of the yard. In reality she'd jumped at the chance to gain a moment's privacy—a moment to relive her conversation with J. T. Delaney.

"Another buyer, my left foot," she muttered as she wheeled her load across the grass. "J.T. probably stands for Jerk the Tenant."

She upended the barrow and carefully shook the coals onto the last reminder of the tree that had towered over the yard until a January ice storm brought it down. The hiss and spit of the embers as they hit moist wood was nothing compared to the hissing and snarling she longed to indulge in now that she had the chance.

Except she couldn't.

Oh, she was mad, that was for sure. Angry at the way her new security was being yanked out from beneath her, frustrated that these changes were being forced on her, scared silly whenever she considered the money she would have to dredge up. That line about there being another potential buyer, well, that was just the whipped cream on the latte. Honestly. Did the man really think she would fall for that?

She pulled the wheelbarrow away from the stump and sighed. She was ticked at her new landlord, true. But she couldn't work up as much steam as was currently billowing into the air before her. The man was infuriating, but at the same time, he was so different than she'd expected that she was kind of intrigued. *Different* wasn't something that happened a lot in Comeback Cove. She was usually okay with that. Her life had been thrown into chaos once. Stability and routine were her good friends now.

She didn't want that to change just because J. T. Delaney had skated into town, even if he was the most interesting thing she'd seen in ages.

She gazed up into the blue sky, focusing on a wisp of long, thin white cloud. "Glenn," she said softly, "remember when you bought me that really awesome necklace for Christmas, and then you forgot all about it until I found it, like, two years later? Well, is there any chance you could have done that with some off-shore bank accounts, or—"

"Mommy!"

Lyddie's focus jerked back to earth and the sight of her youngest child bounding across the yard with a cell phone in her hand, pigtails bobbing in time with her leaps.

"Slow down, Tish. These coals are hot. You don't want to fall in them."

"Mommy, I'm not a baby. I'm almost seven. I know how to walk."

"Humor me, okay?" Lyddie walked around the steaming stump and met Tish on the safe side of the yard. "Who's on the phone?"

"Aunt Zoë."

"Thanks, kiddo. Go back inside and tell Sara to start your bath. I'll be there soon."

"Can't I skip? I don't want a bath."

"Nope. School night. Hop to it." Lyddie bestowed a loud kiss on Tish's soft cheek, then patted her daughter's denim-clad bottom before lifting the phone to her ear.

"Hey there, fertile one."

A long groan was her answer, deep and painful enough to make Lyddie's heart do a quick thud.

"Zoë? What's wrong, are you in labor? Talk to me, Zo."

"No."

"No, you won't talk to me, or—"

"No, I'm not in labor." Zoë sounded more like her normal overwhelmed self now. Whew. "It's these stupid Braxton Hicks contractions. Who invented them, anyway? I mean, what's the point of a contraction if you're not in labor? Is this supposed to be like the previews at the movies?"

Lyddie laughed and picked up a long stick to poke at the still-simmering coals. "This is your third kid. You don't need a preview."

"Damn straight I don't. It took me years to forget what labor feels like. I don't need reminders."

"Cheer up. It's going to get worse before it gets better."

Zoë moaned and called Lyddie a name that would have earned her a bar of soap in the mouth if their mother had heard it. Lyddie merely giggled.

"So what's up?"

"Nothing." Her sister's voice was a sound portrait of frustration.

"Nothing? That's why you called?"

"Kevin left early this morning and has a dinner meeting tonight, and Nick has a cold so he's clingy and miserable, and Dusty decided that today was the perfect day to see what would happen if you cook Play-Doh in the microwave for ten minutes on high. I hurt all over. I can't breathe. I've been having these stupid Braxton Hicks all day and it's hotter than Hades here and if this baby doesn't come out the minute Sara gets off the plane, I'm grabbing a knife and giving myself a homemade Cesarean."

Lyddie pushed a coal farther over on the stump. "Congratulations. You're having your eight-month breakdown."

"You don't have to sound so damned happy about it!" Across the miles, Zoë burst into tears. Lyddie sighed and sat on the ground. Might as well get comfortable.

Five minutes of soothing, empathizing and commiserating later, Zoë finally stopped crying.

"You okay now?"

"A bit." Sniff. "It helps to hear another adult voice. I should have kept working right until I popped. I wasn't made to be a suburban housewife. Tell me stories of the real world."

Despite herself, Lyddie laughed. "The real world? Have you forgotten that I live in Comeback Cove?"

"It beats the hell out of the 'burbs. At least people talk to each other there. Tell me—anything. Make something up. Anyone interesting come into the store today?"

This time it was Lyddie's turn to groan.

"That sounds promising. Now use words."

"They won't all be nice," Lyddie warned, and after glancing around the yard to make sure none of the kids were lurking in the evening shadows, she gave Zoë the scoop.

"So that's where I am," she said. "You have a

spare hundred grand or two tucked away with your cookie stash?"

"Sorry, I blew it all last week on nursing bras. But seriously, are you sure you want to buy the place?"

"Yes."

"Why?"

Why? Wasn't it obvious? "This is home now."

"Is it? I mean, I know you like it there, but geez, Lyddie. Do you really want to tie yourself to a place where they call you the Young Widow Brewster?"

Oh. That.

"Not everyone says that."

"But they think it," Zoë pointed out, and Lyddie realized that what had intrigued her most about J.T. was the way he'd talked to her. There'd been none of the deference that characterized so many of her interactions with her fellow residents. Other than his brief condolences, there had been no mention of Glenn, no pity in J.T.'s gaze. It had been, well… refreshing.

Still, even if she sometimes felt a bit stifled by the way people dealt with her, she couldn't discount the way she and the kids had been embraced by the town. "This is a good place. The kids need to be here."

"That's debatable. Sara seems awfully excited about coming here for the summer."

"Sara is fourteen. Of course she wants to get away, it's part of the adolescent code."

"Are you sure that's all it is?"

The question was so un-Zoë, so very much like something her mother-in-law would say, that Lyddie had to laugh. "Did Ruth pay you to do this?"

"Oh, my God. You mean Ruth and I actually agree on something?"

"Not precisely, but…" Lyddie sighed and leaned back until she was flat on the ground, staring at the pink-tinged clouds floating through the darkening sky. "Look, you know why I'm here. I agree it gets a little, um, claustrophobic at times, but everyone is really very nice. Plus it's the closest I can come to keeping Glenn alive for the kids."

"And there's no other way that could be done?"

"Not nearly as well."

There was a moment of silence, during which Lyddie could easily visualize her sister perched on the edge of her bar stool, one finger twirling her hair while the other tapped against the phone—Zoë's favorite thinking position.

"Is he married?"

"Excuse me?"

"The landlord. Is he married?"

"What the heck does that have to do with anything?"

"Because if he's married, I can't tell you to jump him."

"*Zoë!*"

"Oh, come on, Lyd. You said he's kind of James Dean–ish, right?"

Lyddie remembered the shorts, the sass, the smile. The man did have a basic animal appeal. Maybe it was just the shock of seeing someone who obviously didn't care what anyone thought about him—a rare find, indeed, in Comeback Cove.

"I am not going to jump him."

"You sure? It would go a hell of a long way toward improving your negotiating position."

"Positive."

"Then I guess you'll have to start researching mortgages."

The shudder that rippled through Lyddie had nothing to do with the damp ground or the cool breeze coming off the river. Of course she had to get a mortgage to buy the building. It was the only way. She hated the thought of taking on that much debt, but she would do it. Even if it meant working until after she was dead to pay it off.

Her kids had already lost their father. They weren't going to lose one of their strongest links to him, too. Not while she had any say in the matter.

LATE THAT NIGHT, Lyddie stared at the computer, the only light in the darkened den, and tried not to get too depressed as she focused on the sample mortgage payments in front of her. Amazing, how simple squiggles on a screen could generate such worry.

It hadn't been like this before, when she and Glenn had bought their house. That research had been accompanied by giggles, nervous excitement and a bottle of champagne.

This time, each figure she took in seemed more overwhelming than the one before it. It was almost enough to make her seriously consider Zoë's suggestion that she improve her negotiating position by jumping her landlord.

Right. And then she would pull a Lady Godiva in the middle of Main Street.

She minimized the page and clicked on the next bank in the list she'd generated. Maybe this one would have better terms. And maybe she could forget about J.T. And maybe she could even stop Zoë's other question from surfacing every time she printed out another loan application.

Do you really want to tie yourself so permanently to a town where they call you the Young Widow Brewster?

"Yes," she muttered as she stabbed her pencil against the notepad. Concentrate. That's what she had to do now. Focus on the store, on her future, on building a forever life in Comeback Cove. All those other thoughts would have to wait until—

"Lydia?"

Until she dealt with her mother-in-law.

"Do you have a minute to talk?"

Oh, no. Not that tone. Not the I'm-alone-and-lonely voice.

"A minute." She turned away from the computer, not certain if she were getting into something better or worse. "What's up, Ruth?"

"I know you're planning to send Sara to your sister's for the summer, but is that carved in stone?"

Lyddie was tired and frustrated, haunted by questions she couldn't answer and worries she couldn't share, and all she wanted was to check out a couple more banks and then go to bed. She longed to tell Ruth that whatever it was, it would keep until a better time. But in all honesty, between the coffee shop, Ruth's job and three kids needing to be carted around town and/or talked around, that "better time" was about twelve years down the road.

It looked as if she were going to have to get it over with.

"Her plane ticket is bought and paid for. Zoë is counting on Sara to help with the boys after she has the baby. So yeah, it's pretty well definite."

"I see. It's just that…" Ruth paused as she walked into the room and sat in the desk chair beside Lyddie's. "I talked to my sister today. She suggested that I bring the girls along when I go to Florida next month. Ben will be at camp and I thought it would be a nice treat for them."

Florida in July? Ew. Tish wouldn't mind the heat, she thrived on it, but Sara had inherited Lyddie's love of cooler weather. She would wilt in two hours. Besides which—

"Ruth, that's a wonderful offer, but Sara has her heart set on Vancouver. Zoë has arranged for her to have weekly lessons from someone who plays clarinet in the Vancouver Symphony, and you know Sara and music."

"Clarinet lessons? I know everyone is making a big deal over her winning that orchestra award in school, but does she think she's a musical genius now?"

"Actually, I think that being a musical genius is what led to her getting the award." Lyddie spoke a bit more sharply than she'd intended, but tough.

Ruth shook her head. "I didn't mean to dismiss her ability. You know I'm as proud of her as you are. But are you going to let one factor dictate her future?"

"Sara's future is Sara's concern. She loves music. She wants to make a career out of it."

"But that's ridiculous. She has her father's brain— she could easily do anything she sets her mind to do."

"And her mind is set on music." Lyddie raised her hand before Ruth could speak again. "Look, she's fourteen years old. She could decide next week that she wants to be a politician, or an undertaker or even a physical therapist, like Glenn. But right now she's set on music and I have the chance to give my child something that could further her dreams. What kind of mother would I be if I didn't do that?"

"A mother who wants to keep her child safe at home."

In a moment Lyddie's budding anger drained into understanding. Ruth had Lyddie, the children and her sister in Florida. That was it. The core of her world—her husband and her son—had been ripped from her. Lyddie couldn't blame her for wanting to hold on as tightly as she could.

But as much as she felt for Ruth, her needs could not override Sara's.

"Ruth." Lyddie placed a hand on the older woman's arm. "I'm going to miss her, too. It won't be the same without her. But she's at the age when she needs to spread her wings a little. Florida would be wonderful, and I'm sure she'll be torn, but this trip to Vancouver is making her happier than she's been in months. I know you wouldn't want to take that away from her."

Ruth sighed and patted Lyddie's hand. "I suppose not. Just promise me she'll come home in September."

"She'll come home if I have to fly there myself and drag her back by the hair."

"Good." She waited, then said, "What about Tish?"

For a moment Lyddie's own desire to be the one to introduce her child to the wonders of Disney made her hesitate. Then she gave herself a mental slap. Who was being selfish now?

"How long will you be gone?"

"Just over two weeks."

"At the end of July, right?"

"That's right. The second half of the month. The dates are marked on the calendar."

With just the slightest lump in her throat, Lyddie said, "It's up to her, but I think she'd be delighted to go. Let's iron out the details tomorrow, okay? It's been a long day. I'm wiped."

Ruth looked as though she wanted to say more, but Lyddie turned back to the computer. She bookmarked the pages she needed, shut down the computer then dragged herself up the stairs, wondering who on earth had ever thought that a two-story house was a good idea.

Before she could collapse into her own bed, however, she had one more job to do. Barefoot, she padded down the hall for her nightly peek into the kids' rooms.

Ben had fallen asleep with the light on, as always. A copy of Carl Sagan's *Cosmos* lay on the bed near his outstretched hand.

"Good night, my little brainiac." Lyddie eased the book from its landing place and set it on the dresser where Ben would be sure to see it as soon as he woke. She smoothed the hair from his forehead and tiptoed to the door, where she paused to look back again.

"Glenn," she murmured softly, "he's getting too smart for me, hon. I can't understand the things he talks about anymore, and he figured out that I've been faking for a while now. Could you maybe send him a friend? Preferably one who understands all that physics stuff, so he doesn't walk around feeling so alone?"

Book safe, light out, she moved to the big room shared by the girls. Tish had kicked off her covers. Lyddie smoothed the blankets over her once again and kissed the sleeping child gently on the forehead. A glance across the room showed Sara curled in a fetal position, slumbering peacefully under the Clarinets RULE poster she'd tacked above her bed.

Ruth was right about one thing. Letting Sara leave, even for the summer, was one of the scariest things Lyddie had ever done. In her heart of hearts she knew that Sara was going to fall in love with Vancouver, with the opportunities, with the sights and sounds and offerings that awaited her.

She was prepared to do anything—go into debt until she was ninety-two, bind herself to a town where she would always be the hero's widow—to make sure her children had every possible chance to connect with the father they'd lost. But what would she do if Sara didn't want to come home?

Two DAYS AFTER making an ass of himself in River Joe's, J.T. made his first foray to the post office. Conversation dropped a bit when he walked through the door, but didn't come to a dead halt the way it had at the coffee shop. He wasn't sure if that was good or not.

He nodded in the general direction of the room and took his place at the end of the line. He didn't recognize any of the people ahead of him. Of course, from their surreptitious glances, he saw that they certainly knew who he was.

"Morning," he said when he caught the woman ahead of him giving him the once-over. She blushed and inched away. It seemed public opinion had indeed taken his measure and found him wanting, even when he was wearing regular street clothes.

It was kind of like back when Pluto was demoted from planetary status. Science and reason were nothing compared to long-standing opinion. He'd had to endure many a tirade from folks who insisted that Pluto was and always would be a planet, simply because that was what they believed.

He never thought he would empathize with a dwarf planet, of all things, but something about being on the receiving end of those glances had him feeling sorry for old Pluto.

The line moved quickly. J.T. stepped up to order

his stamps but was stopped by a shriek that echoed through the room.

"J. T. Delaney, it's you!"

He blinked and focused on the smiling face on the other side of the counter. It took a second to subtract twenty-five years and about that many pounds from the woman beaming at him, but once he made the connection, recognition flooded through him.

"Tracy?"

If anything, her grin grew wider. "You old dog. What took you so long to come and say hello?"

"How about, I was saving the best for last?"

It wasn't until he saw her smile that J.T. realized how much he'd needed a friendly greeting. It was nice to know that at least one person remembered him with something other than loathing.

Tracy laughed and swatted his shoulder. They passed a couple of pleasant minutes playing catch-up before the door opened to admit the next customer.

"Oh, geez," Tracy muttered. "Incoming."

J.T. glanced over his shoulder to a most unwelcome sight. Jillian McFarlane was advancing on the counter with a smile more synthetic than that on any of the themed Barbie dolls she used to collect.

"Hello, Tracy. Hello, J.T. Lovely day, isn't it?"

J.T. refrained from pointing out that the cold front accompanying Jillian would cast a pall over any day. He couldn't believe she'd actually been elected mayor. All he could think was that nobody else had wanted the job. Either that or she scared all the other candidates away.

"Mornin', Jelly. Good talking to you, Tracy. I'd better hit the road."

"Don't be a stranger, J.T." Tracy waved. J.T. thought he was free and clear until he felt Jillian's hand on his arm.

"Hang on. I need to talk to you."

Talk to Jillian? Alone? Not without body armor.

"Sorry. Have to run."

"Tracy, would you excuse us for a moment?"

Tracy crossed her arms and smirked.

"I don't know, Jillian. What if someone comes in? I could be accused of deserting my post."

Jillian shook her head so hard that her hair broke loose from the coating of spray holding it in place. The resulting wave of fumes was probably enough to be federally regulated.

"Honestly, Tracy. Go sort something, will you?"

"Whatever."

Tracy wiggled her fingers in a lazy farewell and ambled to the back room. The minute she was gone, Jillian tightened her grip on his arm.

"I had an interesting phone call this morning, J.T. From Randy Cripps down in Brockville."

It sounded familiar, but for the life of him he couldn't place it. Jillian heaved a major-league sigh.

"You know. Cripps Chips?"

Oh, right. The potato-chip guy who had been

interested in buying the coffee shop. "Why did he call you? Complaining that I'm taking so long to get back to him? I thought I'd wait until I heard from Lydia Brewster before I—"

"He wasn't complaining. He wanted me to listen to his plans for expanding here."

"Oh. Well, good for him, but I'm not doing anything until I hear from Lydia."

"J.T. Pay attention. Lydia Brewster is a very nice woman who had a very rough time. I've had no problem encouraging the town to support her and Ruth, and she's become an active, valuable member of the community. We're glad to have her." Jillian raised a finger. "But she runs a very small operation with only two permanent jobs and a handful of seasonal helpers. Cripps wants both buildings—River Joe's and Patty's Pizza. One would be a retail outlet and one would be a production site. Do you know how many jobs that could bring in?"

"Wait. Neither of those properties is big enough to put a factory in it."

She sighed again, this time speaking as if he were a particularly obtuse toddler. "It's a small-batch company. They don't need a huge amount of space. But he wants to expand, get his product in front of a larger audience so he can begin to add new markets. We have enough tourists to make that possible."

"Okay, so, good for him, good for the town." He crossed his arms. "But Lydia has first crack at it."

"But—"

"Don't waste your breath trying to talk me out of it, Jelly. River Joe's has been there forever. If she wants to keep it there, she should have that right."

"We'll help her find a new place."

"Where? You know as well as I do that the river-front area is full up. That was probably your doing, and if so, then let me be the first to say, good job, Madam Mayor." He meant it. No matter what had or had not happened in the past, he still wanted the town to thrive. "Lydia deserves that tourist traffic just as much as Mr. Crispy does."

Jillian's eyes sparked and she spoke through a jaw so tight he could probably bounce a loonie off it. "We will take care of Lydia. We owe her. But you owe this town, J.T., and this is your chance to help make things right. Think of it as balancing your karma."

"My karma's in great shape right now. Giving a widow the heave-ho just to bring someone else into her place, well, that sounds like something a whole lot more likely to feng my shui and all that jazz."

"But you—"

"Need to get going. You're right." He waved his stamps in the air, but with Jillian about to blow her top, he wondered if he was just wiggling a mata-dor's cape in front of an enraged bull. "My dad's old boathouse is available. Some cabins, too. If Mr. Chippy is interested in any of those, let me know. Otherwise, sayonara, Jillian."

THE NEXT MONDAY, Lyddie hung up the phone in her so-called office and tried to keep from either screaming, swearing or sobbing. All were appropriate reactions to the news she'd just received, but none would do a bit of good.

She balled up her apron and threw it into the far corner. It hit the wall with a highly satisfying smack before slithering down to the floor.

"Damn, damn, damn…"

Her volume increased with each utterance, forcing her to clamp her lips tight before she totally lost it. If she started yelling now, she knew it would be heard in the dining room. The last thing she needed was Nadine asking questions. Not yet. Not until she'd had a chance to vent in private.

Lyddie marched to the front of the kitchen and forced herself to take one of those deep, cleansing breaths that the Lamaze instructor had insisted would get her through the worst contractions. It had proven to be a bald-faced lie during labor, but at least now it enabled her to maintain some control as she pushed open the door to the dining room. When she peeked in she was relieved to see that business was still light. The midafternoon lull meant this was her best chance for escape.

"Nadine, will you be okay alone for a few minutes?"

"Sure thing, boss. You got a hot date you have to squeeze in?"

"Yeah, Ryan Gosling's yacht is passing through and he has a few minutes free for a quickie. Call me if you need me. Otherwise I'll be back in a few."

Without waiting for Nadine to respond, Lyddie retraced her steps through the kitchen to the back door. She shoved it open and was hit by a blast of humid heat, the scent of fresh pizza in the air and Jimmy Buffett begging for a cheeseburger in paradise. If she hadn't been in such a pissy mood she would have reveled in the assortment. As it was, she turned to glare across the parking lot at the reason for her dismay—Patty's Pizza—then cursed in frustration.

She needed to get away. Needed to vent. Alone.

Something near Patty's caught her eye. It was a man. A tall, confident, complicate-your-life-beyond-reason man, walking down the street without so much as a glance at the people he was passing.

"Typical," Lyddie said, and booted it until she was in J. T. Delaney's face.

"Hold it right there," she said without preamble.

He raised his focus from the sidewalk to her face, clearly startled. Something like pleasure flashed in his eye. It was gone in the instant it took her to scowl.

"We need to talk. *Now.*"

"Is it something I said?"

"More like something you didn't say. Get in my car. We're going for a drive."

"I love a woman who takes charge," he said, but

followed obediently as she fished her keys from her pocket and led him to her minivan.

"In." She pointed to the front seat, not even bothering to clear away the pile of library books Ben had left for her to return. This was a grown man. He could push books off the seat as well as anyone else.

She let herself in her side, slammed the door and had the car out of the parking lot before he had his seat belt fastened.

"I never pegged you for the dominatrix type," he said over her squealing tires. "Guess you never can tell."

"This is not a good time for jokes."

"Fine. No problem. Can I ask where we're going?"

She stared out the window, bit her lip. "I don't know."

"You said we need to talk."

"Yes."

"You want privacy for this discussion?"

She swallowed hard, nodded. "Yes."

"Fine. My dad's old boathouse is empty and I have the keys. You know where it is?"

She did. She passed it every day on her way to and from work. She didn't bother to answer, just stepped on the gas and carried them out of town and down River Road in record time.

She parked the car in the lot and hopped out, crossing the rutted dirt and gravel in long strides, letting her anger build as she waited by the door. For a second she realized that if anyone were watching—and in Comeback Cove, that was more likely than not—then the gossip network would soon be buzzing with the news that she and J. T. Delaney had been alone together in a deserted building.

Well, that would be one way to get folks to stop calling her the Young Widow Brewster.

It took J.T. a minute to find the right key, another couple of tense seconds to convince it to work in the stubborn lock, but at last the door was open.

"Careful," he said as she stepped inside. "I haven't been in here yet. It might not be in the best shape."

His warning was justified. Standing behind her in the half-open door, J.T. blocked a good deal of the sunshine from outside. Dust motes danced in the weak light of the sole unshuttered window, drifting slowly down to earth. Deep shadows hovered outside that small patch of light. The mingled scents of grease and gas and the sound of water lapping at boards reminded her that this was a boathouse—meaning one wrong step in the unfamiliar darkness could land her in even deeper water than she faced already.

"Hang on." J.T.'s voice, low and subdued behind her, was oddly reassuring considering he was the reason for her misfortune. "I doubt there's any electricity, but I'll try the light—wait—no, nothing.

There should be a flashlight up on the shelf. Just give me a…"

The door slammed closed, plunging them into darkness.

Lyddie yelped. J.T. cursed.

"Don't move," he said.

"I won't."

"Let me get the door open again." He moved slowly behind her. Something warm—a hand, probably—grazed the small of her back. And all of a sudden, it wasn't nervousness about the dark and the water that was making Lyddie's heart do double-time in her chest.

For the first time in four years, she was alone in the dark with a man. And all she could hear was Zoë's voice, laughing on the phone, telling her to jump him.

Oh. Dear. God.

Four years of zero interest in anything sexual ended in the space of a breath. Every erogenous zone roared back to sudden, urgent, demanding life.

She must have made some sort of sound, for in an instant he stopped his slow walk.

"Mrs. Brewster? Are you okay?"

"Fine." Except she kept remembering the way he had looked when he first walked into the shop, before she knew who he was. And the way he grinned. And the slight suggestion in his voice when she told him to get in the truck and he said he liked a woman who took charge.

Most of all she kept feeling that touch on her back, over and over. Heat pooled low in her belly. Her skin prickled with awareness. Even without contact she felt him moving. Every hesitant footfall echoed through her, pulling her focus back to that spot where she could still feel him. And each time it replayed in her mind her breath came a little faster.

"You're sure you're okay? You sound like you're hyperventilating or something."

Hyperventilating? More like panting with excitement. All she had to do was turn around and he would be there.... It could happen. It would be so easy. In less than a heartbeat she could be running her hands up that chest, pulling his shirt up to feel hot flesh against her, around her, maybe even in her....

"Lydia?"

"I'm fine. Really." At least she would be, if ever there was some light to break this spell. "Can you find the door?"

"Hang on. It's a little stiff. One good shove should—there!"

With a grunt from him and a squeal from the hinges, the door gave way. Light poured back in. Lyddie squinted against the brightness and saw J.T. outside, hunting on the ground, then propping a rock against the door.

"There." He brushed off his hands and stepped back inside. "Sorry about that. Caught me by surprise."

He wasn't the only one.

"It should stay open now, but if you'd rather go someplace else, I wouldn't blame you."

"No, I…" *Oh, great.* She was so befuddled from the hormone surge that she could barely remember why she'd brought him here. Was this how it felt to be a man, left temporarily brain-dead when the blood headed south?

Breathe, Lyddie. You are not some idiot teenager in the middle of her first infatuation, you're a grown woman with an adult job in front of you. Get with the program.

"It's hot in the sun. Let's stay here."

"You're sure? I don't dare offer you a seat. I didn't expect it to be so dusty. It's not the way I remembered it."

For a moment she forgot about the sale. This was the first time he'd been in his father's boathouse since Roy's death. Probably the first time he'd been here in twenty-five years.

Her heart ached for him. She knew all about those firsts.

"I'm sorry. We can leave if you'd rather."

He shrugged, but without any of the cockiness she'd noticed in their earlier encounters. "I had to come back sometime."

That he did. And that, too, she understood, all too well.

"So what was on your mind?"

She dragged her gaze away from his face—that way lay danger, which she could tell by the low current of warmth still humming through her when she looked at him—and focused on the patch of sunshine in the far corner.

"I called my lawyer today. I asked him to read over my lease and see if I had any rights of first refusal on the property."

"You don't. I already checked."

Give the man credit. At least he wasn't gloating.

"I know that now. Anyway, he let me in on another little item he thought I should know about." She crossed her arms as the memory stabbed her once again. "He told me that all sales in the business zone must be approved by the planning board."

"Right."

"*And* that they would never let me buy just my building, because I share a parking lot with Patty's Pizza."

"You're kidding."

Another bonus point. He sounded truly, sincerely astonished by this news.

"Are you really surprised, or are you just a great actor?"

"You thought I knew?"

She turned to face him. Mistake. The swaggering

jokester had disappeared, replaced by a sincerity that made her catch her breath. She had a feeling that she was seeing the real J. T. Delaney for the first time. And it was a damned intriguing sight.

She spoke carefully, uncertain how to proceed. "It's your property. It would make sense that you would know."

"I've looked at some of the papers, but not everything yet. I never had to know this before."

That made sense. Damn.

"So I guess the price of my building has just jumped."

He hesitated before nodding. "If this is true, then yeah. It will have to."

Her throat tightened. She could have managed payments on her building alone. But hers and Patty's? The possibility was looking slimmer by the minute.

"Let me guess. You just got off the phone when you ran into me in the parking lot."

"Right in one."

"That explains a lot."

He was being way too understanding. Though maybe she could twist that logic for her own benefit. Maybe that overwhelming desire she'd felt when the lights went out had nothing to do with him. Maybe it was just a by-product of the frustration she'd felt, a kind of emotional leftover that misfired.

She risked another glance at him—strong arms, firm chest, a mouth that begged to be explored.

Nope. Not a leftover.

She sighed. "I need to get back."

"Maybe we could—" He stopped abruptly, then ducked his head. "You're right. We'd better go."

They walked to the van in silence, which persisted through the drive back up River Road. Despite the circumstances, it was a surprisingly comfortable silence. Lyddie almost wished for the pure, hot anger she'd felt a few minutes earlier. That was a lot easier to understand than the mix of despair, hopelessness and residual lust still swirling inside her.

She pulled into the lot that was the source of this latest dilemma. They were sure to be spotted. If she acted like there was nothing to hide, maybe the gossips would go easy on her.

She reached for the door handle, then stopped. It had to be said. "J.T.?"

"Yeah?"

"I'm sorry I dragged you off the way I did. That was wrong."

"Don't worry about it. I've been expecting to get lynched ever since I walked back into town."

That sounded more like the J. T. Delaney she knew. Especially when he slid out of the van, then poked his head back in to flash her that killer grin and added, "But if I'd known it was gonna happen in broad daylight with a pretty woman, I would have offered myself up a whole lot sooner."

CHAPTER FOUR

THREE DAYS AFTER Lydia Brewster kidnapped him, J.T. drove his mother downtown to help him pick out paint. Not that she was going to make it easy on him.

"You're working too hard," Iris said as they walked through the double-wide doors of McCoy's Hardware. "You don't need to paint the cabins. You should take some time off, have some fun."

"I am having fun, Ma. Those fumes will do it every time."

"Oh, you." She swatted his arm playfully, but he saw the way her lower lip trembled as they made their way to the paint aisle.

That, in a nutshell, was the problem. Iris refused to believe he was really going to make her move. Rather, she believed it, but let it be known at every possible opportunity that she disagreed vehemently with this decision. No matter how much he talked about Tucson, she insisted that he could stay in Comeback Cove if he would only try. The fact that she was the one who couldn't stay—not without risking her life—seemed completely irrelevant to her.

It was almost a relief when the owner hurried around the counter to greet them.

"Morning, Iris. J.T. What can I do for you?" Steve McCoy, son of the McCoy who'd run the store in J.T.'s day, spoke to them both but kept his focus on J.T. It was that assessing gaze that worried him. Steve wasn't giving J.T. the "potential shoplifter" once-over that his father had perfected all those years ago. Instead, the expression on Steve's face could best be described as...wary.

"We need paint," Iris replied. "White. With some yellow and green for trim."

Again, Steve's attention was directed at J.T. "Is this for the coffee shop? Anything to do with Lyddie gets a discount."

"Nope." J.T. ignored Iris's elbow in his ribs. He still wasn't sure if the rule regarding shared parking lots had been on the books for years or if it was something Jillian might have shoved through to tip the scales in Mr. Crunchy's favor. In any case, he wasn't about to discuss that property with anyone other than Lydia, Iris and his lawyer.

"The cottages," Iris explained after frowning at her son. "Roy had some cottages upriver that we used to rent out. They need freshening up before we can sell them."

J.T. suppressed a snort. They needed a hell of a lot more than freshening. There were floorboards to replace, wallpaper to strip and steps that were lawsuits in the making. He would have his hands full getting them fixed up by the end of summer.

"Gotcha. Well, then." Steve pulled out a few paint chips. "Here's some popular yellows and greens. Why don't you look them over, Iris? And J.T., would you mind giving me a hand with a load of mulch in the back?"

J.T. had no doubt that the "load" waiting for him had nothing whatsoever to do with mulch. But before he could say something about a bad back, Iris beat him to the punch.

"Of course he'll help. J.T., you've been showing off those muscles since you got home. Go put them to use."

God save him from mothers on a mission.

He followed Steve into the back room. But as he'd expected, Steve had something else in mind.

"Hang on there a minute, will ya, J.T.?"

J.T. came to a halt between a shelf loaded with potting soil and another one overflowing with hose heads. He hoped he could look reasonably surprised by this request.

Are you really surprised, or are you just a great actor?

He frowned in an attempt to chase Lydia's voice from his memory. He couldn't deal with that particular problem now.

'Course, he'd spent the whole night telling himself that. It hadn't done a bit of good then, either. No amount of rationalizing had made him forget that moment in the dark when she had made that little sound he could swear had nothing to do with fear and everything to do with—

"So listen." Steve pulled open a box of hammers and began stacking them on the closest shelf. "I hear you've got a full plate ahead of you, selling and packing and such."

"You're very well-informed," J.T. said wryly.

"Small town, big mouths. Speaking of which, I have to ask—how long do you think this is gonna take?"

It was a good thing he bore no illusions about his standing in this town. He could get a complex from people asking how long he planned to stick around.

"I'll wrap things up as fast as I can, but you know it's not all up to me." Then, because it was Steve asking, and at one time he and Steve had been pretty tight, he risked a guess.

"People getting nervous because I'm here?"

"Some."

"They think I'm gonna start another fire?" J.T. paused, watching Steve carefully. "Or do you think I'm going to start talking about what really happened that night?"

"Look." Steve swallowed hard as he placed the next hammer on the shelf. "I know you got a raw deal back then. You don't know how many times I wished I'd had the guts to stand up for you, tell people the truth. But I didn't. I'm not proud of it, but what's done is done, and now I—"

"Easy, Steve." J.T. couldn't take much more of watching the guy fall all over himself. "Look. I'm not here to dig up old memories or start any rumors. None of that crap. As far as I'm concerned, the fire is ancient history."

"A lot of folks don't feel that way."

"Sure. A lot of meddling old busybodies with nothing better to do than—"

"A lot of customers who live here year-round and keep my business going. Folks who make it possible for me to make my child support payments and keep some other people employed, too."

Oh.

"Let me get this straight. You're saying that because I came back, people are talking about the fire again. And that's a conversation that some folks—say, you, and Mike Smithers, and Larry Brown and Tim Pattinson and some others—would rather didn't get started again."

Steve's head bobbed in what J.T. assumed was agreement. "That's about it."

"I see."

J.T. rocked back on his heels, staring out at the yard. If he moved slightly to the right he could catch a glimpse of the river in the distance, the blue calling to him like an old lover.

"They're all still here in town?"

"Some. The ones who aren't still have family here."

He thought back to the new stores on the streets, the names taking on deeper meaning.

He hadn't been alone the night of the fire, but he'd been the only one spotted at the scene, the only one to flee town. The others had stayed. Stayed, and kept silent.

And helped the town rebuild.

"Steve. Look. I'm not trying to stir up anything. And I'm not—okay, for a while I was pissed that no one said anything, but seriously, it wasn't like we could undo what happened."

"So you're not trying to set the record straight?"

He sighed. "I am here to sell off the properties and get my mother packed up and move her to Tucson with me. That's it."

Relief flooded Steve's face.

"Right. Well, then. Let's get you some paint."

"Got anything that'll whitewash the past?" J.T. asked, and followed Steve back into store.

LYDDIE HAD COME a long way in the years since Glenn died. The pain of losing him was always there but manageable now, the jagged edges blunted by time. But some days still ripped her. Today was one.

"I hate Father's Day," Tish said. Lyddie bit her lip and concentrated on working through the snarl in Tish's long auburn curls.

"Why do we have to go? It's yucky. You get sad

and Gram cries. And it's hot there, and you won't let me run. I have to be a *laaaaady*." She wrinkled her nose at her reflection. "It's not like Daddy can see us or anything. Are you almost done? I want my hair short. Can I get it cut soon?"

"We'll get it cut when school is out. I'll be done in another minute—faster if you hold still. And as for why we're going to the cemetery…" But for this, Lyddie had no easy answer. How to explain to a seven-year-old that some things are done just for the sake of doing them, for the assurance that you've done what you could even when you know it won't make a bit of difference?

"We're not going for Daddy." She flipped the comb around and parted Tish's hair down the middle. "We're going for us. So we can remember."

Silence. Then—

"But I don't remember him, Mommy."

Lyddie closed her eyes and concentrated on the feel of her daughter's hair, soft and curling in her hands. "I know, sweets. You were too little when we lost him. But it's a way of remembering that you had a daddy who loved you. That's important for you to know."

"I know *that* already," Tish grumbled, but she didn't sound quite as reluctant. "Are you doing regular braids or fancy ones?"

"Fancy."

"Oh, great." Tish slid down in the chair, and blew

out a drama-queen sigh that had to have come from her sister. Lyddie snickered and concentrated on the intricate weavings of a French braid, grateful that Tish had given up her protest.

An hour later, standing on the soft ground in front of Glenn's headstone, she would have given anything to be snickering again. Ruth had left them, overcome by tears as she always was on these outings. It was just Lyddie and the kids in an artificially quiet circle. Even Ben had consented to hold Tish's hand. And once again, as always happened, Lyddie looked from the tombstone to her children and wondered what she was supposed to say next.

She'd read all the books on helping kids deal with grief. But in real life, standing with the hot sun beating down on them and the murmurs of other visitors in the background, none of those well-meaning suggestions ever sounded helpful. Especially when the kids seemed more bored than sad.

"Are we done yet?" Tish asked.

"No." Lyddie had no idea what they should do, but she knew Glenn deserved more than three minutes of awkward silence.

"But we gave him the flowers. And the sandwiches."

"I know, sweetie."

Tish dropped Lyddie's hand to twist the sash of her pink eyelet sundress. "Why do we give him sandwiches, anyway? He can't eat 'em."

"Tish!" Sara had the adolescent eye-roll mastered.

Ben spoke up. "The ancient Egyptians used to leave food with the mummies. They thought it would be needed in the afterlife. And they left money and pets, and sometimes slaves were even—"

"Enough, Ben." Lyddie could already imagine the nightmares Tish would conjure up that night. "Why don't you tell Tish about the peanut butter sandwiches?"

Ben squinted behind his glasses. He opened his mouth, then closed it. "Uh, well…"

No. This couldn't be happening. Ben had the best memory of any of them. Lyddie refused to believe he could have forgotten.

Sara jumped in. "Daddy ate a peanut butter sandwich every day, Tish. With fluff and black-berry jam."

He always said I was the jam and he was the fluff, and the peanut butter was the love.

She reached for Tish's hand once again, gave it a little squeeze and looked at Ben. "Did you really forget, bud?"

His Adam's apple bobbed as he swallowed once, twice. "I guess I did. Sorry, Mom."

"Don't apologize, honey, you didn't do anything wrong. I just wish… What do you remember?"

Ben shrugged. "Um…well, stuff. He read me stories at bedtime. And he taught me how to skate. That was fun."

"Sara? Can you tell Tish a story or two about your dad?"

Sara frowned and twisted the daughter's ring Lyddie had given her on her thirteenth birthday. "Okay. Well, I remember one time when we were in church, and I was bored, and you were working in the nursery, and he took a five-dollar bill from his pocket and folded it so it looked like a man's shirt. That was cool." She frowned. "Then Ben yanked it away from me and it ripped."

"Did not."

"You did, too."

"I did—" He stopped, flushed. "Maybe I did. I don't remember."

"It's okay," Sara said after a moment's silence. "You might not have grabbed it. I tell myself that story a lot. So I might have changed it a bit."

"Why do you tell yourself the story, Sara?" Lyddie had planned to stay quiet and let the kids lead the way, but she had the feeling this was important.

"Because…well… Promise you won't get mad?"

Oh, God.

"Promise."

"Okay. Well. Sometimes, I kind of… It's hard to remember him. You know?"

"Because it makes you sad?"

"No." Sara lifted her head, looked directly at Lyddie with the wide-set eyes she'd inherited from her father. "I mean, I can't remember. Not what he was really like. Just the stories I tell myself."

Lyddie had the same feeling she'd had the year she mistakenly wore spike heels to the cemetery: like she was sinking into something better left untouched, but she had no choice because she was already stuck.

"You really can't remember him? But you were almost ten. I thought—I hoped you were old enough…"

"I remember some stuff. And sometimes I get this feeling, like I'm doing a Daddy thing, but I can't really say why. It's just like I said. It's all stories now that I tell myself to make me remember." She looked down again. "And sometimes I'm not even sure if it's really something that happened at all or if it's a whole bunch of memories I put together in my head."

Ben nodded. "Me, too. It's like he was a story, not a real person."

This was wrong. So, so wrong. Of course Tish had no memories of Glenn, but for Sara and Ben to be losing him, too… Glenn had adored his children. They needed to know who he was and how much he had loved them.

Tonight, she thought. Tonight she would sit down and go through the photo album and start writing stories to go with all the pictures. And everything else she could remember. But she'd already told them all her stories. They needed to see him in a new light, as a person who was once a kid like them, not a fading memory.

Lyddie glanced around the cemetery. For the first time she focused on the other visitors walking the gravel paths and laying flowers on graves. Father's Day had brought out the crowd. Surely, somewhere in this quiet place of remembrance, there was someone who could tell her children something new about their father.

"Mommy, can we go? I'm bored."

"No, Tish. Not yet." There. On the other side of an ostentatious marble angel, there was Harley Prestwick, town historian. He'd lived in Comeback Cove forever. Surely he would have a tale or two.

"Wait here," she ordered the kids. "I'll be right back."

Gravel flew from beneath her sensible pumps as she walked double-time down the path. For a man in his seventies, Harley could move. It wasn't until she reached out to tap his shoulder that she realized her request might seem a bit bizarre, or that Harley might not be up for company at the moment. But Harley had never been known to suffer in silence. And surely the needs of three children couldn't be ignored.

"I have a favor to ask," she began, and explained her request as quickly as possible, stopping a couple of times to catch her breath. She really had to make time to exercise.

Luckily, Harley was not only agreeable, but he also seemed eager to have someone to talk to on this sunny afternoon. Lyddie walked beside him back to the kids and sent up a prayer of thanks.

Within minutes, Harley was seated on a granite bench, Tish beside him, Ben and Sara leaning against a pair of flowering crabs.

"Well," the old man began, "your father was a couple of years behind my boys in school. But I remember him well. Always a nice fellow, even back then, you know. Polite. And good-hearted, too, looking out for the little kids…"

Harley droned on. Lyddie checked the kids' faces and saw what she feared: the initial curiosity had dwindled to bored endurance. Once again, they were only hearing what they'd heard a hundred times before. Glenn the saint, Glenn the selfless one, Glenn the hero.

Maybe this hadn't been such a great idea after all.

She turned to see if there were any other possibilities wandering the cemetery and found herself almost face-to-face with J. T. Delaney.

"Oh!" She stepped back, flushing at the realization that her breasts had been about two inches from his chest. Memories of the boathouse engulfed her. She looked away, fast, before she could start blushing. Or worse—imagining.

"Sorry," he said. "Didn't mean to scare you."

"It's okay. You just caught me by surprise."

"I cut across the grass." He grinned. "Years of practice playing graveyard tag."

"What a lovely pastime." He looked rather lovely, too, she had to admit. The tight shorts and chest-hugging shirts had been abandoned today in favor of a yellow-striped short-sleeved shirt and gray cargo pants. Not exactly Sunday-go-to-meeting clothes, but it gave him a far more respectable air. Almost like an adult.

Which made her wonder...

"How old are you?"

"How old am I?" His eyes sparked with familiar mischief when he grinned. "To borrow a line from the song, old enough to know better, but still too young to care."

Lyddie felt the heat rise to her face once again. She must be as pink as the blossoms on the crab tree. At this rate, she could pose for the "before" pictures in an ad for sunscreen.

"I'm sorry. That was incredibly rude. It's just, I was wondering—did you know Glenn? My husband? Back in school, I mean."

He seemed to tense for a second, though so quickly that Lyddie was sure she had imagined it. "Sure I did. Not really well—he was a year ahead of me—but we were in the church senior-high group together for a while."

Two facts registered at the same time: if he'd been a year behind Glenn, then she and J.T. were probably the same age. And the thought of the Comeback Cove hellion in a church youth group was almost enough to make her snort with laughter.

"I have a favor to ask." She spoke quickly to cover her giggles. Once again she outlined her request. Surely even a church group had to have had some wild times with J.T. involved.

SHE SPOKE SO quietly that he had to lean close to catch all her words. Not that he minded. The nearer he drew to her skin, the more aware he was of a subtle perfume even more alluring than the crab apple scent filling the air. There was a warmth that surrounded her. Maybe it was all that pink—the faint rose that washed her cheeks, the deeper hue of her dress.

He'd never seen her in anything but work clothes. The long shorts she usually wore were definitely all business. But this skirt that kind of drifted around her shins, well, that lent a whole different interpretation to the bit of leg visible below. The pant things said *go no further.* The dress—

"So do you think you could help me out?"

Damn. She'd caught him unprepared. "Sorry?"

"Okay, I guess I garbled that. I need a story or two. About Glenn. One in which he's something less than a saint."

Could he tell tales on Glenn? Hell, yeah. Including at least one that he could guarantee she had no desire to hear.

The irony of her request made him look away. He could well understand her desire to have her kids learn some new things about their father, but cripes, Glenn had died saving this town. Nothing would be served by telling them things that would minimize what he had done, what they had lost.

But surely he could come up with something. And to tell the truth, he was feeling a bit lost himself after paying his respects to his own father. He would be grateful for the chance to make some kids smile.

"Lead the way."

He followed her to the group beneath the tree. Harley Prestwick wouldn't take kindly to being replaced, but tough. If the kids' slumped shoulders and glazed eyes were any indication, this crowd had checked out a long time ago. He was pretty sure the only things holding them in place were inertia and good manners.

"...and I looked at my boy Jeff and I said to him, yes sir, you watch that Brewster boy and you'll be in great shape." Harley beamed at his audience, then caught sight of J.T. His mouth twisted as if he'd tasted something sour. "Hello, J.T."

"Afternoon, Harley. Hi, guys. I'm J. T. Delaney, and I know you've all heard about me so you can stop pretending to be polite when I know you want to stare." That got him a grin from the boy, who said his name was Ben. The oldest girl, Sara, blushed as she introduced herself and stared off in the distance, just like her mother. The little girl eyed him up and down.

"I'm Tish. What's J.T. mean?"

"It's my initials. Justin Tanner. But around here it means Just Trouble."

Well, that certainly wiped the smile from Lydia's face.

Tish studied him again, then propped her hands on her hips. "I don't believe you. You're too nice for that name."

Damn. Outed by a kid. Did she get that ability to see beyond the surface from her mother?

"So I hear you guys want to hear about your dad when he was a kid."

Harley stirred from the turtle-in-the-shell pose he'd taken up when J.T. started talking. "We're fine here, J.T. I told them all they need to know."

More like he'd turned a good but human man into a candidate for sainthood, from what J.T. had seen.

"I'm sure you told them all the important stuff, Harley, about what a great guy Glenn was. But with all due respect—"

Harley snorted. Behind him, Lydia slapped her hand over her mouth as if to suppress a sudden urge to break into laughter.

God, she was cute.

"With all due respect, I think I knew a side of

Glenn that you never saw. Did you guys ever hear about the time he almost poisoned the science teacher?"

"No way!"

That got them. All three kids inched closer. Even Lydia seemed surprised.

All of a sudden, J.T. wished he'd spent more time with Glenn Brewster. Not just because he'd been a great guy, but so that J.T. could keep spinning stories to bring that soft glow to Lydia's eyes.

"Okay. This was way back. I was going into grade twelve, so your dad would have been heading into grade thirteen."

"Grade thirteen?" Ben gave him a dubious look.

"Uh-huh. Back then, we could finish up after grade twelve, or stick around for an extra year. It was supposed to get us ready for university." He winked at the kid. "'Course, I never got to do that year, but your dad did. Anyway, it was just before school started. Your dad was helping out down at the coffee shop and…"

In the middle of the tale, J.T. realized that Harley had disappeared. By the end of the saga of Glenn's adventures in trail riding, he noticed that Lydia had joined Tish on the grass, pulling the little one onto her lap and sharing in the laughter. She had a great laugh. It was full and throaty and brimming with life, and he'd lay money that she didn't get to use it nearly as often as she should.

He wished he could do something about that.

Somewhere around the fourth account, right around the time he noticed that Sara was casting some mighty curious glances between him and her mom, he stumbled over an unexpected truth.

"...so Glenn gave the guy the coffee, never even asked who he was even though this crowd had followed him in, and then—"

And then, he got it. It was so clear that he wondered how the hell he'd missed it before.

He didn't realize he'd stopped talking until Ben scrunched up his nose and shoved his glasses higher up the bridge.

"J.T.? Is something wrong?" Lydia's laughter was gone. The frown lines between her eyebrows were back, and he gave himself a mental kick.

"Sorry." He pulled himself together. "I, uh, just remembered something. Anyway, the guy went to pay and he pulled out his credit card and then..."

Lydia didn't care about the location of her business. Well, maybe she did—she wasn't dumb, she knew what a prize spot she had—but that wasn't it. She wanted the building itself. Lydia Brewster wanted to hold on to the building because her husband used to work there and she was trying to keep it for her kids. Just like she wanted stories that would make him seem real. She wanted to make sure her kids—Glenn's kids—would have every chance to know the person he had been. Not just from pictures and memories, but by walking the floors he'd walked and doing the things he'd done.

At that moment he vowed that he would do whatever it took to make sure Lydia got to keep her building. After what she and her kids had gone through, they deserved that much. After all, a hero should be remembered. Not sainted, not idolized, but remembered.

Even if that hero had been part of the group that had almost destroyed the town twenty-five years ago.

CHAPTER FIVE

A COUPLE OF days later, Lyddie stood dumbfounded in front of the bank manager's desk and tried to make sense of what he was telling her.

"You're kidding, right?"

Ted McFarlane—sometimes known irreverently as the First Man, in reference to him being married to Mayor Jillian—shifted in his chair. It was obvious that he didn't like being the bearer of bad news.

Tough.

"Lyddie, if it were up to me I'd approve the loan. I know you're good for the money. But I have other people to answer to, and they don't understand—"

She huffed out her disbelief. "Spare me the song and dance, Ted. Jillian doesn't want me to buy the building, does she?"

He tugged at the tie that always seemed out of place around his thick jock neck. "Jillian has nothing to do with bank business."

"Really. So it's just a coincidence that my request was turned down two days after I heard that the potato-chip guy from Brockville was dropping hints about a major donation to the school upgrade fund if he got the building?"

"You heard that?"

"Loud and clear."

"It's merely a rumor at this point. And as I said, that has nothing to do with your loan."

Like hell it didn't. Nadine had been a steady source of reliable gossip. She'd dropped a couple of hints over the past few days that Jillian wasn't happy about the possibility of Lyddie buying the buildings. Her Worship wanted River Joe's to continue, but she wasn't averse to a move if it meant stable jobs.

In all honesty, Lyddie couldn't blame Jillian. The mayor had to put the good of the town first. But no one else knew what that building meant to her. There were mornings when she could still picture Glenn's head popping around the door after they stopped in to see his dad, days when she could still see him lounging in the chairs by the fireplace. He *lived* in that building. Letting it go wasn't an option.

"You know, Lyddie, the only problem is the amount of the loan. If you were to ask for less— say, enough to buy just one building that isn't on the waterfront—I'm sure we could work something out."

Of course he could. Jillian would approve of that.

"No, thanks."

"I am sorry about this. You know how much the town appreciates all you've done over the years."

There it was—the opening she needed. It was

impossible to miss the guilt in Ted's voice. He was being manipulated by Jillian, no doubt, and Lyddie would bet her last dollar that he was looking for an excuse to reverse his decision. Ted wasn't a bad guy. One mention of Glenn's name, one tear down her cheek, and the money would be hers.

Do you really want to tie yourself so permanently to a town where they call you the Young Widow Brewster?

Enough. She would find another way—one that didn't involve losing her self-respect.

"Goodbye, Ted. I'll see you around."

"I…uh… Will you be okay, Lyddie? Can we talk about a smaller loan?"

"No, thanks. Rumor has it there are other banks. Even some that aren't in Comeback Cove."

J.T. TURNED OFF the highway onto the road to the Cove after a long day in Cornwall taking care of assorted business matters. All he wanted was to go home, get something to eat and avoid getting suckered into watching another episode of *Downton Abbey* with his mother.

Then he realized what he'd been thinking, and had to laugh. When was the last time he'd thought of this place as home?

He cranked some classic Guess Who and slowed for the infamous Maple Road Bend in front of the high school, checking twice to make sure no idiots were out to prove their manhood by flying through with their lights—

"What the hell?"

He jammed on the brakes, sending the car swerving. Something had just raced across the shadows of the school lawn.

Probably a deer. But as he switched off the engine and opened the door, he knew there was nothing doe-like about what he'd seen.

He stood silent with his hands braced on the car roof, peering into the darkness. The sky was clear but moonless—great for stargazing, not so good for picking out activity. He forced himself to be patient, waiting for his eyes to adjust. Soon, he knew, whatever was hiding would move again.

There! Beside the row of oaks that marked the property line, a burst of movement and an abbreviated gust of laughter gave him his answer. Kids. At least three of them. Given the time of night and the speed with which they were fleeing, they were undoubtedly up to no good. The question was, had he spotted them before or after it was mission accomplished?

If he had half a brain, he would get back in the car and drive straight home. Pulling over in the lot and walking around the school in search of damage was nothing short of idiocy. If there were damage, and if he were found at the scene—highly likely, given his history—then he'd be looking at a hefty fine, minimum, for destroying public property. The town would finally get the chance to pin something on him.

Another movement caught his eye. Something was in the bushes by the flagpole.

Walk away, Delaney.

He meant to. He did. But a low sound drifted toward him, like a muffled moan of pain, and in a second he was sprinting across the grass. If some little jackass had got himself hurt—

But it wasn't *any* little jackass, as he saw the minute he pushed aside the fragrant cedar branches and took in the frightened face before him.

"Ben?"

The kid bit his lip in a gesture that seemed all too familiar. His eyes were bigger than J.T. remembered. And he was crouching, as if he couldn't quite bear his own weight.

"Come on, Ben. I know it's you. J. T. Delaney, remember? I talked to you guys at the cemetery the other day."

Ben's brave expression did a slow crumple.

"You hurt yourself?"

A nod. At least it was a response.

"Okay. Let's call your mom and get you home. Think you can walk?"

There was a crackle of twigs and dry leaves as the boy moved—then a small yip as he lurched forward and landed heavily against J.T.'s side.

"Whoa, buddy. Is it your ankle?"

"Yeah."

All of a sudden, *Downton Abbey* was looking a lot more appealing.

Ten minutes later, J.T. pulled into the Brewster driveway. Ben spoke only to give directions that J.T. didn't need, but pretended otherwise just to haul a few words out of the kid. There was a story here and he was pretty sure he understood it. Too bad he couldn't get a little corroboration.

As he killed the engine he saw a figure hurrying down the porch steps. Lydia probably started watching out the window the minute he called. The leap of pleasure he felt when he saw her was a welcome surprise. The fact that she smelled like vanilla and made his heart beat a little faster was a bonus.

She beat him to the passenger side of the car.

"Oh, Benjie. What happened?"

The boy mumbled halfheartedly. "Nothing."

She frowned. J.T. felt oddly jubilant, glad that she wasn't taking the attitude in stride.

"Let's get you inside and have a look at the ankle." Her tone shifted. "Then we'll talk."

He helped Ben out of the car. Lydia braced the boy on the other side. It seemed like a good system until their hands met somewhere in the middle of Ben's rigid back, sending a *zing* straight down his arm.

"Sorry." Lydia curled her fingers away from his, but he wasn't ready to lose that touch yet.

"Actually, it will probably work better if we hold hands. Or at least grab wrists. We'll be more stable that way."

"Oh. Okay." She extended her hand and he circled her wrist with his fingers.

She felt… He wasn't sure how to describe her. Soft, but strong. Pliant, but not something he could shove around.

Holding Lydia's wrist, he decided, was probably a sneak preview of how it would be to hold her in his arms.

"Ready?" She sounded slightly breathy, the way she had in the boathouse. Damn. Did she feel it, too?

Good.

Soon they deposited the boy on a sofa in an exceedingly cluttered family room. Here in the light, J.T. could clearly see the paleness of Ben's face. He was one hurting puppy.

"Let's have a look." Lydia kneeled on the floor and tugged on the lace of Ben's sneaker.

The slump of her shoulders made him frown. It must get damned tiring, being the only parent 24/7.

"Here. Let me have a look." He moved in and probed the ankle with experienced fingers. "How's it feel here? How about here?"

"You sound like you know what you're doing."

"I ran cross-country in school. I've dealt with a few ankles in my time." Her vanilla scent was making it damned difficult for him to think clearly. "I bet that if you ice it and keep it elevated overnight, it should be a lot better by morning."

"Sounds good." Lydia was back to her usual brisk efficiency. "We'll deal with the ankle tonight. The rest will wait."

J.T. hid a grin as he straightened. He wouldn't want to be in Ben's half-laced sneaker in the morning.

"Need me to get him up the stairs?"

The look she sent him was so filled with gratitude, he felt like he'd just rescued a drowning kitten. "That would be wonderful. My mother-in-law is at bingo tonight, and this lug is getting too big for me to manage on my own."

"My pleasure."

And it was, even though the presence of a banister for Ben to lean on meant there was no excuse to touch Lydia. By the time he got Ben to his room— one so filled with geek apparatus that it could have been his own at that age—Lydia had joined them with ice packs and extra pillows. He headed back down, listening to the soft rise and fall of their voices while he waited for Lydia. Only because he needed to tell her about the circumstances surrounding Ben's injury, of course. When she crept down the stairs, her smile was weary but still welcoming.

"Let me guess," she said softly. "He didn't get injured while helping a little old lady cross the street."

"Only if she's a hell of a runner."

"Okay. You'd better give me the whole story." She nodded toward the door. "Let's go out on the porch so I don't wake anybody when I start to fume. Can I get you anything? Some coffee, or a beer, or—"

"I'm good, thanks."

And he was. Despite the fatigue creeping in after a long day of driving and meetings, despite the dread he felt at needing to give her news she didn't want to hear, just the thought of spending a half hour on a secluded porch with Lydia made him feel inordinately cheerful.

Once outside, he settled himself in the rocking chair she indicated. She sat in the chair beside his, kicked off her flip-flops and propped bare feet on the railing, sighing as she leaned back. He was tempted to throw off his sandals and follow suit. The question was, would he be able to resist a game of footsie?

"Okay." She spoke without looking at him, head tilted back, eyes closed. "Give it to me straight."

He summarized the events and his suspicions, stressing that Ben had not acted alone. He didn't want her to think that her kid was the only budding juvenile delinquent in town. Especially when he mentioned the cans of spray paint he'd spied in the bushes.

When he finished, she sat in silence. She was so quiet, her breathing so steady, that for a moment he thought she might have fallen asleep. He watched the rise and fall of her breasts and felt an unexpected contentment creep over him. What was it about this woman that felt so damned right?

At last she spoke. "I'm glad you were the one to catch him. Someone else might not have been so willing to give him a second chance."

Did she mean that only someone with his history would be willing to cut the kid some slack? Honor among thieves, and all that? He hoped not. He wanted her to see that there was more to him than a lousy reputation.

But they weren't talking about him, and neither did he want to go down that road at the moment. So he settled for saying, "Yeah, well, they get kind of protective about old Maple Road School here in—"

She made a strange sound, like a smothered cough.

"What did I say?"

"It's not Maple Road School anymore."

"It isn't? When did they—oh. Right." He remembered now. The school had been rechristened a couple years ago. It was now known as Brewster Memorial.

So not only was the kid out to vandalize public property, but he was also going after something dedicated to his father and grandfather. Wouldn't Freud have a field day with that one?

"You can tell me to take a hike," he said, eyes firmly fixed upward on the stars that he'd been watching since he was Ben's age, "but I remember summers around here when I was a kid. Boring as hell. Still the same?"

"Afraid so. There's day camp, but he's too old for that, and he's too young for a job."

"So he spends his day plotting trouble with his friends?"

"It sure looks that way." She sighed. "I didn't think… Not to sound like a bragging mom, but he's smart. Really smart. Which is great except that he's kind of outgrowing everyone around him, so when he started hanging out with those kids, I hoped… well…" She pressed her fingers to her forehead. "He's not a bad kid. Really. He's just… It's a hard age, I guess."

If she hadn't said that, he might have been able to say good-night and walk away. Might have. But how many times had he overheard his mother defend him to his father using those same words?

"Is he any good with his hands?"

With that, she finally stirred, lifting her head to face him. "Excuse me?"

"Can he hammer a nail and handle a paintbrush?"

"Sure, but—"

"I have three cottages to fix up before I can sell them. I could use a set of extra hands." Yeah, like a hole in the head.

She sat upright, staring at him with a gleam in her eyes visible even in the darkness of the night. "You want to hire Ben?"

"If he's interested. I'd pay him a few bucks a day and work him hard."

"Hard enough that he'd be too tired to go out and make trouble at night?"

"Hard enough to cramp his style, at least. It's tough to totally wear out a kid that age."

"Why?"

He had half a dozen answers, most of which were so ill-formed and illogical that he couldn't speak them aloud. How to tell her he wanted to ease some of her burden, smooth the worry lines from around her eyes?

He settled for the one reason that made sense, the one that had hit home when he saw Ben's room. "He reminds me of myself."

Too late, he realized that might not be considered a compliment in certain circles. Luckily, Lydia didn't seem to care—at least if the way she almost bounced out of the chair was any indication.

"I honestly don't know how to thank you. That's so generous, I—"

"It's pure selfishness. I'm getting too old to keep bending over, picking up dropped nails."

"It's a lot more than that to me. And Ben." She gave a short laugh, as if in disbelief. "Give me a minute to catch up. Um, when do you want him to start? What exactly would he be doing? Oh, and he'll be gone for three weeks later in the summer, is that a problem?"

"I can work around it. Maybe we'll be finished with the cottages and ready for something else by then. Where's he going?"

"Science camp in Toronto. It's his big summer adventure. Sara went to Vancouver, he gets to be a total geek for three weeks and Tish is going to—"

She stopped abruptly.

"Let me guess. Tish will be going to spy school and you forgot that you weren't supposed to tell."

"What?" Again she laughed, higher this time, almost nervously. What had caused that? "No, no, she's going to Disney with Ruth. I just... I'm sorry, I just realized something for the first time. Anyway. Ben. Thank you." She leaned forward, placed a warm palm on his forearm as if to pat it, then pulled back abruptly. Damn. He'd been looking forward to a couple more seconds.

"Um, J.T., since you're here and we're talking about unpleasant things already, I have to tell you. There's a problem with the sale."

Crap. "What is it?"

"My loan request was turned down."

Jillian. "You're kidding."

"I wish."

"Did they give you a reason?"

Her laugh was bitter. "Oh, yeah. Ted said—"

"Hang on," he said, all vengeful thoughts of the mayor momentarily knocked aside. "Ted McFarlane?"

"Mmm-hmm. He's the manager down at the bank."

"*Ted* is a bank manager? Do you know how many times he had to take grade nine math?"

Her laugh was far too short. "To his credit—well, maybe not—anyway, I don't think he's the one really responsible for turning me down."

"Of course not. It's Jillian. She wants some potato-chip guy to get the buildings. She can't get it through her head that she has no say in who buys my property."

"Bingo. She believes she's doing what's best for the town, and if that means I have to move, she'll do whatever it takes to make sure that happens."

"She always was a determined one." And no way in hell was he going to let her do this.

"Yeah, well, so am I. I'll apply to another bank. It's going to slow things down, I'm sorry, but—"

"Do you want to move?"

"No."

"Even though you know that you're going to end up on Jillian's naughty list?"

"At the moment, I couldn't care less." She stared into the night, the tight curl of her toes negating her casual air. "Well, yes. I do care. But I'm not giving up. Not that easily."

"What would you think of me holding the mortgage?"

Her feet thunked to the floor as she twisted to face him. Surprise widened her eyes, brought a joy-

ful light to them for a fraction of a second before
something shuttered them down.

"No."

"No? Lydia, I'm offering you the perfect way out
of this. You can tell Ted and the rest of the town to
do whatever they want. If you want to buy the properties, they're yours."

"I said no."

"Are you—"

"Damn it, J.T., no!"

Well, hell. He could understand it if she'd said
she didn't want to have to deal with the fallout. Or
that she wanted a regular mortgage, or had changed
her mind about the whole thing. But this made no
sense. She acted like she was pissed as hell, and it
was directed at him. "Can I ask why not?"

"I don't trust your motives."

Crap.

He took a deep breath and leaned forward, giving
himself time to get the words right. "Okay, look. I'm
not going to pretend that I don't find you attractive.
I like you, Lydia. But if you think I'm offering this
to try to get you to—hell, you don't think I'm that
much of a jerk, do you?"

For a second she did nothing but stare at him with
her mouth slightly open. Then she went very, very
red.

Crap squared.

"Oh, my God. That's not what I—oh, geez, I

messed that up so badly, I…" She buried her face in her hands and kind of shook for a moment. He had the awful feeling she was crying. He hated watching women cry.

But when she raised her face to look at him, he saw no tears glinting in the porch light—just total mortification.

"Um…J.T., I'm sorry. That's not what I meant."

Great. He'd just admitted an attraction to a woman who didn't think of him that way at all.

"Well, this is awkward."

She leaned back in the chair—probably so she wouldn't have to look at him—and stared up at the sky as she spoke.

"I don't think you're a jerk. Okay, maybe a little that first day when you came strutting in doing your king-of-the-castle thing. But since then, no. You're on my side and listened and you're helping with my kid and you…well, you've done everything right. But it's too much. I can't accept anything else."

"Lydia—"

"Lyddie. Please. Only my mother-in-law calls me Lydia."

"Okay, Lyddie. Everything I've done has worked to my advantage, too. Selling to you is easier than to someone else. Having Ben help will get me through my work faster. Holding the mortgage is financially good for me, since I'll be getting the interest."

"Those are fringe benefits. You know that's not why you're doing any of this."

"And you have a window to my mind that lets you see my thoughts? Even those that I seem to be missing?"

"I don't need a window." Her voice hardened. "I'm living it. And it's getting to me."

"You want to tell me what I'm doing so wrong, since I'm clueless?"

"You bought in to the guilt."

Glenn. She had to be talking about Glenn.

"You think I'm doing these things because I feel sorry for you."

She seemed to pull deeper into her chair, as if withdrawing from his words. "Essentially."

Oh, shit. How was he supposed to answer that one?

Did he feel sorry for her? Well, yeah. He didn't belong to the cult that practically worshiped Glenn— after all, the guy was another of the ones who had left him to face the fire all alone—but still, he hadn't deserved what had happened to him. Neither did Lyddie.

So when did it become wrong to give a helping hand to someone who could use it?

"And if that was my sole reason—which it's not— why would that be a bad thing?"

"Because…well… Do you have any idea how people talk about me here? Poor Lydia Brewster. She's so brave. Carrying on after her husband died making sure we were all safe. She's so noble, so strong, we owe her so much—"

She erupted from the chair, holding her arms rigidly across her chest as if she were afraid she would explode. "I'm so sick of it. So damned tired of being put up on a pedestal like some unfeeling statue. I'm real and human and I'm afraid if it keeps up I'll—"

Again she stopped. This time, though, he got the feeling she wasn't about to say more. This time he was pretty sure she thought she'd said way too much.

What she didn't know was that she'd spilled her guts to one of the few people in town who could understand.

"You're afraid that if you keep living with that reputation, you'll start believing it yourself."

She plopped back into the chair like a marionette whose strings had just been severed. "How did—"

"Been there, done that."

She opened her mouth then closed it again, fast, before looking away. Embarrassed, most likely.

"Look, Lyddie. Here's the truth. Yes, I want to give you a hand. Not because I think you're some kind of martyr," he said quickly when she started to bristle. "But I meant what I said. It makes sense. It's the easiest course of action. Yeah, I think you got a raw deal, but since it helps me to help you, I don't see the point in not doing what's best for both of us."

She started to say something, then stopped and pulled her knee up, hugging it close to her chest.

"You might call that pity," he said softly when it became apparent that she was thinking over his answer. "But in my book, wanting to help someone I like sounds more like friendship."

"Friends?"

She seemed to appreciate that idea. For a moment he debated telling her the truth about Glenn. Would it help? She'd said in the cemetery that she wanted her kids to know who he'd really been, and hell, learning that he'd been one of the fire gang would sure twist his image around.

But she'd said nothing about Glenn himself tonight, just about her and what she was living. And there was a world of difference between hearing that someone had almost accidentally poisoned the science teacher and learning that even a hero had once been guilty of cowardice.

After all, the last thing people want to change is their minds.

So he pushed thoughts of Glenn aside and nodded. "Friends who can help each other. Can you handle that?"

"Promise you'll never say I'm being brave?"

"Promise."

She chewed on her lip for a second before nodding. "Okay. I'll call my lawyer tomorrow."

"Me, too."

Her sudden grin all but made her face shine in the night. "Should we swear a blood oath, or is a handshake enough?"

"I'll pass on the blood, thanks." But the thought of one more touch was too tempting to resist. He swiveled to face her and crooked his little finger in her direction. "Forget the handshake. There's no contract more binding than a pinky swear."

She laughed, a wave of delight that made him tilt a little closer to her. She slipped forward on the edge of her chair and linked her finger through his—and then the laughter erupted for real.

"What's so funny?"

"This is silly."

"I disagree. Pinky swears are sacred."

She shook her head. "So, do we say some special words, or what?"

"I think…" But that was as far as he got. She was so close. Their knees were just millimeters apart, their fingers entwined in a tease of contact. The vanilla scent that clung to her reached out to him, drawing him even nearer. The precise steps of a pinky swear were long lost in his memory, but he suddenly knew exactly what he wanted to do next.

He wanted to kiss Lydia Brewster. Wanted to taste her, to touch her, to pull her close and feel her softness against him.

And from the way her breath had started coming faster, he'd bet she wanted it, too.

Her lips parted.

His hand twisted to make full contact with hers, palm-to-palm, skin-to-skin, heat-to-heat.

Her eyes opened wide. Not with fear or dread, but with something that looked like anticipation.

His knee brushed hers. They both jumped, but neither pulled back....

Until he remembered what they were doing.

This was a business deal. They were forging an agreement that would benefit both of them, true, but it was still business. If he kissed her now she would never believe what he'd said about not wanting to help her just to score points.

If he gave in and kissed her now, he would kick himself forever. He didn't want to pair a first kiss with a mortgage.

He was going to kiss her someday. But it was going to wait for its own time, with no talk of mortgages and deeds to complicate the issue.

So he let his hand slide a bit more against hers before closing the grasp and turning the touch into a quick handshake.

"Well, then." He was still holding her hand when he stood, but he let go as quickly as he could. "Right. I'll be in touch. Soon."

She rose more slowly, moving like she was shaking off a particularly strong anesthetic.

"Okay. Um, J.T.?"

He halted midway to the steps, hoping she wasn't

going to slow his flight. If he didn't leave now he didn't know how much longer he could maintain his honorable intentions. He had his limits.

"Do you… Would you like…?"

Yes, he did. And hell, yeah, he sure would.

She inhaled sharply and squared her shoulders. "What time should I get Ben to you tomorrow?"

"Don't worry about it. I have to go past here to get to the cottages, anyway. I'll pick him up, say, around eight-thirty." He dredged up a slightly rakish grin. "Warn your mother-in-law."

"I will. Thanks. Again."

"My pleasure," he said, and realized those were probably the truest words he'd spoken since he walked back into town.

CHAPTER SIX

WHACK!

Around half-past dawn the next morning, Lyddie wrestled the ax from the fire-softened wood of the stubborn old stump and hauled it over her head once again.

Lift, aim, *whack!*

She hadn't expected to sleep. Once J.T. vaulted off the porch and drove away, she fully expected to spend the night counting ceiling tiles in a futile attempt at calming herself enough to doze off. But to her amazement she'd fallen into a swift, deep sleep. No dreams she could remember—though depending on the subject, she might have welcomed them—but she slept so soundly that when she woke abruptly around four-thirty, she was up for the day. Wide-awake, jumpy and buzzed enough even without caffeine that she could put herself out of business.

Then, of course, the memories flooded in. Memories…and more. Because she couldn't keep herself from imagining what might have happened if J.T. had leaned forward instead of jerking back.

As soon as it was light enough to see, she'd pulled

on shorts and an old T-shirt and headed out to the
yard to work off some of the restlessness. Tish's and
Ben's bedrooms faced the backyard, and Ruth had
been known to sleep through children shrieking right
outside her door, so Lyddie felt safe in taking out this
strange mood on the stump.

Whack!

She would never want to return to the days when
chopping wood was a necessity, but there was something soothing in the work. You lifted the ax, you
swung, it hit. Sometimes it bounced a bit, sometimes
a chip flew a bit too close, but as long as you were
careful, that was as exciting as it got. It was predictable. It warmed the muscles and calmed the spirit.

It was nothing like J.T.

The first time she met him, he'd seemed so bad-
ass, skating into the shop and making it obvious that
he wasn't there to court favor with anyone. Yet here
he was doing everything he could to make sure she
could stay in the building.

She should have been grateful. She *was* grateful.
Except…

She stopped, breathing heavily, and wiped sweat
from her forehead. Except, she admitted, she was
afraid that despite his assurances otherwise, he'd
fallen into the Young-Widow-Brewster mentality.
That he was cutting her a break, not because of her,
but because of Glenn and all that had happened.
That he pitied her.

God, she hated pity.

And the thought of being pitied by J.T. was worst of all. She didn't want the widow card to factor in to her interactions with him. She wanted the building, welcomed his assistance, but only for the right reasons. Like, he respected her business ability. Or for the reason he stated, that he understood her desire to keep this connection to Glenn for the kids. Or—if she were being honest, since it was damned hard to lie to herself at dark-thirty in the morning—because he was hot for her bod.

Whack!

Okay, it was probably better that something had made him back off. Necking on the porch like a teenager wouldn't have been a great idea, especially with Ruth due home at any moment. But still—she hauled the ax up again—still, it had been four years since she'd felt anything resembling interest in a man. Now she'd felt it twice in a month, both times with him. It had been kind of nice to experience that reawakening.

Maybe she should have a fling with him. Partway through the discussion last night it had hit her that everyone was going to be gone for a couple of weeks. She was going to be alone. All day, and all through those hot summer nights. What better way to pass the time than playing Sleeping Beauty to J.T.'s Prince with a Crooked Crown?

That would make folks stop thinking about her as the Young Widow Brewster, for sure.

Of course, it would be even more difficult to shake off a label like town tramp, but at least it would be a hell of a lot more fun.

She snickered aloud at the thought—Lydia Brewster having a wanton fling—and raised the ax for one final blow. She'd made progress on the stump and made good use of the nervous energy. Not as good as if she had J.T. here, of course, but—

"Lydia!"

The sound of Ruth calling her name interrupted Lyddie's wayward thoughts, replacing them immediately with worry. Her mother-in-law, wrapped in a red plaid flannel robe, hurried toward her.

"Ruth? What's wrong? Is it one of the kids?"

"No, no." Ruth shook her head, dislodging one of the fat pink curlers she wore every night. She reached into her pocket and pulled out the phone. "You have a call. Zoë."

"The baby?"

Ruth's smile was tired but indulgent. "Talk to her and see."

Lyddie pulled the phone to her ear. "Zo?"

"Congratulations, auntie. You finally have a niece."

Zoë sounded tired but happy as she relayed the details of little Emily Suzanne's arrival. Lyddie walked slowly to the house as she listened, not at all surprised to learn that her sudden awakening had happened right about the time Zoë started pushing. She and Zo had always had a special bond that alerted them when something was up with the other.

And it was a lot more comforting than thinking she had jolted awake merely because of the memory of J.T.

"How's my Sara?" she asked when she reached the garage. She twisted to hang the ax on its hooks without losing grip on the phone.

"Having a blast. And she's so good with the boys, a real godsend. I'm going to hate to lose her in the fall."

Lyddie winced. "Zo, this isn't like when you borrowed my favorite jeans back in school. You have your own daughter now. You can't have mine, too."

"I know, I know. But she's a great kid. Oh, and the clarinet teacher said she's one of the most gifted she's ever seen. She's hunting for someone closer to you who can keep teaching Sara, even just once or twice a month."

The words brought both pride and pain. Of course Lyddie wanted Sara to excel, wanted to know that her daughter could do well at something she loved so dearly. But could she, Lyddie, nurture that gift the way it required? Especially here in Comeback Cove?

"Oops, I have to go. Kevin just got back from the cafeteria and, God love him, he found me a cheeseburger! Call you later."

Lyddie hung up and hurried back to the house. She was going to be late unless she got moving.

Ruth sat in the kitchen, hunched over a cup of tea. She looked up when Lyddie entered.

"Is everything all right?"

"Wonderful. A girl. Seven pounds twelve ounces. Emily Suzanne."

"What a lovely, old-fashioned name."

"It is, isn't it?" Lyddie considered heading straight to the shower but decided she needed a bite first. She opened the fridge and rooted among the leftovers.

"Sorry she woke you," she called over her shoulder. "Zoë knew I'd be up already and wanted to catch me before work. She figured I'd get it before it disturbed anyone."

Ruth waved her hand dismissively. "Don't worry about that. I never minded losing sleep for a baby. But I did get a bit of a start when you weren't in the house."

"Of all the mornings, huh?" Lyddie grabbed a bowl of leftover mac and cheese. She decided against mentioning her bond with Zoë. Ruth would find it too woo-woo for words.

Besides, there was another matter to discuss.

"Ben had a little excitement last night." She gave Ruth an abbreviated version of the evening's activities, focusing on stabbing her macaroni whenever she had to mention J.T. She ended by saying, "So anyway, J.T. will swing by around eight-thirty to pick him up."

"Are you sure that's wise?"

Lyddie had an idea what was coming. "It seems like an ideal solution to me."

"Lydia, if you want the boy to stay *out* of trouble, I hardly think J. T. Delaney is the man for the job."

"I don't know. Maybe he'll be able to anticipate what Ben might do and head him off at the pass. You know, that whole past-experience thing?"

"This is hardly a joking matter. Surely you don't want that man having an influence on Glenn's son?"

He's my son, too. Lyddie smothered the thought beneath a mouthful of pasta. This was an old bone between her and Ruth, and she had neither the time nor the desire to get into it again.

She bought herself a few seconds to cool down as she chewed and swallowed. Then she said, "You know, everyone talks about him like he's the devil incarnate, but he seems pretty normal to me." Maybe as *hot* as the devil when he wore those tight shirts, but was that such a sin?

Ruth compressed her lips into a thin, very straight line. "You weren't here back then. You have no idea what he did to this town."

"Actually, I do. And I agree, it was pretty awful. But you know, he was never charged, which makes me think there was no proof other than his reputation. And—" she pointed her fork in Ruth's direction

"—it's been twenty-five years. He was just a kid. Didn't anyone else in this town ever do something stupid or crazy?"

Two spots of red appeared in Ruth's cheeks. She stared at the table. "Not like he did."

"He's an adult now. He could have changed."

"He *could* have." But there was no doubt that Ruth considered that about as likely as snow in August.

She was tempted—so tempted—to tell Ruth about the building, and the mortgage. But until she and J.T. ironed out the details, she didn't feel right discussing it with anyone else. "Well, all I know is he's being very generous to me and Ben. And now I'm going to shower and check on that ankle before letting our resident delinquent know that he gets to do an honest day's work today."

Ruth sniffed the way she did when she wanted to say something but was forcing herself to stay silent. For her part, Lyddie fought down a most inappropriate grin—but only until she cleared the kitchen. Then, she grabbed the lowest railing on the hall banister and swung herself onto the bottom step, arms outstretched like a dancer.

She had a niece. Ben was heading off to his first job. She was going to buy the building.

And J. T. Delaney had been *this close* to kissing her.

If ever there were a day to start making changes, this was it. She refused to spend the rest of her life trapped in an outdated reputation like J.T. had been forced to do. He would be leaving at the end of the summer. She wouldn't. So from here on in, she was letting the town know that there was more to her than just what they wanted to see. Goodbye, Young Widow Brewster.

Of course, once people found out that J.T. was holding the mortgage—and since this was Comeback Cove, that would be common knowledge before the end of the week—she might not have to worry. There would be more than one tongue insisting she was sleeping with the enemy, and not just in the metaphorical sense.

She could only be so lucky.

EAGER TO START the transformation she had decided she needed, Lyddie took the opening steps right away. She raced through a shower and was about to pull on her usual wardrobe of capri pants and a polo shirt when she stopped. Why not wear something different? Sure, it was a cliché, but if she wanted people to stop thinking of her as a dowdy aging widow, she would have to stop dressing the part.

She knew she'd succeeded when she walked into the shop and jolted Nadine out of her early-morning stupor.

"Whoa. What are you all dolled up for?"

Lyddie brushed the crinkly turquoise skirt and tugged at the matching tie-dyed T-shirt. It had been one of Glenn's favorite outfits. "Nothing. I just felt like doing something different."

"Different. Right." Nadine smirked behind the rim of her mug. "What time's your hair appointment?"

"I haven't made one."

"Yet?"

Lyddie conceded defeat. "Okay. I left a message on Marsha's machine begging her to work me in this afternoon. How did you guess?"

"You've been acting jittery lately. I figured you were either bored or planning to spike Jillian's morning coffee."

Lovely. She put her soul on her sleeve and it was dismissed as homicidal. "Strawberry muffins today." Lyddie reached into her supersize purse and brought out the pack of pinecone-shaped candles Sara had given to her on her last birthday. Nadine snickered.

"You changing the music, too, boss?"

"Honestly. You think I'm so predictable." Lyddie closed the bag before Nadine could spot the handful of CDs she'd grabbed from the car. "For your information, I'm celebrating. My new niece was born this morning."

"Congratulations. Does she know her aunt is a nutcase?"

"Her aunt is not a nutcase. Her aunt is just…well… tired of people looking at her and thinking 'Glenn's widow' when they should be thinking just 'Lyddie.'"

Nadine set the tray back on the butcher-block table

and came around to where Lyddie stood, running her finger around and around the rim of a sugar bowl. Lyddie braced for one of Nadine's infamous grab-'em-by-the-shoulders-and-shake-some-sense-into-'em lectures. To her surprise, the older woman pulled her into a long, hard embrace.

"Well, it's about time," Nadine said softly.

"What's that mean?"

"You've been here, working in Bud's place, living with Ruth, for four years now. That's more than anyone should have to handle." Two hard thumps to her back brought tears to Lyddie's eyes. "We'll miss you, but it's better for you."

"What?" Lyddie pulled herself from the hug that was suddenly a lot less comforting. "What are you talking about? I'm not leaving, I just want to change the way people think of me."

"Then you're gonna have to leave. Once this town has you pegged, that's it."

"No way."

"You see anyone cutting J.T. any slack? That boy went out and made something of himself. Iris says he's a teacher now, a respectable man, but does anyone ever mention that?"

"That's different. I haven't done anything to live down. I just want people to see there's more to me."

"You're wasting your time."

"I'm committed to spending the rest of my life here. I need to make sure I don't go crazy in the process."

"You sure? Insanity makes the winters a hell of a lot easier."

"Nadine…"

"Fine. Okay. Here's my best advice. If you want people to see the real Lyddie Brewster, the first thing to do is ask yourself who she is."

"That's easy. I—"

Oh, damn.

"As I suspected." Nadine hoisted the tray on her hip and headed for the door. "Think about what's important to you, kid. What you'll fight for. Then go for it."

Lyddie watched Nadine leave, then watched the kitchen door swing back and forth, slower and slower until it came to a stop. The sight of it at rest made her shiver. She could be that door—starting off at a good clip, gradually losing her steam until she ground to a complete halt.

No frickin' way.

She gathered the tray of condiments and headed for the dining room. When she hit the door, she kicked it so hard that it slammed open, cracking against the wall loud enough to make Nadine shriek.

Lyddie grinned. That smack was nothing compared to what was going to happen next.

SHE BIDED HER time, waiting for the perfect moment. It arrived at precisely nine-fifteen, when Jillian rushed into the shop. Nadine stepped up to take the order but Lyddie zoomed away from the cash register and elbowed into place.

Behind her, Nadine groaned. "This is not a good idea, Lyd."

Lyddie simply smiled. "Good morning, Jillian."

"Morning. Medium hazelnut, no—"

"No cream, no sugar. Got it."

Jillian's eyes widened slightly. "Oh. Right. Thank you."

"It's not that hard to remember."

"No, I suppose not." Jillian laughed. "Does this mean I'm becoming predictable?"

"No, Jillian. It means I pay attention. I put things together. Like, people with their favorite orders. Or rumors of donations, with loans being refused."

Nadine muttered an "aye yi yi" and ducked into the kitchen. Jillian looked somewhat surprised, but quickly put her official mask in place. "Lydia, I understand you're distressed, but town business and bank business are two separate entities. Your loan was denied, but—"

"Spare me the song and dance. I already listened to the Ted version."

Jillian's eyes sparked with something that Lyddie could swear was anger, but in a second it was gone—replaced not by Jillian's trademark politician mask, but by something a lot more infuriating. Something that looked a lot like pity.

"Lyddie. Listen to me. I know you have a—a fondness for this building, and that's understandable, but you know, we all have to make concessions. If you can work with me on this, I'm sure we can ease you into a new location. We'll take care of you. I promise."

The hell with that.

Lyddie's heart was doing a double cha-cha and her palms were so sweaty she didn't dare pick up anything breakable, but other than wanting to throw up, this felt good. She pressed on. "No, thanks, Jillian. No concessions, either. I'm not going down without a fight. I've got alternate financing, and I'm buying this building."

"Fine, Lyddie. You do that." Jillian's smile was so sweet it made Lyddie's teeth ache, but at least it seemed closer to the way Her Worship would act with anyone else. "Remember, though, the sale can't go through without planning-board approval."

"There's no reason to refuse it. I'm buying both buildings. I'm complying with all the regs. The only thing I'm not going to do is give up." She handed Jillian the coffee, in a paperboard cup instead of the usual ceramic mug. "Here you go. It's on the house. I took the liberty of making it to-go."

Jillian hesitated only a moment before accepting the cup. Her cheeks flamed but her voice was steady as she said, "I see."

About damned time. Lyddie did her own version of the fake-smile thing. "I'm so glad we had this chat. It's good to clear the air once in a while, don't you agree?"

"The only thing clear to me," Jillian said, "is that you have gone totally and completely out of your mind."

With that, she turned and walked away. The tinkle of the bell seemed to linger in the silence that hung in her absence.

Nadine poked her head out of the kitchen. "Is it safe to come out?"

"Yes."

"Did it feel as good as you hoped?"

Lyddie thought for a minute. "Yeah. I don't like being screwed over." *Or pitied.*

"Well, hold on to that good feeling, girl. You're going to need it when Jillian takes off the gloves."

"I've lived through worse," Lyddie said, though to be honest, she wasn't so sure. The room was awfully quiet. A woman could have a hell of a lot of second thoughts in this kind of silence.

All of a sudden, she had a really good idea of how it felt to be J.T.

BY THE END of the day Lyddie was only too happy to throw the lock and flip the Open sign to Closed. Closed, as in minds, she thought sourly as she walked back to the counter. She couldn't wait to have a few minutes alone.

"Thank God this one's over," Nadine said. "I kept

waiting for Jillian to come back and stab you with an eyebrow pencil."

"She's more of a poison gal, I think. No blood on her suits." Lyddie made a shooing motion in the direction of the door. "Everything is set in the back. You go ahead, go home."

"What about you?"

"Paperwork calls."

Nadine wrinkled her nose. "Don't let it suck up too much of your time, kid. Your days might be numbered. Better have some fun while you can."

The memory of J.T. on the porch in the moonlight jumped into her head. She pushed it aside just as swiftly. "I'm taking the kids to the movies tonight. We'll get double butter on the popcorn."

"Be still, my heart." Nadine vanished into the kitchen, reappearing almost instantly with her jacket and purse. "See you tomorrow, Lyd."

"See you."

Lyddie locked the door behind Nadine and turned off the lights. Immediately the room was plunged into shadows cast by the candle still burning on the mantel above the fireplace. The transition from bright and cheerful to calm and soothing was both instantaneous and seductive.

Lyddie hadn't lied: there was a pile of paperwork on her desk. She also needed to call Sara, check in with her lawyer and place a supply order, all before leaving to grab Tish from day camp and getting her haircut. But it could wait.

Fifteen minutes of peace. That was all she wanted.

She popped into the kitchen and set the timer before retreating to the far end of the dining room. With a blissful sigh, she lowered herself into one of the overstuffed chairs, then propped her feet on the coffee table. "God, this feels good."

She closed her eyes and snuggled deeper into the chair. Peace. Quiet. Exactly what she needed.

So her first attempt at kicking her image to the curb had turned around to kick her back. It was just one day. She had two weeks looming on the horizon, two weeks in which she could take a chance or indulge her wildest fantasies, and she had yet to decide what to do.

"What do you think, Glenn? Jogging? Pilates? They have classes at the Catholic church now. Or maybe those scuba lessons we always—"

Tap, tap, tap.

Someone was at the door.

"There are three hundred million doughnut shops in this country. Go find one," she said into the silence.

Tap, tap, tap.

She opened her eyes. From where she sat, she could see the door, but the shadows would keep her hidden until she chose to expose herself. And she didn't want to do that. She only wanted to know who was being so damned—

Oh.

It was J.T. And he was alone.

Spurred by concern, Lyddie made the return trip across the room a hell of a lot faster than the first.

"Hey, there," he said. "I didn't mean to disturb you."

He looked so casual with his palms splayed against the door frame and his face smiling in the sunshine that she relaxed immediately. Still, she couldn't keep from asking, "Where's Ben?"

"At the hardware store. We had to come back for supplies. Officially, he's there to order more paint and call me when it's ready. Unofficially, he's being allowed a few minutes off for good behavior."

"It went well, then?" Lyddie leaned against the frame and hoped she sounded more casual than she felt.

"Pretty good. He didn't say much, but he was steady and helpful. Perked right up when I started talking nanophysics."

"You're kidding. You understand that stuff? He tries to explain it to me, but it's so far out of my league that he ends up muttering about needing someone smarter to talk to."

"A-ha."

Did he have to grin that way every time she saw him? "A-ha, what?"

"I told him I teach physics and astronomy. He must think I'm his best chance at geek talk until school is back in session."

Silence descended. Lyddie squinted against the sun to get a clearer look at his eyes. She hadn't noticed the color before. Too busy trying to *not* look at his mouth, perhaps. But now, when both his mouth and eyes were crinkled in something that looked like delight, she could spare a moment to check.

As soon as she had, she regretted it. J.T.'s eyes were the same rich brown as her favorite café au lait. And she had the distinct impression that he would taste just as rich and smooth, if she ever—

She needed a reality check, and fast.

"So. A teacher, huh?"

His eyes widened a bit, but his voice stayed light. "Well, that's what I tell my mother."

"A cover story?"

"Could be."

"So in reality, you're either CIA or an underwear model."

As soon as she said it she wanted to slap her hand over her mouth. Of all the idiotic, half-brained, dumb-ass things to say.

"Can't say I ever posed in my jockeys. At least, not for a camera."

She struggled to regain control despite the all-too-vivid pictures forming in her mind. "That leaves the CIA. And if you tell me, you'll have to kill me, right?"

His grin grew wider. Her heart rate accelerated a notch.

"How about, I'd have to find a way to keep you quiet for a while."

Hoo boy, the things she could imagine...

She lounged against the door frame, arms crossed, feeling saucy and funky and just a little bit like pushing the envelope. Kind of like when she'd confronted Jillian, but without the desire to throw up. "So, Mr. CIA Man, will you be driving past the school again tonight? Because you never know. It might be my turn to spray-paint a few buildings."

His eyes gleamed, but he shook his head. "Sorry. I have a hot date with a caulking gun."

Lucky gun.

"Okay," she said. "In that case, I'll skip the painting party and go drag racing on the back roads instead."

"You like living dangerously, huh?"

"Oh, yeah. Every night I tuck the kids into bed and head out on a crime spree. The cops don't even ask for my statistics anymore. They have everything memorized."

The grin deepened, bringing out a dimple in his left cheek. She had a totally inappropriate thought about dragging him to the kitchen, grabbing lemon pudding and filling that little cleft so she could lick it clean.

"Never thought I'd meet anyone here who could rival my record."

Lyddie tossed her head indifferently. "Sorry, J.T., but you're history. Hope that doesn't bother you."

"Bother me? Hell, no. I'm inspired."

So was she.

"So," he said, leaning against the wall in an exact mirror of her pose. "After the cops let you go and you're free, where does the owner of the only coffee shop in town go when she wants to get a cuppa joe with a friend?"

Lyddie's heart did a strange little combination between a flutter and a thud. Her stomach clenched. Was that an invitation?

A loud beep pierced her panic. She jumped before reality kicked in and reminded her that she'd set the timer.

"Let me guess. I asked the wrong thing and set off your alarms."

He was too close to the truth for comfort. "No, I—that's the timer. I set it before I sat down. I—" This was the coward's way out and she knew it, but there were times when it would be foolish to pass up the perfect escape once it was presented. She might want to change her image but that didn't mean she had to jump in both feet first.

"You have to go, right?"

"That's about it."

The timer beeped again, long and insistent. Lyddie shook her head and hoped he wouldn't think she was a wuss. "I, um, I have to get Tish. I'd better turn that off and hit the road."

"Gotcha." He nodded. "I'll drop Ben at your place around four. Have a good one."

Without another word, he sauntered back down the road. She closed the door but didn't move until the next beep from the timer dragged her into the kitchen. She punched the button with a fist full of frustration.

No wonder she couldn't make the town see beyond her reputation. She was so nervous, so out of practice at being anything other than the Young Widow Brewster, that she panicked at the first hint of someone showing interest in Lyddie the woman. This was going to take a hell of a lot more than a change of clothes and a new haircut.

She didn't know precisely how she was going to pull this off. But as she grabbed her purse and locked the door on her way to the van, she couldn't deny the creeping suspicion that whatever she did, J. T. Delaney was going to be a big part of the process.

CHAPTER SEVEN

HOUNDING A KID to find out what was up with his mother was one of the cheapest tricks in the book. Luckily, J.T. had no problem being cheap when it came to Lyddie.

Something was going on with her. It was more than the swing of her newly short hair, though that was entrancing him far more than was wise, all things considered. Ever since he'd sort of tried to ask her out for coffee, she'd seemed almost shy around him. No, that was the wrong word. More like…nervous. Skittish, his mother would say. Like she was waiting for something she either wanted or dreaded.

He had yet to figure out which emotion would win.

In the meantime, he'd talked to the lawyer and got the ball rolling on the sale. He needed to go over some details with her but he wanted a hint as to what was up before they met. If her nervousness was his fault, he wanted to know now before it messed up the sale.

Or anything else.

Right?

So when he and Ben finished the first coat on the inside of the cottage-in-progress just before lunchtime, he decided to serve a little subtle interrogation alongside their sandwiches.

"Hey, Ben. What's the big excitement around town these days?"

"Nothing." Ben heaved a giant sigh. "Was it this boring when you were around?"

"Worse. No internet, no Wii, no cable."

"Sucks."

"Tell me about it. That's half the reason I got in so much trouble. Nothing else to do."

Ben shrugged and crammed another bite of tuna sub into an already full mouth. J.T. read the back-off signals loud and clear.

Tough. For once, they were going to discuss something other than supernovas and nebulae.

"I always thought this place would be more exciting once I grew up, but I guess I was wrong. Either that or I just haven't found the hot spot yet. What does your mom do for fun?"

"Mom? She doesn't do any— I mean, she doesn't have time for fun stuff. That's what she tells us, anyway."

As he'd suspected.

"She never goes out with her friends, just for a good time?"

"She goes to bingo with Gran sometimes. I don't think she likes it."

Having endured one bingo night with Iris in the not-distant-enough past, J.T. knew the feeling well.

"You think she'd like to kick back and have a good time once in a while?"

Ben sighed and set his sandwich down on the step. "Look, if you're planning to hit on my mother, just tell me."

So much for the theory that geeks were totally clueless when it came to interpersonal affairs.

"I'm not gonna hit on her." Maybe. Definitely not yet. "But she seemed kind of…fluttery, the last couple of days. I thought she might be worried about you."

"PMS."

Whoa. "Aren't you a little young to be talking about that so casually? When I was your age I couldn't even walk down *that* aisle of the drugstore without wanting to puke."

Ben shrugged and reached into the bag of potato chips that lay between them. "Can't help it," he said. "I got Mom whining about it all the time, and when it's not her, it's Sara."

"Lucky you."

"I just throw chocolate at them and they shut up and leave me alone."

Smart kid.

Since Ben seemed to prefer the direct approach, J.T. decided to roll with it, starting with the subject that had afforded the most luck thus far. "If I did hit on your mom, would that bother you?"

Ben smiled.

"What? I don't like that grin. Does that mean it's okay, or what?"

"It means good luck."

"You don't think she'd give me a shot?"

"I wouldn't bet on it." He took another handful of chips and added, "It's not you. She says no to everyone."

"Everyone who?" And why did that bother him so much?

"I dunno. Tourists, mostly."

"Well, I can understand that. Only an idiot goes out with a tourist."

"That's what she says. And she's always telling me and Sara to stay away from them." He switched into a high-pitched imitation. "Be polite, be helpful, but don't be stupid. Don't fall for someone who's going to leave."

Ah, damn. He was going to leave. He'd made no bones about it, right from the start. Did that mean that he, too, was forbidden?

Not that he was looking to get involved. God, no. But it was only the day after Canada Day, and he was probably going to be around until mid-August. It would be nice to spend some of that time with Lyddie.

But whether his chances were good or lousy, he had to tend to business first.

"Listen to your mother about the tourists. She knows what she's saying." He snatched the bag of chips before the boy could dive in once again. "And stop eating these. They'll stunt your growth." He reached in for a handful himself, savoring the grease and salt that had been banished from Iris's cooking.

"So, you gonna hit on her?"

"Is that any way to talk about your mother?"

Ben sighed again—damn, this kid loved to sigh—and said, very slowly and precisely, "Pardon me, sir, but are you planning to ask my mother out on a date?"

"Smart-ass."

"So are you?"

"Tell you what. I'll answer that one if you tell me where you got those cans of spray paint I found with you."

The teasing curiosity in the boy's face slammed closed faster than any door J.T. had ever seen. "Bought 'em."

"Where?"

"Store."

"Isn't that interesting." J.T. leaned back, bracing his elbows on the step behind him. "Wonder how you managed that, what with the town passing that by-law that made it illegal to sell spray paint to a minor."

Silence.

"Okay, so you don't want to talk about it. Let me tell you one thing, and then I'll drop the wise-old-man act. I was just about your age when I started acting like an idiot. I had some fun, no doubt about it. But I paid for it, big-time." Ben opened his mouth to say something, but J.T. shook his head and continued. "I'm not going to tell you what to do. I'm not your mother. But I'll tell you this—there's a difference between me and you. I was the one leading the trouble. You're following someone else. Which means it's a lot easier for you to get out of it than it ever was for me."

"You think I'm some dummy who does anything they say?"

"'Course not. You're too smart for that." He paused. "At least, that's what you tell yourself."

Ben shook his head. "Like you said, you're not my mom. I don't have to listen to you."

"No, you don't. You can think I'm the biggest nitwit in three counties if you want. Free country and all that. But make damned sure you know that when everything goes to hell, not one of those kids will stand up for you. They'll run faster than they've ever run in their lives and leave the last one out to hold the bag."

"Bull—"

"No, it's not. Been there, lived that." *And your dad was one of the ones who ran.* Not that he would ever let that slip. It would accomplish absolutely squat.

Worse, the last thing Ben needed to hear was that his own father had had some moments of testing limits. No point in encouraging him to see juvenile delinquency as an acceptable option. "If you don't believe me, then tell me why nobody stayed with you at the school the night you got hurt."

Ben flushed and stuffed wax paper into his sandwich bag. His jerky movements told J.T. he'd hit a nerve, but he sure didn't feel like celebrating.

"One more thing," he said as Ben stood up.

"Yeah?"

"If you really don't want anyone to know that you got the paint from the kid whose dad owns the hardware store, you might want to be a bit more subtle next time you run into each other."

The slight flush on Ben's face was all the confirmation he needed.

Ben gathered up his trash and headed to the cottage. J.T. waited until the kid was out of earshot before indulging in a heartfelt curse. His own misspent adolescence wasn't nearly enough preparation for this kind of situation.

J.T. had worked with a lot of kids in his time and had pulled a hell of a lot of numbskulls back from the brink. He was no novice at getting through to a kid.

But he'd never had a kid get to him the way Ben did.

Like mother, like son.

J.T. GOT A BIT CLOSER to understanding Lyddie's skit-tishness the next night, helping Iris separate linens into boxes—Pack, Toss, Donate. She chattered about Lyddie taking down Jillian, all while moving items from one location to another whenever she thought J.T. wasn't looking.

"...then Jillian left. But as Tracy said, you know she's not going to let things drop."

No, she wouldn't. J.T. tossed a handful of mono-grammed napkins into the donation box and scowled. Damn Lyddie. Why did she have to start at the top? Couldn't she have found a slightly less threatening victim on whom to test her new claws?

He had no doubt that there was a boatload of anger simmering under that slightly frazzled exterior she presented. How and why she let it loose was none of his business, of course. But he hated to see her get hurt. And try as he might to talk himself into be-lieving this could work, the sour feeling in his gut told him Lyddie had made a major-league mistake.

"What are you doing?" Iris asked. He pulled him-self from his thoughts and realized he was standing frozen with an ancient tablecloth in his hands.

"I'm—uh—deciding. Figuring out whether to keep this or not."

"You're keeping that, of course. And the napkins." She pulled them out of Donate and threw them into Pack. "These were from your father's family. You can't give them away."

"Ma, let's get real. I'm not a linen kind of guy. And you might have forgotten, but my initials are not *PC*."

"All right, so they're from your father's mother's family. They're still quality pieces. You won't find that kind of detail today."

"We can't keep everything."

Iris smoothed the fabric in her hands. J.T. looked at her wrists and winced. She was still so damned thin.

Not for the first time, he asked himself if he were doing the right thing. Staying in Comeback Cove could kill her...but taking her away could, too.

He took the napkins and set them gently in the keeper box. "We'll hold on to these."

Iris nodded quickly. He saw her blink once, twice, then swallow and shake her head.

"The other thing I heard is that you are being blamed for Lyddie's sudden change," she said.

He grunted. "No surprise there."

"People say you've been spending a lot of time with her."

"I'm selling the buildings to her. Her kid works with me. Of course I spend time with her."

"Are those the only reasons?"

He saw the hope she didn't dare speak. Another piece of his heart broke off.

"Ma, I'm sorry, but I'm not going to fall in love

with Lydia Brewster and move back here. Don't even go there, okay?"

"I never said you were."

But she had been thinking about it. Probably hoping and praying, too.

It was just like when he was seventeen. But then he'd deserved the guilt of knowing he was hurting her. This time it wasn't all his fault. And damn, that felt even worse than having only himself to blame.

"This is the hardest part," he said softly. "It gets easier as you go."

She nodded, head down. "I said that to you on your first day of school."

"And the first day of band, and at football tryouts, and the first time I got hauled in front of the cops." He hesitated. "And even though you weren't with me, it's all I heard the night I left town for good."

Iris grabbed one of the monogrammed napkins and pressed it to her eyes. J.T. waited, knowing this had to happen, hating being unable to help.

"I don't want to leave. I don't want to have to leave. It's not... Why do these things have to happen? Why do I have to be so stupid and weak?"

"You're not stupid, Ma. Or weak. Being sick doesn't make you either of those things."

"Sick." Bitterness twisted her face the way she twisted the napkin. "Other people can cope with this—this *thing* without losing their homes. I could manage it when your father was here to help. Why can't I do it now?"

There was no point in even trying to answer. They'd been over this ground too many times, shed too many tears already.

"I've been thinking...." She lifted her head, dared to look at him. "Summer isn't bad for me here. Maybe we don't have to sell the house. Maybe I could be a snowbird, staying here in the summer, going to Tucson in the winter. I think...I think if I could do that, it would make it easier. If it wasn't all or nothing."

It was a good solution, one he kicked himself for not considering earlier. "That could work," he said cautiously. "And if it would make it easier for you to spend the winters with me, then we should make it happen." At the sudden brightening of her face, he added, "But I don't think it would be practical to keep this house. We should still sell it, maybe keep one of the cabins for—"

But she was shaking her head, shaking away his words.

"No. J.T., you don't understand. I want to stay *here*."

"But—"

Then he got it.

"Because of Dad. Right?"

She inhaled, ragged and shaky. "I miss your father so much."

"Me, too."

"I told him not to go out on the water that day. I told him it was too rough, but he just laughed and said he'd seen worse...." She pulled the napkin away and he could see it all, the loneliness and hurt she'd been holding back since he walked through the door. "How can I leave? This is our home. This was where we raised you, this was where he walked and laughed and... I can't go. He's here, all around me. I can still feel him watching me, I know what his voice sounded like in this room and in the backyard and...I can't... If I leave here, how will I remember him?"

He couldn't give her the answers she needed. All he could do was step over a pile of towels and hold his mother tight as she broke down and cried.

A COUPLE OF hours later, when the tears and the talking were over and an exhausted Iris had taken herself to bed, J.T. found himself wandering the house. He couldn't settle down yet. Everything was too raw, too recent to allow him to sleep.

He needed to move.

He peeked in on Iris, then, satisfied she was okay for the night, sat on the front steps and strapped on his Rollerblades. As soon as he hit the road he knew he'd made the right choice. The streets were quiet, the air, cooling, and the night beckoned.

He stayed away from the river, away from downtown. He didn't want to see tourists tonight. He skirted the lights and the noise and glided down the back roads, losing himself in the rhythm of his feet skimming over the deserted pavement. He used to ice-skate on the frozen river when he was a kid. When he moved to Tucson he'd feared his skating days were lost forever. The day he'd discovered in-line blades was one of the best of his life.

He didn't know what to do for his mother. He didn't know how to make her believe she would be able to go on. But as he pushed himself to go faster, crouching and hurtling into the night and the stars, he realized there was someone who could help.

And he was only mildly surprised when he looked around and saw that he'd unconsciously skated almost to her doorstep.

It wasn't until he was picking his way carefully among the gravel of the driveway that he realized this might not be good timing. Lyddie could be busy. Her mother-in-law would probably be there, ready to give him one of those glares she dispensed every morning when he came for Ben.

But he had to give it a shot. The women in this house knew what Iris was living. He couldn't help, but they could.

He sidestepped his way up the porch steps and clomped past the chairs where he and Lyddie had sat and struck their deal—the first time he'd been tempted to kiss her. He couldn't let himself think of that now. He needed to keep his head on an even keel, stay focused.

Though that might be a lot easier said than done.

A knock on the door brought the *slap, slap* of rapidly approaching flip-flops. In a moment little Tish came to a dead stop in the hall.

"Hi. Is your mom home?"

Tish looked him up and down. She was off at day camp before he arrived in the mornings, so she was probably trying to figure out if he was friend or foe.

Her and a lot of other people.

"Who are you?" she asked.

"A friend of your mom's. Is she around?"

She squinted. "I know you."

"That's right. You do. I'm J. T. Del—"

"Oh!" She lunged forward and reached for the door. "Graveyard man!"

Okay, so it wasn't the best thing he'd ever been called, but neither was it the worst. And it got him inside.

"Mommy's in the kitchen." Tish pointed toward the back of the house, then started to run upstairs.

"Wait! I can't just walk in on her. I'll scare her. Could you tell her I'm here, please?"

She gave a heavy sigh that conveyed her opinion of useless adults. "I guess."

With a roll of her eyes, she flounced off. J.T. finally released the grin he'd been holding back. That was one little lady who would never let the world boss her around.

In an instant Lyddie hurried into the hall, her surprise matched only by his pleasure at seeing her. He'd expected to feel relief, or maybe nervousness at the topic he had to broach, but instead he slipped into the comfort that always seemed to surround him when she was near.

At least, he was comfortable until he realized she was wearing some of the best-looking cutoffs he'd seen in a long time.

"Hi." She seemed flustered. "What's up?"

"I wanted to talk to you about something."

She pressed her lips together but her expression said it all too clearly: *Now?*

"I'm sorry, I should have called first, but it was kind of an impulse thing. I can make it another time if—"

"No, that's okay. I just—" she looked down, brushed at a smear on her shorts with a briskness that made him ache "—we're making jam. Can we talk while I work? The pectin has been sitting and I need to mix it now."

"Not a problem. Thanks."

He unlaced the blades and padded after her into the kitchen where the table and counters were cluttered with measuring cups, bowls, a sack of sugar and box after box of shiny strawberries. It was a sight straight out of Norman Rockwell—

—until the refrigerator door, which had been open, closed to reveal Ruth glowering at him.

"Evening, Mrs. Brewster." He would stay respectful tonight if it killed him.

"J.T." She nodded. Why did everyone do that? Was it their secret code, the greeting they all used for an outcast?

"I'm sorry to intrude, but I need some help. From both of you, actually."

"What is it?" Lyddie asked. Ruth merely tightened her lips.

"It's my mother. She's… I'm dealing with things that are out of my league."

"What do you mean?" Lyddie emptied a small saucepan of pectin into a stainless steel bowl filled with strawberry mush.

"Stir, Lydia. What have you done now, J.T.?"

God, if he made it through this intact, the rest of the summer would be a cakewalk. Lyddie looked pissed but he jumped in before she could attack Ruth the way she had Jillian.

"This isn't like when I was a kid, Mrs. Brewster. We were talking about my father, and the house, and she kind of fell apart on me, and I need to know— God, there's no way to ask this without sounding like an idiot, but—"

"You want to know if it's normal for her to still miss her husband so much that she can't breathe?"

It was more sarcastic than he would have liked, but probably all he could expect from Ruth.

"That's about it."

Lyddie and Ruth exchanged glances across the bowl of mush. Ruth attacked a bowl of whole berries with a potato masher, employing such vigor that he had the feeling she was imagining his head in there. Lyddie stopped stirring and focused on him.

"Yes. It's normal."

Such simple words, yet they carried a world of hurt in them.

"I thought so. But it's been a while now, and sometimes she still seems like it just happened."

Ruth sighed. "They were together for almost fifty years. She's not going to get over him in a couple of weeks."

He felt his shoulders tensing at the condescension in Ruth's voice, but again he forced himself to stay steady. Ruth didn't know that Iris was dealing with much more than her grief. And nobody knew how much he worried that she could end up suicidal again.

Instead, he asked the question that had pushed him through the door. "What can I do to help her?"

Ruth gave him a look so filled with amazement— and not the good kind—that he took a step back. It was all there in her face. Accusation, judgment, condemnation and the certainty that he was somehow the cause for all that had gone wrong in his mother's life.

The hell with that. He had a lot to answer for, and he knew he'd caused his share of grief back then, but not now. And if he wasn't going to get any advice, he was out of here.

"Okay. I guess this was a mistake, so I'll—"

"Wait." Lyddie's cheeks were almost as red as the berries in the bowl, though whether from anger or embarrassment, he couldn't tell. She set her spoon on the counter and addressed Ruth. "I'd like to talk to J.T. alone for a while. You want me to finish up the jam, or do you want to do it?"

"Lydia—"

"Ruth."

"Fine." Ruth undid her apron, then tossed it over a chair. "Go ahead and have your little chat. But you might want to remember that it's easier to prevent a problem than to cause it in the first place."

With that, she pushed open the screen door and went outside. J.T. watched her go with a mixture of relief and regret. He should have known.

Though to be honest, Ruth Brewster had never been this hostile when he lived here. She hadn't condoned his actions but he had always sensed a kind of boys-will-be-boys vibe from her back in the day. Now, though, she seemed almost eager to remind him of his guilt, to push him away.

He could think of only two explanations. The

first and most likely was that the sheer magnitude of the fire and its fallout had erased any tolerance she might have ever had for him.

The second was that she knew he hadn't been alone that night. That she knew—or suspected—that Glenn had been in on the action. And that she was terrified he might tell folks about that before he left.

If he knew for sure that she knew, he would let her know she had nothing to fear. There was nothing he could gain from tarnishing Glenn's reputation. But if she didn't know—well, he couldn't broach the topic. If he'd guessed wrong, and she had no idea, he would rot in a well-deserved hell if he were the one to shatter her heroic image of her son. She'd lost enough. He couldn't take that cold comfort from her.

"Here." Lyddie pushed the bowl to his side of the table, bringing his focus back to her. "Harley insists on giving us berries every year, way too many. A guilt offering. We can barely keep up. Make yourself useful and start mashing."

He picked up the masher, looked at Lyddie and raised his eyebrows.

"Is this to help you or to vent my frustrations?"

"Both. I'm sorry about Ruth. She was in a wicked mood already. Sara—my daughter—"

"The one in Vancouver, right?"

"Right. Well, she called, and everything is fine,

but she's having so much fun that Ruth is afraid she won't want to come home when summer's over. Which is no excuse. But I thought you'd like to know it wasn't all about you."

"Thanks."

"Good." She gave him another one of those grins that tested his resolve to stay away from her until the negotiations were complete. "Now get mashing."

"Yes, ma'am."

He set to work, watching the berries squish into a pulpy mess while waiting. She wasn't ignoring him. He might not know Lydia Brewster nearly as well as he'd like, but he knew this: she would talk to him. And listen. And help.

So he bided his time while she scooped the contents of her bowl into plastic containers. She worked with no hesitation, comfortable with both her activity and with him—as he was with her.

When she had settled the lid on the last container she carried them to the green linoleum counter, setting them beside four other tubs of jam. Then she wiped her hands and walked slowly back to him.

"Ruth was right about one thing," she said. "Iris isn't going to get over this in a matter of months. But that's not what's really worrying you, is it?"

"No. Are these mashed enough?"

She peeked into the bowl. "Give them another minute. So what's bothering you?"

He frowned at the berries, measuring his words.

"I guess it's an issue of quality, not quantity. She'll miss him for the rest of her days. So will I. But I'm worried that it seems just as strong now as it was when he first died."

"It's probably worse."

That made him glance up, uncertain he'd heard her right, but she was spooning sugar into a measuring cup and didn't return his gaze.

"Here's the thing, J.T. Everyone thinks that grief starts off horrendous and then gets gradually easier, like going down a slide. But it doesn't. At first you don't really know what you've lost. You know he's gone, you know nothing will ever bring him back, but it doesn't hit home until you try to get back to reality and find that nothing is the same."

He set the masher gently to the side of the bowl, focusing only on Lyddie.

"It's in all the little things. Having to take the garbage out all the time by yourself. Turning on the hockey game and yelling to him that the Leafs are winning for once, but he's not there. Walking through a store and seeing a sweater that would have been perfect for him, then remembering he's not home to wear it."

She looked so alone as she spoke. He wished he had the right to hold her the way he'd held Iris—not for pleasure, but for comfort. "Does it ever get easier?"

She shrugged. "Depends on how you define easy.

You get used to it. After the first few times of breaking down in Wal-Mart you remember that it's all changed. And then, just when you think you're going to be okay, something new will pop up, like somebody losing their first tooth or someone in town giving you a free carwash just because they feel sorry for you, and then it starts all over again."

"No forgetting, no escape, huh?"

"No. And there shouldn't be, really. Because when you really love someone and you lose him, it should hurt. You know what I mean?"

"Yeah."

Okay. He was still unsure what to do, but at least he knew that Iris wasn't slipping beyond his reach.

He waited while Lyddie carried the saucepan to the stove and started it heating. "So, anything special I should do to help her?"

"Talk about him. Keep the memories alive. Listen. Really listen, not just to what she's saying, but to what she doesn't say, too. That's going to tell you more than you'd imagine."

He nodded. Who had listened to Lyddie when Glenn died? Who had held her close while she wept out her grief?

Or had she been so busy getting her children and Ruth through the loss that no one had ever done that for her?

"She's afraid that when she moves, she won't remember him the same way."

A sad smile tugged at Lyddie's lips. "I know."

"Yeah, I figured. Any words of wisdom on that count?"

"I'm not the one to ask. Yes, I moved here, but I was coming to a place where there were even more people who shared my memories. It wasn't the same as it will be for Iris. But…"

"But?"

She swiped her face, leaving a smear of red across her cheek, drawing his attention until she spoke again. "Okay, obviously I believe in staying with the memories. But when you've loved someone as long as your mom loved your dad, well, I think that person is too much a part of you to ever be completely lost."

That sounded like something Iris would say—like something she would believe. He could give her that hope.

"I don't know if that makes any sense, but—"

"It's fine. Perfect. Thanks." He peeked out the back door. "Do you think Ruth is plotting something vile against me?"

Lyddie rolled her eyes and grinned. "Ruth believes in action. If she hasn't killed you by now, you're safe."

"That's a comfort." His focus was drawn to the smudge on her face. It started high on the cheekbone then curved to point directly at her mouth. He really didn't need that kind of distraction. "You, uh, you have something on your cheek."

"I do?" She reached up, scrubbed at the wrong side with her finger. "Did that get it?"

"No, it's on the other— Stop, you're making it worse. Here." He was probably going to hell for giving in to temptation this easily, but he couldn't stand and watch any longer. If helping her meant he had to touch her, well, he'd suffer the consequences.

He grabbed a towel and ran the corner under water. At his approach she turned off the flame beneath the pot and looked up at him.

He stopped when she was barely within reach, not trusting himself to go closer. He told himself this meant nothing as he raised the towel and dabbed oh so gently at the jam. But even as his fingers brushed her skin, her scent reached out to him—strawberry and vanilla and a hint of sweat, just enough to make his mind jump to other activities that could leave people perspiring.

His hand dropped to his side. "There. Got it."

She stood very still, eyes wide. She bit down on her lip, quickly, then took a short breath and said, so softly that he could barely hear, "Are you sure you got it all?"

She stepped closer. And lifted her face to his, tilting slightly to reveal the cheek that was still pink from his earlier efforts.

There wasn't a bit of jam in sight, but damn, he was only human.

"You're right. Looks like I missed a spot." He ran

his finger gently across her cheekbone, longing to cup her face in his hands and kiss her. One side of his brain whispered a reminder that he should keep his distance until the sale papers were signed. The other side was busy shouting that if he didn't kiss her, he'd be the world's biggest idiot.

She lifted her head slightly so his brief touch began to resemble a caress. He saw the pulse leaping at the base of her neck. If he ducked his head he could put his lips to it and feel her pounding through him.

She leaned closer, leading with her breasts. His fingers slipped lower, his thumb flicking against the corner of her mouth. Her eyes closed, but from the way she parted her lips, he didn't think she was trying to block him out. Anything but.

He might fry for all eternity, but his thumb grazed the edge of her bottom lip. She inched closer. He leaned forward and reached toward her with his other hand—

"You said you weren't going to hit on her."

Lyddie yipped and jumped back about two feet. J.T. whirled to face Ben, tense and glowering in the doorway with an expression of supreme revulsion on his face. It seemed that things couldn't get any worse.

Then a noise from the other side of the room made him turn just in time to see Ruth walking rapidly away from the screen door.

CHAPTER EIGHT

SHE COULD DO IT.

Lyddie sat at the kitchen table the next night looking over the list of supplies Ben needed for camp but her mind wasn't on shorts, windbreakers and binoculars. Even as she made check marks next to the items he already had and highlighted those she would need to buy, all she could think of was the same subject that had occupied her mind for the past twenty-four hours: that moment in the kitchen right before Ben opened his mouth. The moment when she knew J.T. was going to kiss her.

The moment when she knew she wanted more.

She told herself, as she had a hundred times since, that it was good they'd been interrupted. She could still tell Ben that J.T. had merely been cleaning her face. Okay, so neither of them believed it. Ben spent the day avoiding her. Ruth stayed silent, pressing her lips together and appearing on the edge of tears whenever Lyddie came near.

But worse than putting up with their reactions had been the knowledge that if J.T.'s lips had actually brushed hers the way she ached for them to, she would have been all over him like chocolate ice cream on a toddler. They would have needed a chain saw to get her off him.

And all night and all day, a little voice kept whispering in the back of her head that soon, she would be alone. For two glorious weeks. Fourteen days and fourteen long, hot summer nights.

She could do things. Things with J.T., things that would definitely make her feel like anything but the Young Widow Brewster. And nobody would be around to stop them.

The possibilities made her shiver.

Tish glanced up from her puzzle on the other side of the table. "Mommy, are you cold?"

"No, sweetie."

"Why did you do that quiver thing?"

Because I'm imagining how it would feel to have J. T. Delaney underneath me. "Oh, you know. Just a chill."

Tish considered that. At least *she* was still speaking to Lyddie. It was nice to know she wasn't a total outcast.

"Mommy?"

"Yes, sweetie?"

"When will the teacher letters come?"

"You mean the one that tells who your teacher will be next year? Just before school starts."

"Oh." Tish frowned at her puzzle piece, turning it aimlessly in her hand without trying to fit it into the opening in front of her. "I hope I don't get Miss Lockhart."

"Why not? She's supposed to be good."

"I don't like her. She makes me feel funny."

"Funny ha-ha or funny strange?"

But Tish must have decided she'd said too much, because she merely rolled her eyes and shrugged. "I don't know. Can I call Millie?"

"Who?"

"Millie. From camp."

"Sure, I guess. Why?"

Tish gave one of her best drama-queen sighs. "So I can talk to her."

Lyddie laughed and held out her arms. "That makes sense. But it'll cost you a hug and a kiss."

Tish consented to a hug and offered her cheek for a kiss. She even allowed a quick tickle before squirming out of Lyddie's embrace and skipping to the phone. Lyddie coached her through dialing and the welcome, then slipped out of the room when it became obvious that Tish no longer needed her.

She ran upstairs, passing the closed door to Ruth's room. She considered knocking, then shook her head and moved on. Glenn was dead. She wasn't. She had done nothing she needed to explain or apologize for.

At least not yet.

On impulse, she ran to her room, dropped the list on the quilt-covered bed and grabbed her wallet off the dresser before rapping sharply on Ruth's door.

"Ruth, I'm running out for milk. I'll be back soon."

There was a moment's silence, followed by a reproachful admonition to do as she wished. Lyddie shook her head but refused to stop now. She told Tish to head upstairs with her grandmother and flew to the car before anyone could stop her. Her daughter wasn't the only one who needed to talk to someone.

Five minutes later, she pulled into the parking lot of the library, knowing full well that it was closed at this time of night. She locked the doors, waited for the radio to finish playing "Call Me Maybe"—grinning at the irony even as she sang along—then punched numbers into her phone with a prayer that this was a good time.

"Hello?"

Lyddie breathed a sigh of relief. Prayer number one had been answered.

"Zoë, it's me. I know things are crazy, but have you got a few minutes?"

"If you don't mind slurping noises and the occasional burp."

"Oh, do I remember those days. Not a problem. How's she doing?"

"She's perfect, and I slept six hours straight last night, and Sara is a godsend and the boys are actually cooperating. But that's not why you called. What's up?"

Lyddie glanced around the deserted parking lot

and slumped lower in the seat. "Um, see, there's this guy...."

"No!" But unlike Ruth, there was nothing but delight in Zoë's denial. "Really? That's wonderful! Tell me."

"Well, he used to live here. He's home for the summer. And he seems kind of, um, interesting."

"What's his name? No, wait, I don't want to know. I might have met him."

"You haven't. But Sara has."

"Well, then, if you want to talk freely, he should stay anonymous. Mr. X."

"God, Zo, are you stuck in high school?"

"High school is better than what I'm doing now. This kid has suction that could put vacuum cleaners out of business. So what does he look like?"

"Dark hair. Black with a little gray you only see in sunlight."

"Forget sunlight. You want moonlight."

She thought back to the night on the porch and grinned. "Actually, in moonlight it looks raven."

"Holy crap, you've done moonlight already?"

"Is that any way to speak in front of an innocent child?"

"She likes it. Her little eyes are telling me she wants more excitement from Aunt Lyddie. Tell me more."

"Well, let me think. His eyes crinkle when he smiles. He smiles a lot, at least around me. He has this mouth that makes me remember things I thought I'd forgotten, and wonder about things I thought I'd never wonder again."

For a moment the only sound was muffled breathing and gulping. Lyddie assumed Zoë was tending to the baby until she heard a sniff.

"Zoë? Are you okay?"

"Yes. I can't help it, I'm still hormonal."

"What's wrong?"

"Nothing. I'm just so damned glad to hear you happy again, you know?"

Lyddie closed her eyes and smiled over the lump forming in her own throat. "Yeah. I know."

Zoë sniffed again, then blew out a long breath. "Okay. I have to stop bawling, I'm dripping on the baby. So, has he asked you out? What are you going to do?"

"That's the problem. See, like I said, he's only here for the summer. Which is good, because it's not like I need anything permanent. But it turns out I'm going to be alone for a couple of weeks, everyone will be gone and he seems interested, so I keep thinking maybe—"

"Oh, my God. Are you thinking of doing him?"

Lyddie winced as she stared into the darkening lot once again. "Don't say that. It sounds so trampish."

Zoë hooted with laughter, then immediately shushed the baby, who had started to wail at the sound. "Shh, Emily, sh. Mommy didn't mean to scare you. But Aunt Lyddie said something too funny!"

"I'm glad you think it's cute. I'm dying of mortification."

"Come on, Lyd. You've been alone for four years. You were faithful to Glenn forever. Unless you were the campus slut back in college, I don't think you have to worry about being a tramp."

Lyddie ran one finger around the rim of the steering wheel, staring out at the river. It was dark tonight, heavy with the anticipation of approaching rain.

Anticipation. That, she could empathize with.

"So, you gonna jump him?"

She snorted into the phone. "Please. I wouldn't even know how to start. What do I do, hand him a cup of morning roast and say, 'Coffee, tea or me?'"

"If you want to do it, you should. It's not like you're a high school kid who has to worry about her reputation."

If only Zoë knew just how much *reputation* was factoring in to this decision.

"You have to, Lyd. It's perfect. You'll be alone. You know how to be subtle. The kids will never know their mother is a slut."

"Geez, Zoë. Like that's the kind of thing I need to hear right now?"

"I'm in public relations. I know how to use words.

And we're talking the height of tourist season, right? Isn't that when the gossip network dies way down?"

"Not really, but…" Lyddie spoke slowly, unsure whether to go along with Zoë's reasoning or not. But she had a point. In tourist season Lyddie could probably have sex in a convertible on Main Street and the main concern would be whether or not it drew a paying crowd.

"So do it."

"Yeah. Right. I'll add it to my to-do list. Buy Tish new shorts, get Ben's health forms for camp and proposition J. T. Delaney."

Zoë groaned. "So much for keeping it anonymous."

"Whatever. Look, we both know I'm not that kind of woman. I can't sleep with a man I barely know. That kind of thing can get a gal killed these days."

"So here's what you do. You have about two weeks before everyone leaves, right?"

"Ten days."

"Not like you're counting or anything. Anyway, you screw up your courage, you ask him if he's involved or busy, you ask him to do a test right away. You can buy them over the counter."

"You're kidding."

"Not about that. Go across the bridge into New York. You can get mouth swab tests and blood ones there, though I think you have to mail in the blood ones. You're a worrywart, so get both. You'll trust the results more if you do. Do the tests, get the answer and if he's good to go, heck, you go, girl."

Phrased like that, it sounded almost possible. Except—

"And then, after sleeping with this man for two weeks, I'm supposed to drop him, just like that?"

"After two weeks, they're all boring, anyway."

"Does Kevin know that?"

"Kevin is the exception. So was Glenn. But that's not the important part."

"I can't wait to hear what you think *is* the important part."

"It's this, kiddo. You have the time, you have the opportunity and you have the potential partner. You're an adult woman with adult needs. What would you regret more? Taking the chance on doing something wild and crazy just for you? Or passing up this chance and saying 'shoulda, woulda, coulda' for the rest of your life?"

THE GHOST OF almost-kisses haunted J.T. from the moment he walked out of Lyddie's house, followed him as he walked the streets of town and dogged him now as he slapped a final coat of paint on the last cottage.

He should have kissed her while he had the chance. Shouldn't have dallied. Should have stayed far away. Should never have asked Ben about her in the first place.

Would regret both missing out and putting her in an awkward position for the rest of his days.

Ben poked his head around the corner from the bedroom where he'd been assigned to work. "I'm done in there."

It was the first comment other than a grunt that J.T. had heard from the kid since getting caught pre-kiss. He'd let it slide, figuring that some solitary painting would do them both good.

But now, with the bulk of the work behind them, it was time to talk this over, man to kid-trying-desperately-to-be-a-man. He hoped he hadn't blown things with Ben. The kid was basically all right. A little messed-up in his choice of friends, but it wasn't like he had much of a selection in the Cove.

"Okay. This wall is almost done. You finish it, and I'll start cleaning."

Ben lingered a moment, then slowly peeled himself away from the door and joined J.T. and grabbed the roller and tray.

"Nice to see these places looking decent again." J.T. eased into conversation over the rhythmic squeak of the roller. "My dad always kept them in good shape when I was a kid. I can't believe he let them slide like this."

"Huh." Ben frowned at the paint.

Okay, that didn't go so well. At least they were in the same room.

"Of course," he continued as though this were a

normal conversation, "you never can tell if you're remembering things the way they happened or not. When you're the kid, you don't always see things the way adults do."

Ben's snort told J.T. his subtle approach had been less than successful. Time for Plan B.

Unfortunately, Plan B was an outright, "So you walked in on something you didn't like last night." And while he would use that tactic if he had to, he had the feeling it wasn't the best way to handle Ben. This was a kid who still bristled at being told what to do. If he could find a way to give Ben the opening, he suspected the going would be a lot smoother.

"Yeah, my dad was a stickler about doing things the right way. Probably just trying to drum something through my thick head, but I remember him telling me how to do things over and over, the same directions until I could practically puke. 'Course, I never forgot them, so maybe he knew what he was doing."

Shrug. Then, very casually Ben asked, "What happened to him?"

"My dad? I guess he didn't have as much energy once he got older. It takes a lot to keep all these places up."

"No. I mean, what *happened* to him."

Ah, damn. This was gonna be a hell of a way to get the kid to open up.

"He went out on the river in a storm."

"Did he go overboard?"

"No. He made it to an island, but then he had a heart attack." The thought of his father dying alone, slowly, half-drowning in the driving rain, was still enough to make J.T.'s voice falter.

Ben nodded. "Thought that's what it was. I heard stuff back when it happened, but no one would talk about it in front of me." He switched to a sarcastic falsetto. "Shhh. The *children* might hear you."

A-ha. A chink in the armor. Ben resented being kept out of the loop, treated like a little kid. Maybe this conversation could be worth the cost.

J.T. tossed rolls of masking tape in a paper bag in the middle of the floor and asked, as casually as he could muster, "Did you know my dad?"

"A bit. From church and stuff. He was nice to us." He shrugged. "Everyone is nice to us."

From the way he said it, it was clear that Ben shared his mother's feelings about excessive niceness from the town.

"I'm sorry if you thought he was too nice, but I'm glad you had the chance to know him. He was a good guy." He waited a beat, then added, "Just like your dad."

"My dad got shot." It was flat, almost accusatory, as if J.T. had done something wrong by bringing Glenn into the conversation. Tough. Glenn was part of what lay between the two of them, and now that they'd started, J.T. wasn't about to back off.

"I know. I'm sorry."

Ben made a sound that sounded like a cross between a cough and a snort. "Oh, yeah. If he was still alive, you wouldn't be kissing my mom."

Finally, an opening.

He pulled a strip of masking tape away from a dry wall and spoke as if they hadn't just made a giant leap forward.

"I'm not gonna play games with you, bud. You want answers, speak up."

Silence. No surprise there. J.T. didn't know how he would feel if he caught someone doing a lip-lock with Iris, and he was supposed to be an adult.

"You ever realize how complicated life is, Ben?"

"Nope." And the way he was driving the roller into the wall made it clear that Ben didn't particularly care if he ever did.

"Well, it is. And one of the most complicated parts is when you feel two apparently opposite emotions at the same time." *Go for it, J.T.* "Like the way I can feel bad about your dad and still want to kiss your mother."

Ben scowled at the paint. "You said you weren't going to hit on her."

Gone was the bravado of the earlier night. All that remained was a confused boy who'd already dealt with too much in his life.

"You want me to stay away from her?"

A too-casual shrug lifted the skinny shoulder.

"Or are you pissed because you think I lied to you?"

A smack of the roller against the wall seemed to confirm that theory.

"You have a drip on your right. See it? Good." J.T. stared at the runaway paint. "Look, I wasn't really lying. When we talked before, I wasn't planning to do anything. But things change. I know this will make you want to hurl, but your mom is a very special woman. I like spending time with her. You gonna give me a hard time about that?"

"What about when you have to go?"

Newspaper crunched in J.T.'s tightening fists.

"Your mom and I are adults. We both know I have to leave at the end of summer. If we decide to spend some time together before I go, have a few laughs, that's our choice."

Listen to him. Going on about choices and fun when he hadn't had so much as an hour alone with the woman. Damn it, once again he was taking the heat for something he hadn't done. Not that he hadn't wanted to, of course....

"She likes you." Ben's white-knuckle grip on the paint roller made it clear that this was an accusation, not a compliment. Good thing he didn't know that J.T.'s gut did a little flip thing at this bit of information.

"I'm not trying to make her like me. But—" He stopped, unsure how much to say, then decided he could take the chance. "Listen. You ever have a time when everyone treated you like dirt?"

"Sort of." The words came slowly, then in a great gush, as if a dam had been breached. "Not dirt. But after my dad—it was like the guys didn't know what to do with me. You know?"

"Exactly." His heart ached for the kid. "So when that was going on, was there maybe one person who made you forget it all, who made you laugh and feel normal again?"

The roller slowed. "Yeah."

It was the most cautious agreement J.T. had ever heard. He wasn't sure what to make of it until he saw the faint color in Ben's cheeks.

If he were a betting man, he'd lay money that the person who had helped Ben was a girl. If he wanted to make any progress whatsoever with the kid, he had better stay far, far away from that topic.

"Okay. So, I know your mom probably doesn't talk about me in front of you, but you have to know I'm not this town's favorite son."

"I heard things."

I just bet you have, bucko. "First, most of what you've heard is bull. Second, you have any questions about me, you ask me. Not your mom, not your grandma, nobody else. Got that?"

A slight nod.

"Good. Now this is the big one. Your mom hasn't treated me like the others have. She gave me a chance. I can relax with her." Except when he was trying to hold back from kissing her. "I hang out with her because she's one of the only people here who lets me be me. Believe it or not, even us bad guys want to be liked once in a while."

Ben frowned and concentrated on the paint. There seemed to be some sort of mental tug-of-war going on, and J.T. held his breath, waiting to see how it would come down. Finally Ben turned to face him.

"But what about when you leave?"

This time the question wasn't delivered with anger or blame. It was filled with need and a hint of lone-liness, overlaid with a plea, and J.T. cursed himself for not realizing that, in helping Ben, he may have set the kid up for yet another loss.

Ben wasn't worried about his mom. Well, some, yeah, but that wasn't all of it. *Ben* was the one who liked J.T., the one who liked hanging with some-one who understood. He wasn't worried about what would happen to Lyddie when summer ended: he was worried about himself.

Another autumn. Another loss.

No wonder the kid had been so concerned about J.T. kissing or not kissing Lyddie. If there was no kissing, Glenn's position in the family would remain unchanged. But if there was kissing going on, maybe J.T. would stay.

This was almost worse than making Iris face the truth.

"When I leave…" He took a moment to yank up a strip of tape, trying to figure out how to ease the truth.

"Is it for sure that you're going?"

"I'm not gonna lie. I have to go back to Tucson. Staying here isn't an option for me."

"Because they all hate you."

"That's part of it. But there's other people involved. It's not all about me."

Ben shrugged as if to show how much he didn't care about those other people. "You could try to make people like you."

"Too much water under the bridge, buddy. It's not gonna happen. And like I said, there's those other people."

"Yeah. Right."

"Look, when you go to camp, do you make new friends, and maybe wish you could have more time with them?"

"I guess. Sometimes."

"When you're with them, do you spend all your time worrying about how hard it will be to say good-bye, or do you have as much fun as you can while you have the chance?"

A slight understanding dawned on the boy's face.

"This isn't exactly camp for me, Ben, but it's kind of like that. I know I have to leave. So does your mom, and…and anyone else who might wish I could stick around a bit longer." God help him, he would never have believed that someday, someone other than his mother would want him to stay. "As long as we all know the score going in, we can all make the most of the time we have together, and nobody gets hurt."

"Yeah, but—"

"Saying goodbye will be hard. But it's always better to have fun with people you like while you have the chance, instead of shutting them out so it won't hurt when it's over. Does that make any sense?"

"Some. Maybe."

"Good." He waited a beat. "By the way, I'll have some time left in town when you get back from camp. These cottages are almost ready and I know I'll need an excuse to get away from my mother once in a while. I don't suppose you'd take pity on an old man and go fishing with me once or twice before I leave, would you?"

Ben turned back to the wall, but not before J.T. spotted the pleasure shining in his eyes. "Yeah, I could probably manage that."

"Good. I haven't been fishing all summer. If I try to go back without getting out on the water at least once, I'll probably get arrested."

Ben snorted. J.T. took advantage of the good mood to add, quietly, "And by the way—you might want to know that I didn't kiss your mom the other night."

"Were you gonna?"

"Maybe. Hard to tell about these things sometimes."

Okay, that was a lie, but it was the first out-and-out falsehood he'd uttered all day, so it was allowed. He'd had every intention of kissing Lyddie. Every intention and every desire. It was just his own worries about letting loose with her—well, that and Ben's intrusion—that had stopped him.

But he hadn't been blowing smoke when he said it was better to have fun while the chance was there. It was good advice. Good for adults, too.

He had a little over a month left in town. Maybe he could let Lyddie come a little closer. Maybe a lot closer.

The hell with it. Next chance he got, he was asking her to dinner. If he were going to be blamed for something, then damn it, he should at least have the fun of doing it.

CHAPTER NINE

A WARM FRONT moved in overnight, leaving the dawn too sticky for even the river breeze to cut. Judging from the number of people staggering in and ordering oversize iced coffees in place of their usual hot double-doubles, it seemed half the town had spent most of the night hunting for relief from the humidity.

"Give me a blizzard over this any day," Nadine snapped as she lifted her apron to wipe her face.

Lyddie knew the feeling. Comeback Cove could handle the worst winter Mother Nature produced, but a stalled tropical air mass was enough to wilt even the pleasure-seeking tourists. Nothing moved on a day like this. Well, nothing except tempers.

Tempers, and Lyddie's ever-increasing jitters about whether or not she should approach J.T. By lunchtime she felt ready to break.

She should never have talked to Zoë. Now it all seemed so...*possible.* And that was the most terrifying part of all. To know that all she had to do was work up her courage and—

"Holy doodle, she actually eats?"

Lyddie set down the cream pitcher she'd been refilling and looked in the direction of Nadine's amazed glance. At the end of the counter, Jillian perused the chalkboard menu. Lyddie was glad of the distraction. Wondering about Jillian was a lot easier on the nerves than wondering whether or not she might get lucky in a few days.

A few moments later, the reason for Jillian's unusual behavior became obvious when Ted strode into the shop.

Tracy Potter paused in the middle of paying to lift an eyebrow in Lyddie's direction. "Uh-oh. Ted must have caught Jillian breathing in the presence of another man again."

"As long as they don't get into a shouting match or go all kissy-kissy on us, I don't give a rat's ass what they do." Nadine nodded toward the happy couple, holding hands and whispering to each other as they pointed to the chalkboard. Lyddie knew she was in bad shape when she caught herself in a momentary spurt of jealousy.

She took their orders—club sandwich and coffee for Ted, naked salad and a skinny iced latte for Jillian—and had just finished loading their tray when the heat-dampened hum of conversation dropped in half. Everything in Lyddie went still. There was only one person in town that had that effect on business.

She fumbled through giving the First Couple their change and held her breath, waiting for J.T. to approach the counter. He seemed edgy somehow, sitting at one table, hopping to another, glancing in her direction before moving on.

If jitters were measured on the Richter scale, hers would have officially progressed from minor tremor to major trauma.

Finally he seemed satisfied. He left his soft leather briefcase on a table by the big bay window and approached the counter. Lyddie gave silent thanks that Nadine was in the kitchen. This way, she didn't have to do anything suspicious like shove the older woman aside in order to serve J.T.

"Hey," she said, only slightly breathless. "Where's my kid?"

"Packing for my mom. I was told in no uncertain terms that I was in the way and should go get lunch." He grinned, and for a moment he seemed like his usual casual self, not the man who had run his thumb over her lip and left her weak-kneed for the past two days. "I think Ma just wanted me gone so she could pack every pot and pan she owns without me telling her they sell cookware in Tucson."

"At least she's packing."

"In theory. Could I have some soup, please?"

"Coming right up." Soup. Great. How was she supposed to serve soup when her hands kept shaking and the sight of his muscled forearms resting on the counter only made it worse? Lyddie grabbed a bowl, took a steadying breath and lifted the lid of the pot. "What do you mean, 'in theory'?"

"Well, she says she's getting ready to go, but the number of boxes doesn't seem to be increasing. I think she sneaks down at night and takes stuff out."

"Seriously?"

"Maybe."

Lyddie ladled soup into the bowl, wrinkling her nose against the extra heat and tomato-scented moisture. "You think she's just pretending to agree while she has a different agenda?"

"I'm almost positive."

"What do you think she really wants?"

"Easy. She wants to stay." He grabbed a bottle of water from the cooler. "Both of us, me and her."

Lyddie's stomach did a funny little contraction. J.T.? Stay? In Comeback Cove? That would play hell with her love-him-and-let-him-leave plans, for sure.

On the other hand, life was definitely more interesting since he had swaggered back into town. The idea had a certain appeal. Well, except for the way it made her stomach twist.

She added a spoon and two packets of crackers to the tray. "But there's no chance of that happening, right?"

"About the same chance of a snowstorm blowing through here in the next hour."

That should make her feel a whole lot better. *Should* being the operative word.

He slapped money on the counter. "Anyway, I was wondering…"

Lyddie glanced up. The edginess was back, hovering just below the surface of his voice. He seemed almost as jittery as she felt. Almost like a fifteen-year-old who was getting ready to ask a girl out for his first date.

Now, there was a wonderful prospect. Maybe he would make the first move.

"Yes?" she asked, hoping she didn't sound too eager.

"Would you be interested in— I mean, would you have some free time later today? I have some papers for you."

Oh.

Lyddie's hopes fell as the heat rose in her cheeks. Business. He wanted to talk business. The man was *this close* to two weeks of a virtual male fantasy— no-strings sex with a woman who had four years of celibacy to make up for—and he would rather talk business.

She stared at the briefcase on the table, sure that the heat of her glare could burn right through the leather. From the corner of her eye she saw Ted and Jillian whispering in a way that boded no good, but for the moment, she really didn't care.

"Lyddie?"

Back to reality. She let her hands drop below the counter so he couldn't see the way she was curling them into fists of frustration. "Sure. This afternoon. Right."

"Great. I'll be here." He tossed his change on the tray before carrying it to his table.

Nadine bustled through the door, a fresh tray of muffins in her hands. "Did I miss any excitement?"

Argh.

Lyddie slipped through the kitchen and locked herself in the bathroom. Once there, she ran the water until it was icy, filled the sink, then closed her eyes and dunked her face as deep as she could without drenching her hair. Maybe the shock would knock some sense into her.

"Damn it!" She came up sputtering, groping blindly for paper towels. She didn't feel any more sensible, but at least she was awake enough to smell the coffee.

Unless she worked up a boatload of courage real soon, the temperature was the only thing that was going to make her break a sweat.

J.T. STARED AT the papers before him and tried to remember why he'd thought this was a good idea.

The morning had been pure hell. Iris insisted on packing everything, Ben chattered nonstop about fishing and there was enough humidity to make him long for the dry heat of Tucson. Add in the fact that he seemed to have forgotten the basic steps in asking a woman to dinner, and he was left with a knot in his gut and a bad taste in his mouth.

Oh, he remembered the essentials. Grin, get her smiling, lower the voice so no one else could hear, deliver the question. If this were anyone but Lyddie he would have been fine. But somehow, the usual steps didn't feel like enough with Lyddie. He didn't want to drop an invitation into the middle of a conversation about packing and soup. Silly as it seemed, he wanted to do this right. A little more privacy. A few less ears to overhear.

For now, though, he was stuck eating a bowl of soup that he barely remembered ordering and couldn't decide if he liked or not. There was something green floating in it. Spinach? Not that it mattered. He was too edgy to eat. He shuffled the papers and tried to look serious while spooning up broth. If he were lucky he could keep this up long enough for everyone to return to their previously scheduled lives, and he could leave without everyone watching.

He turned a page, opened the crackers and frowned as the light dimmed. For a second he hoped a cloud had rolled in. Then a footstep grabbed his attention. He glanced up to see Ted McFarlane looming over his table.

Damn it to hell.

Ted had always loomed. He seemed to think it made him seem intimidating. Good thing he didn't know it just made it easier to notice the slight bend in his nose that had been J.T.'s last and only gift to him.

"Mornin', Ted."

"Afternoon, J.T."

J.T. winced. So much for appearing cool and collected.

"Something I can help you with?" he asked, hoping Ted wanted nothing more than a donation to a local charity.

"Sure can."

Every muscle in J.T.'s shoulders seized tight.

"You can call off your dogs."

Ah, damn. Every head in the place had turned in their direction. Even Lyddie's, as he saw when he instinctively glanced her way. For a second he felt bad that this was going down in her shop. Then he realized that while everyone else was staring at him in morbid fascination, like something about to be thrown to the lions, Lyddie's expression alternated between fury—when she looked at Ted—and encouragement, when she looked at him.

Lydia Brewster was cheering him on.

"There's only one dog in my house, Ted. It belongs to my mother, and the most I've ever seen it move is to lift its head to eat. Other than that, I have no idea what you're talking about."

Ted shifted. "Your buddies. The ones harassing my wife to fast-track approval for your sale to Lyddie."

What the hell? "Thanks for the compliment, Ted,

but you're giving me way too much credit. I haven't asked anyone to do anything for me except sell me paint and soup."

J.T. purposefully kept the words low and mild. Nonetheless, they raced through the store like an urban legend on the internet.

Ted's face reddened slightly. "Right. That's why my wife has people coming up to her on the street, telling her to approve your sales and get you out of town."

He remembered Steve's nervousness in the hardware store. *Damn.*

J.T. sat back in his chair and feigned indifference, though it took every ounce of his willpower to do so. "Sorry that I'm overstaying my welcome, but I'll be gone as fast as I can. Meantime, believe it or not, all I'm doing is minding my own business."

Ted laughed, short and disbelieving. "Right. Tell me another one, J.T."

Three tables over, he saw Jillian watching, her lips slightly parted as if in anticipation of a kiss. *Oh, lord.* Ted needed to impress Jillian, and he was doing it by coming after J.T. It was high school all over again.

"Sit down, Ted," he said with more fatigue than rancor. "It's too hot for this crap."

"Fine. Just tell me what kind of trouble you're trying to stir up." Ted lowered his voice to what he probably thought was a menacing growl. He jerked his head toward the counter. "And why you had to drag Lyddie into it."

"First, I don't drag people into situations against their will. Anyone who's with me is there because they want to be." He pitched the words loud enough to carry to Jillian and the rest of the room. Lucky for her, he was probably the only one who noticed the way she paled.

"And second," he continued, "you know as well as I do there's nothing illegal about this sale."

"Just because it's legal doesn't make it right."

"It's right for me. And for Lydia."

"But not for the town."

He didn't even try to stop the snort. "You think that's gonna make me change my mind?"

"Would it kill you to do the decent thing for once?"

"Hell, no. I can be as decent as the next guy. I'm selling a great property to a long-standing tenant at a fair price. What could be more decent than that?"

"Call off this sale. Help Lyddie move on. Let Cripps Chips come here." Ted's fists tightened. "Think of it as making up for what you did."

"You think I owe this to the town."

"Damned straight."

"And what about Lydia?"

The stubborn expression on Ted's face never wavered. "We'll take care of her, just like always. We'll make sure she gets something good. Something newer, where she can—"

"I don't want another place," Lyddie said quietly from behind Ted's back. J.T. let loose with the grin he'd been holding back since he'd spotted her stalking toward them, tucking a towel in the pocket of her apron as if she planned to use it to whack some sense into someone.

To give Ted his due, he didn't get flustered or angry. He simply smiled gently at Lyddie, the way he undoubtedly would to a small child incapable of understanding a complex problem.

He was so dead.

"Lyddie, come on. You know you don't want to do this."

"I don't?"

Ted shook his head. Obviously he had missed the flatness in Lyddie's voice. "Of course not. You understand that we're not trying to be the bad guys. We just want to do what's best for everyone."

"How nice." She smiled sweetly. J.T. shivered. He wouldn't want to be on the receiving end of this. "And what if I told you that nobody is allowed to accost anyone else in my establishment?"

Whoa. Who would have thought there was a hellcat hiding inside Lyddie?

Ted blinked. "Huh?"

Lyddie kept her voice very quiet, but there was no doubting the force of her words. "I mean it, Ted. You can't attack anyone in my store and you definitely can't tell me what to do with my business."

"I'm not trying to—"

"Oh, yes, you are. And while you're generally an okay guy and I have no doubt you believe you're doing what's best for everyone, the fact is, I'm not willing to let you choose the course of my life. So right now, I suggest you apologize to J.T. and go eat your sandwich before I turn it into humble pie."

Ted's face took on an expression of such horror that J.T. almost burst out laughing. He couldn't recall the last time someone in the Cove had stood up for him—in public, no less—and it was turning into a mighty fine experience. If he hadn't been hungry for more of Lyddie before, he was now.

"Don't worry, Ted. I'll spare you the effort." J.T. rose slowly, both to prolong Ted's agony and to give himself more time surrounded by Lyddie's vanilla perfume. He offered a formal bow. "Mrs. Brewster, on behalf of Mr. McFarlane and myself, let me offer my sincere apology for acting like two buffoons in your shop."

Ted mumbled something that sounded like agreement.

"Apology accepted." Lyddie glowered at them both for a moment, then let it soften into something warmer.

"You're both welcome to stay. *I'm* not in the habit of telling people what they should do or where they should go."

Ted had the grace to flush.

J.T. shook his head. "That's okay. Time for me to get back to work, anyway." When a roomful of curious eyes glanced his way, his smile narrowed. "Show's over, folks. See you later, Lyddie."

THE SHOP EMPTIED soon after J.T. left. Most of the witnesses made sure Lyddie knew they hoped she would be okay, and that they were pleased to know she wouldn't be moving. She nodded and bit her tongue to keep from reminding them that she wasn't the one in need of apologies.

Jillian, however, was another story. No sooner had J.T. left than she whipped a notebook from her purse, ignoring her husband while furiously jotting notes. Nadine muttered something about lawsuits and running people out of town. Lyddie's blood boiled. When she walked past to wipe down a table, she couldn't keep herself from bumping against Her Worship's arm. The ensuing scrawl across the page was a reward in and of itself.

"Oh, Jillian, excuse me. I lost my balance for a second."

Jillian looked highly aggrieved, but she forced a smile. "Don't worry about it."

"I hope it wasn't anything important." Lyddie tried to catch a glimpse of the words filling the page, but Jillian snapped the book closed.

"Nothing you need to worry about." When Lyddie shrugged and went to move on, Jillian added, loud enough to carry, "Though if I were you, Lydia, I wouldn't be so quick to stand up for J.T. People notice those things, you know. They're bound to talk."

A month ago, even a week ago, that might have worried Lyddie. Not today.

So when Jillian followed her oh-so-helpful words with a knowing smirk, Lyddie merely leaned closer and said, "I doubt it, Jillian. They're too busy laying odds on whether or not that vacation you took last winter was really a cruise, or if it had something to do with the sudden lack of wrinkles around your eyes."

Jillian froze, Ted coughed and behind the counter, Nadine dropped the mug she'd been filling.

By the time three o'clock arrived, Lyddie couldn't wait to lock the door on the day. All she wanted was to kick off her shoes and collapse in silence for a few minutes before she had to go home.

Then she remembered that J.T. was coming back to talk to her. Suddenly, she didn't feel so exhausted after all.

"Go home, Nadine," she said as the older woman tossed her apron in the laundry hamper by the back door. "And cross your fingers that tomorrow is easier."

Nadine shook her head in that slow way that always warned Lyddie there was a lecture ahead. "I'd say that's mostly up to you."

"Me?"

"Yeah, you. Something's going on with you, missy, and I wish you'd get it straightened out before the rest of us have to pay any more than we already have."

Lyddie's stomach tensed. "What do you mean?"

"Come on, Lyddie. Your moods are flying all over the place, you're turning red all the time, you keep closing your eyes like you're trying to hold it together and today you lost your brains long enough to insult Their Royal Highnesses. It's obvious to anyone who takes the time to put it together."

"It is?" Lyddie forced herself to keep her eyes wide open as she reached back to brace her hands on the butcher-block table. There was no way Nadine could know about her supersecret fantasies for the upcoming weeks—but it sure sounded as though she had an idea.

And if Nadine had figured it out, then half the town already suspected her of sleeping with J.T.

Which was an oddly cheering thought, actually. If everyone believed it anyway, then what was left to stop her?

"Ah, Lyddie, come on. There's no shame in it anymore. It's not like it used to be when women tried to hide it."

"Of course not."

"So have you done anything about it yet?"

"Uh…"

Nadine frowned. "You really should. It's only

going to get worse the longer you wait, you know, and there's no point in suffering when you don't have to. Especially when the rest of us have to feel the fallout."

Oh, dear God. Had Nadine just given her permission to jump J.T.?

"What do you suggest I do?"

"Well, get to the doctor first."

"Of course."

"And then do some research for yourself. You can find anything on the internet these days."

The memory of her web search on over-the-counter HIV tests the previous night brought heat to Lyddie's cheeks. She was just about to admit that she'd already handled that task when Nadine took one look at her face and groaned.

"Another one coming? Go splash some water on your cheeks before you turn into a lobster."

Lyddie's embarrassment did a one-eighty and turned into confusion. "Another what?"

"Well, another hot flash, of course."

Lyddie stared stupidly, replaying the conversation in her mind. Symptoms…doctor…moods…

"Oh, my God. You think I'm going through menopause?"

"Well, what the hell did you think I was talking about?"

"I… But…" Holy crap. Her brave attempts to

turn her life around were being dismissed as nothing more than *hormones?*

"You honestly think that's the problem?"

"Don't see how it could be anything else. There's no way you could be pregnant, you're the right age, and you—"

"I'm only forty-two!"

"That's plenty old. I knew a girl over in Morrisburg who started in her thirties."

"Lucky her," Lyddie mumbled. *Menopause.* Never mind that Nadine was calling it all wrong. The very word made her feel old and broken, like she should be reaching for a sweater. Plus it irked the hell out of her, knowing that she was seen as such a permanent widow that people couldn't even come up with anything juicier to pin on her. She didn't want to be the town tramp, but come on. Did they honestly think she was that meek, that undesirable, that only raging aging hormones could drive her to action?

A soft rap sounded at the back door. Nadine cursed. Lyddie started and her gaze flew toward the sound.

It was J.T., giving her that smile that only she seemed to see. Everything in her that had felt momentarily withered and discarded bloomed into sudden life, pulsing through her.

"What's he doing here?" Nadine asked.

"We have some papers to discuss."

He pointed at his watch, but Lyddie was way ahead of him. It was time to meet. Time to act.

Time to make her move.

CHAPTER TEN

LYDDIE WAS VAGUELY aware that Nadine had said goodbye and slipped out. But mostly, now that she'd made her decision, all she could focus on was J.T., in all his glorious flesh.

She moved fast through the kitchen, not allowing herself to think. She'd done nothing but *think* for too long now. It was time to start doing.

She saw his surprise at her approach, saw the way it quickly shifted into a gut-melting grin of welcome when she opened the door, and from the top of her head to the tip of her quivering toes, she knew that if she could get up the nerve to go through with this, she would end up with the best how-I-spent-my-summer-vacation essay ever.

He stepped closer. "How are you doing?"

"Holding on. You?"

"Par for the course." He shrugged. The movement hiked his T-shirt higher. He was in the bike shorts again, a second skin that hugged every dip, every line, every God-knows-where-that-leads curve. Any last doubts were pushed aside by a drive far more primal.

"I'm sorry about what happened this afternoon." She forced her gaze back to his face, gauging his reaction by the narrowing of his eyes, the twist of his lips.

"You didn't do anything wrong."

"It's my place. Anything that happens here is ultimately my responsibility."

He crossed his arms and gave her the half smile she already knew meant he was in full tease mode. "So, if I told you I had the time of my life, would you take responsibility for that, too?"

"No. But I would say you were a damned good liar."

His laugh was low and husky, intimate and enticing. Lust erupted within her, fast and hot and urgent. Every inch of her skin itched to press against him. She wanted to taste his lips and tangle her feet with his and inhale the scent of afterglow off his chest. She wanted to whimper and moan and lose herself in the overpowering urge to move closer, harder, faster. She wanted to feel alive in every pore, every molecule.

And then she wanted to laugh and whisper and hold him tight until it started all over again.

She pointed to the briefcase resting by his feet. "You have some papers for me?"

"Uh...papers. Right."

He seemed awfully distracted for someone who was supposed to be here for a business meeting. She hoisted herself onto the corner of her desk, putting herself level with his shoulder, and smiled. "You know. The papers you were reading before Ted went all Neanderthal on us."

"Oh. Those." A wry smile quirked the corner of his mouth. "Would you believe I don't remember a thing I read?"

Simple words. Innocent, even. But the way his voice dropped when he said them made her ever more certain that she wasn't alone in this.

It had been a long time since Lyddie played this game, but she remembered the next line. "How come? Were you preoccupied?"

"You could say that."

"Couldn't wait to see if Ted could speak without Jillian's hand stuck up his...back?"

He stared for a second, then burst into laughter, richer and deeper than the strongest Colombian. Lyddie realized that while she'd seen him grin and even heard an errant chuckle, this was the first time she'd heard his belly laugh. It seemed to take him over. It was strong and vigorous and made her think, *damn,* as soon as she stopped being terrified, this was gonna be fun.

He shook his head, shoulders still heaving. "God, that felt good. You know that's the first time I've really let loose since I came back here?"

"I don't know whether to feel sad for you or proud of myself."

"How about if you skip them both and go for a chuckle or two of your own? Say, at dinner with me tomorrow night?"

If life were an Elvis movie, this would be the moment when one or both of them would burst into song. She hadn't been wrong.

Of course, if life were an Elvis movie, she would have a script so she wouldn't have to figure out what to say next.

"Tomorrow night? I—"

He held up a hand. "Wait. That came out wrong. Let me start over." He took a couple of steps toward the window before turning back to her, hands outstretched, face more serious than she had ever seen.

"If you think that I was staring at my work the whole time I was there, then I'm a hell of a better actor than I thought. The only thing I remember—except for Ted—is sitting at that table, watching every move you made and wishing everyone would leave so I could be alone with you. But since that wouldn't be good for your business, I thought I'd come back when they were gone." He leaned forward, hands resting lightly on her shoulders. It was all she could do to keep her knees from turning into Slinky toys. "I would like to see you tomorrow night. Very much."

The fact that she remembered how to swallow was proof that the body's reflexes are a wonderful thing indeed. He was so close. She saw the slight nervousness in those eager eyes, the way his T-shirt stretched with every rise of his chest. When she breathed she inhaled him, warm and strong, fresh like the river, dappled with a hint of pine.

He lifted a hand to her cheek. Lightly. One finger, maybe two. She could have been more certain if she hadn't been staring at his mouth, wondering what would happen if she leaned forward and helped herself to a taste of what promised to be even more delicious than a lemon poppy muffin.

But she couldn't. Not yet. No sensual dessert allowed until she ate her vegetables.

"Tomorrow. Okay, this is, um, complicated. And I've never done anything like this before, so bear with me?"

He drew back a little. Good. But bad, too, because there was now a curious tilt to his lips, negating all the calm she'd regained by his moving away.

What the heck was she supposed to say now?

"Tomorrow night will work. But I have, um, a couple of requests." She ran though the mental list drawn up after the previous evening's online research. "We need to go across the bridge, into New York. We need to leave in separate cars, because I don't want my family to know what I'm doing, and I know that sounds silly, but I'll explain later. Once we're out of town we can ditch one car in a parking lot somewhere and ride the rest of the way together. And when we get across the border…"

Oh, geez. Now she was getting to the really tricky part.

Devilment glittered in his eyes. "Do you always think this fast, or have you been planning this?"

"If I admit to planning, will you still respect me in the morning?"

"A woman who knows her own mind and goes for what she wants is always worthy of respect."

As long as he kept thinking that way, this might turn out okay.

"So don't keep me in suspense. What happens when we cross the border? We go wild at the duty-free shop?"

Lyddie closed her eyes, then forced them open again. No hiding.

"Before we go to dinner, if you're willing, we go to a drugstore to buy a do-it-yourself HIV test."

Well, *that* sure wiped the smile from his face.

Lyddie wasn't sure she had ever seen anyone's jaw actually sag before. His eyes widened and he inhaled, short and sharp, before letting loose with a choked bark of something she assumed was supposed to be laughter.

"Okay. Well." He huffed out a breath, much as she had when Ted told her she wouldn't be getting a loan. "You know, I was thinking an ice cream sundae would be enough for dessert, but if you have other ideas…"

Okay, so she blew that one big-time.

"This is why I told you I've never done anything like this before."

"What, exactly, have you never done? Dinner, or an HIV test?"

"Both. Either. I mean…shoot, I'd better just blurt it out, right? It can't get any worse than it already is."

"Backing up a couple of steps would probably be a better idea than saying anything new, at least for the moment. I need a second here to catch up." He stepped around where she was doing her best imitation of a statue and cupped her chin in his palm. The slightest hint of a grin flickered across his face. "But if it helps, you might notice that I'm not running."

The words and the touch managed to both soothe her and heighten the tension all at the same time.

"It's like this. Starting next Tuesday, I'll be alone for two weeks. I'm going to have a lot of extra time on my hands, and I was hoping, maybe, to spend it with you." She gulped. "For, um, some mutually satisfying experiences."

Silence.

Lyddie decided she'd watched him long enough. She'd kept her eyes open for the asking. Surely she didn't have to watch while he debated how to get away from the strange lady.

"Let me get this straight. I want to be sure I'm not misinterpreting anything."

All she could manage was a squeak or two. She settled for a nod.

"If I'm wrong, don't hold it against me, okay? But it sounds like you just asked me to spend two weeks having sex with you."

She nodded quickly before shaking her head. "Not all the time. Only at night."

For the second time that afternoon, his laughter pealed around her. Since it didn't sound derisive or disbelieving, Lyddie let herself relax just a little.

"I'm glad you cleared that up. Performance anxiety was starting to creep in."

She felt the blush creep up her neck and spread across her face. Could she possibly bungle this any more than she already had?

"And the test is in preparation for this, uh…"

"Fling."

"Fling. Right. You want a test so that starting next week, we could have a fling."

"That's about it."

"Not that I'm not flattered, because I am. Very. I'm just a bit…let's say, surprised."

"Oh." So much for those articles that made it seem like this was a regular prelude to intimacy these days. Betrayed by the internet once again.

Some of her mortification must have shown because he placed a tentative finger beneath her chin and raised her face to meet his gaze. "I have done them before. Don't panic—everything was always fine, and like any good soldier, I've never gone into battle without a shield." The corner of his mouth tipped up. "But I have to say, this is the first time I've had this conversation with someone I've only known a little while, biblically or otherwise."

"But isn't that the whole point? That we don't know each other very well, I mean?" It seemed so common sense, so awkwardly logical to her—but then, she was seriously out of the loop. Maybe she was asking too much.

But no. Not when it came to protecting her kids.

"Look, J.T." She decided that no matter what, she had to get something from this, so slowly rested her hand on his chest. He was warm and firm, slightly damp from the heat and utterly intriguing. It took a moment to unearth her thoughts from the layer of lust that had taken over once again. "I know this is awkward and presumptuous and about a million other things. And I do believe that you are conscientious about taking all the usual precautions. That's not the issue. But the thing is, my kids have already lost one parent. I know it might seem kind of silly and over the top to you, but I have to be super careful."

"Ah."

How he managed to pack so much emotion into one syllable was beyond her. The slight hint of bemusement left his eyes. She braced herself for the pity she was sure would follow, but instead, all she saw was understanding and a most unexpected but still welcome respect.

"Okay. I get it. I see why this is so important to you, absolutely. I guess I would be asking the same thing if the tables were reversed."

Oh, thank God.

"But now I have a question. Is this whole idea, this fling plan, because of me, or because of those things you said on your porch the night I brought Ben home? About you feeling like you were going to turn into your reputation?"

"I… Okay. A lot of it is because of me. I might not be able to change how others see me, but if I can change how I see myself, well, that has to count for something. Right?" She hesitated before deciding she might as well go for broke. "It's also because every time I look at your mouth, I want to outline it with lemon pudding and lick it off, one inch at a time."

"When exactly did you say your family was leaving town?"

Amazing how some things come back to you. Lyddie hadn't heard that trace of desperation in a man's voice in a long, long time, but she still recognized it as being a very good thing.

"The morning of the sixteenth."

"I'll make a note of that."

Okay, that sounded promising.

"Well, I don't expect an answer right away. You should probably think it—"

"Hang on." He hesitated before running his hand slowly along her shoulder. For a moment Lyddie wasn't sure what was happening. He didn't want to start right away, did he? Then she realized he was tugging her hand up to encase it between his own. She hadn't known how cold her fingers were until she felt the heat of his hands.

The shivers running through her at his touch, however, had nothing to do with temperature.

"Again, I'm flattered, Lyd. And humbled. And damned tempted. But—"

In that moment, *but* became one of her least favorite words in the English language.

"But?"

"I have a condition of my own."

Okay, she could handle this. Maybe. "Such as?"

He ran his thumb back and forth across the back of her hand, making concentration all but impossible. "I don't know you as well as I would like, but everything I've seen tells me you take your responsibilities—your promises—seriously."

She tried to nod, but the slight roughness of his thumb was creating a friction that was difficult to ignore. All other tasks became secondary to encouraging the spread of that friction.

"Here's what I'm saying. I don't want you to feel

obligated. I'll run to the store with you tomorrow night, and I'll do the test. But I know this is a big step for you. If you change your mind, I want you to know that it's okay with me. I'll live."

Amazing how his words could be so reassuring and comforting while the simple stroke of his hand was enough to make her believe everything she'd ever heard about him being the baddest of the bad—in the best way possible.

"I won't back out," she managed to say. "But, uh, the same goes for you. If you should, you know, get a better offer, or— You know, I just realized I never asked if you're involved with anyone."

"You want the history? Married at twenty-five, divorced at twenty-eight. No major drama. Turned out we were great at doing college together, but real life was another story. Since then, a handful of relationships, never more than semiserious, always with full precautions. The last one ended about five months ago."

Well, it wasn't four years, but he had some time to make up for, too.

"How about you?"

"Me?"

"I know you were married." He brushed her cheek, a gentle caress that both comforted and created a new rush of sensation.

"That's it in a nutshell."

"Nobody since he died?"

"Nobody."

Both hands now framed her face, thumbs stroking heated lines along her cheeks. "That's a long time."

"Tell me about it," she said, feeling the absence more than ever with each touch.

"You know," he said, leaning closer, "you really should have more information before you make your decision."

"Should I start calling all the girls you went to high school with?"

"I was thinking more along the lines of a free sample."

She jerked beneath his hands. "J.T., I—"

"Lyddie. Breathe, babe. All I had in mind was… this."

As he lowered his mouth to hers, a rapid-fire stream of emotions bombarded her. First came relief. *A kiss! He was only talking about a kiss!* Quick on its heels came a reality check: *oh, my God, he's going to kiss me.* Then the hormones kicked in, doing a little glory hallelujah song and dance as contact was made.

But no sooner had his lips brushed hers than the most dominant feeling of all leaped to the fore.

Different.

After four years, Lyddie could no longer give an accurate description of Glenn's kisses. The memory of his skin against hers had been dimmed by time and pain. The only time she caught his scent anymore was in bits and pieces, soap and rain and garden mud, little fragments of the whole that had been him.

Yet despite the time without him, the years with him had left his mark. His was the last touch she had felt. His was the standard against which newcomers would be judged. And so as J.T. edged closer, teasing her lips with his tongue, all she could think was that he didn't feel right. Not wrong. Just not right.

Her uncertainty must have communicated itself to him, for after a couple of seconds he drew back. One eyebrow lifted ever so slightly.

"I…I'm sorry. It's not you, it's me, it's—"

"It's okay." He lay one finger across her lips. "I told you, anytime you want to stop, you can."

"It's just… When I said there's been nobody, I meant nobody. Not a kiss, not a date, not anything. The most physical contact I've had with any man in four years was that pinky swear."

"So we go slow. Or we stop right now. Your call."

"No, I don't want to… Maybe. I mean… Oh, damn." The lust had ebbed away, leaving only a mix of disappointment, frustration and a slight embarrassment. She bowed her head so he wouldn't see the tears building in her eyes. The poor guy had already taken everything she'd thrown at him and shown nothing in return but consideration, humor and just enough desire to reassure her. He didn't need tears, too.

"Hey." His voice was deeper, his touch on her chin even more gentle than it had been. "You okay?"

She nodded. It must not have been very convincing, because he blew out a sigh and pulled her close, cradling her head on his shoulder. He stroked her hair in a steady, comforting rhythm.

"I'm sorry," she whispered. "I thought…"

"Don't. It's okay."

"I feel so…" *Stupid* hovered unsaid in the air.

"Lyddie. Look at me."

She wouldn't have complied, but he tugged her shoulders back until she had no choice.

"Good. Now listen. You spent, what, ten, twelve years with Glenn?"

"Seventeen. From the time we met."

He whistled. "Seventeen years together, four without him. No wonder you freaked." Again he stroked her cheek, pushing back a strand of hair that had broken free from her eternal ponytail. "I can't imagine the guts it took to do what you did today."

Lyddie thought about saying something regarding the fine line between courage and stupidity but decided it was better to keep quiet.

"I said it before and I'll say it again. No pressure. We do what you want, at your pace."

For the first time since he walked in, she felt a twinge of doubt. Not as to what she wanted to do, but what would happen when the time was up. She had the distinct impression that J. T. Delaney could be highly habit-forming. Could she really end it, just like that? Her stomach clenched.

But she would have no choice. The kids would be home, Ruth would be back and he would be leaving.

"You're being way too understanding," she said. "If anyone finds out, this will be hell on your reputation."

"It's a risk, but I'll manage."

She lowered her head again and let herself enjoy, without pressure, the feel of a strong shoulder beneath her cheek. He rubbed her back. She took a deep breath, reacquainting herself with his fresh-air scent, feeling the equilibrium return. He kissed her hair. She smiled.

"You need to get going?" he asked after a moment's silence.

"Probably."

"You want to take a rain check on tomorrow night?"

Did she? Lyddie thought back to the confusion, the desire, the gentle understanding he'd shown.

Some things took time. She'd learned that lesson the hard way. But while she would always miss Glenn, it wasn't the breath-stealing grief it had been. She was past that. Not just because of the passage of time, but because she'd made a conscious choice to move beyond it. She'd done it mostly for the kids, at least at first. They didn't need to lose their mother as well as their father.

But if she'd managed to move on once, she could do it again.

Slowly, she shook her head. "No rain check. On any of it."

"Lyddie—"

"No. Really. I'm not going to force anything, but this is one of those times when it won't hurt to keep all the options open. Know what I mean?"

He laughed against her, the sound low and rumbling. "Are you always this practical?"

"I wish." She waited the space of one breath, debated for a second then decided if she were going to be determined, there was no time like the present.

"J.T.?"

"Yeah?"

"Could we give that kissing thing one more shot?"

He stilled. "You sure?"

"Only one way to find out."

Good move.

This time, he wasn't entirely foreign. This time she was ready for the differences. This time she was prepared for the greater-than-expected heat of his lips.

This time, as he slowly melded himself to her, she managed to focus on him. Just J.T.

Sensation was all that mattered now: the gentle play of mouth against mouth. The warm strength of his hands cradling her head, sliding lower to rest on her shoulders, tugging her closer to him. The soft hum of pleasure when she tilted her head to increase the contact.

She could do this. She *wanted* to do this.

Lydia Brewster was on her way back.

CHAPTER ELEVEN

Two days after Lyddie offered him the best proposition of his life, J.T. walked through downtown with his briefcase in his hand and an all-too-familiar feeling in his heart: guilt.

Dinner hadn't happened after all. Lyddie had called with an apology to tell him she'd forgotten Ben's pre-camp doctor appointment. But he had made the drive across the bridge anyway, armed with her explicit instructions as to the type and quantity of tests. Now the crisp pharmacy bag was nestled in his briefcase. The fact that it was hidden securely from the view of any passerby did nothing to alleviate his certainty that anyone who looked at him would know exactly what was in the case, what he planned to do with it, and—most damning of all—who he planned to do it with.

For himself, he didn't really care. He had nothing to lose and a whole lot of happy to gain. But Lyddie had to live here. She'd already gone out on a limb, planning to buy the building and standing up for him in public. The town would forgive her, eventually, for defending him. Hanging out with him was pushing it. And if they knew how she planned to spend her two weeks of freedom, well…

Though maybe it would be better if they did. If they thought she'd fallen for him, maybe it would be easier for them to forgive the sale. People always seemed to expect nonsense from a woman who was besotted. They were never quite as understanding when the woman was completely sane.

Interesting theory. He'd have to mention it to Lyddie when—

Ah, damn.

Half a block to go until he reached River Joe's, and who was heading straight for him but Ruth Brewster. The thunderclouds building in the sky had nothing on the ones in her eyes.

He almost shoved the briefcase behind his back. Instead, he switched it to his left hand and raised the right in what he hoped was a casual greeting.

"Afternoon, Mrs. Brewster."

Ruth slowed her steps and glanced up and down the sidewalk. For a moment he thought she was checking to see if he could possibly be speaking to someone else. Then he realized she was making sure no one she knew was in sight. Something was afoot.

"I need to talk to you, J.T."

What was it with the Brewster women accosting him on public sidewalks?

"Sure," he said, all smiles and agreement. "Should we go get a cup of coffee?"

She shook her head. "I've no time to waste on false politeness. There's just two things I need to say to you."

"Yes?"

"First, I'm worried about your mother."

He hadn't seen that one coming. "Excuse me?"

"I've been thinking about her since the night you came to our house. I've been a mite busy and haven't paid her enough attention, but now I see there's something not right with her." Ruth fidgeted with the clasp on her blindingly white purse.

He thought back to those moments in the kitchen before a bit of stray jam had led him deep into temptation. "You said that everything sounded normal."

"It does. But there's something else. Iris was never any bigger around than a cattail, but there's nothing to her these days. And she always seems so tired. That flu she had last winter pretty well wiped her right out. I want you to get her to a doctor."

"She's being treated, but I'll double-check on her appointments," he said cautiously. "Uh…is there anything in particular you think I should be worried about?"

"At our age, it could be anything. The blood gets thicker, the bones get thinner, the heart doesn't know what it's supposed to do anymore. Add in losing your husband, and, well…that kind of shock takes a toll on a body." Her voice wavered, just the briefest of seconds, before she cleared her throat. "Well. Have her checked out top to toe."

He breathed a silent sigh of relief. No mention of emotional problems other than grief. "I will," he promised again.

"I hear you might be keeping one of the cabins for her to spend the summers."

"It seems like a good compromise."

"It is. And I'll give you credit for that. Everything I heard when you first came home said that you were hell-bent on getting her out of here and never looking back, but I think this would be better for her. Nobody can blame her for wanting to get away for winters, but she needs to be here. At least some of the time. I'm glad you're not so shortsighted that you would rip her away from everyone she knows and loves just to make things easier on you."

It was probably the most backhanded compliment he could recall receiving, but he knew what it must have cost Ruth to offer it. He nodded in acceptance.

"Of course, some folks think you're just saying that to get her to go peacefully."

"Really."

She nodded.

He shouldn't have been as surprised as he was. No—he shouldn't have been as *hurt* as he was.

"Mrs. Brewster, I am well aware that I put my mother through all kinds of hell when I was a kid. I can never begin to make that up to her. But even at my stupidest, I never deliberately set out to hurt her. My only concern is what's best for her health and happiness. That's a message I would thank you to deliver to anyone who might be questioning my motives."

She peered at him. "Swear on your father's grave."

He resisted the impulse to raise his hand in a Scout salute. "I swear."

"Good. Now while you're at it, swear that you'll leave my daughter-in-law alone while I'm away."

Now there was the Ruth Brewster he'd been expecting.

"I appreciate your concern, but I really think that what Lyddie does is none—"

"Of my business." She waved her hand, all signs of nervousness gone now. "Of course it is. She's my family and she's been through enough. She doesn't need the kind of heartache you would bring."

He could point out, legitimately, that it wouldn't be up to Ruth, but he knew what she was really saying. He had no reason to make a lonely widow think she was about to lose her last connection to her son.

"I'm not going to whisk her and the children away. I'm not here to upset anyone's life. And believe it or not, I don't make a habit of breaking hearts."

Ruth sighed. "Please. Your poor mother might be down now, but she's a ray of sunshine compared to what she was like after you ran off."

"That was a long time ago," he said stiffly.

"Feels like yesterday to some of us."

"To me, too." And that was growing more unpleasant by the minute. "But that has nothing to do with Lyddie."

"It has everything to do with her. She has to live here, she has to be able to hold her head up without shame. She can't do that if you…if you…"

"If I what? Look at her? Laugh with her?" He leaned closer, hoping he could shock her into silence by stating the unthinkable. "Make love to her?"

Ruth closed her eyes, undoubtedly praying for strength.

"Whatever you would be doing with her, love would play no part in it."

Well, of course not. Love had no place in what he and Lyddie had planned. Respect and affection and good old-fashioned lust, yeah, but that was it.

Though when he remembered the way her voice had softened that night in the kitchen, when she talked about the everyday things that reminded her of her husband, he realized it was a lucky man indeed who would be loved by Lydia Brewster.

"Look." He spoke briskly to shake off his sudden longing. "I appreciate your concern about my mother. I promise I'll take care of her. And I can also promise that whatever business Lyddie and I might have, I'll do nothing to hurt her."

He could easily swear to do no harm. That was

the truth. But he wasn't going to stand in the middle of Main Street with an HIV test in his briefcase and flat-out lie about his plans. That was an invitation to get struck by lightning if ever he'd heard one.

But from the way Ruth's narrow lips thinned a little more, he knew she wasn't the least bit mollified. He braced himself.

But Ruth only shook her head. "When you were five years old," she said, "you could already outtalk anyone. My husband sat down with you in the church basement one Sunday and tried to come up with a question you couldn't answer or a piece of logic you couldn't argue. But you stumped him. No matter what he said, you had an answer for it. Every single time." A sad smile flitted across her face. "You haven't changed a bit, have you, J.T.?"

Lucky for him, a flock of giggling teens swarmed around them then, filling the air with their chatter so he didn't have to try to reply. Ruth gave him one last warning look before marching along in their wake. He moved more slowly as he continued to the water.

Thank God for noisy teenagers.

The blue shingled roof of River Joe's came into sight and he picked up speed. He couldn't wait to be inside, to close the door on the rest of the world for a little while in the one place in town he felt almost like himself.

With Lyddie.

IF J.T. DIDN'T materialize in the next two minutes, Lyddie was going to throw up.

All morning she'd had the shakes. All afternoon she'd wondered wildly what she would do if Nadine decided to linger for another medical conversation. And for the whole long twenty minutes since Nadine had finally headed out, Lyddie paced the kitchen and worried. He was late. Was he having second thoughts? Maybe he'd realized what an idiotic idea this was. Or maybe the town had found out and they were organizing a lynch mob at that very moment.

She pulled out a block of cheese, grabbed a knife and started slicing. Anything was better than playing "what if." And if he walked in and said he'd changed his mind, she had a murder weapon close at hand.

Then the familiar *tap, tap, tap* sounded at the back door and the knife clattered to the butcher block. She gave a nervous little yip, wiped slick palms on her apron and glanced at the door.

It was him. And he looked almost as desperate as she felt.

She hurried to let him in, noting that it had started to rain, glancing quickly up and down the shoreline. No one but a few tourists in sight.

"Hey, there." She refused to look at the briefcase. Not yet.

"Hi."

Silence.

She had no idea what to say next. What was the protocol? Was she supposed to be businesslike, or seductive, or offer him a cup of coffee before they started discussing bodily fluids, or—

He drew in a deep breath. "So, you ready to play vampire?"

She could have kissed him then and there, just for making her laugh. But it seemed too forward, too abrupt. Besides, with a couple of drops of rain still clinging to his upper lip, he looked so damned hot that she was afraid she wouldn't be able to stop. Restraint. That was what she needed. So she nodded toward the butcher-block table and the cheese.

"Let me put this away first."

He followed close behind as she returned to the work area. Even without looking, she was aware of the way they walked in perfect unison, and for one wild moment she wondered if they would find other rhythms so easily.

"Uh, Lyddie?" He reached around her to tap her fist, which was closed tightly around the knife, his breath warm against her cheek, his forearm brushing hers. "The kit comes with lancets, okay? We won't need that to draw the blood."

The hell with restraint.

The knife clattered to the table as she turned in the circle of his arms and dive-bombed him.

Jitters fled at the first touch of her lips against his. Nervousness evaporated as his mouth parted and his arms tightened around her. He pressed her against the edge of the table, kissing her with a desperate heat that told her he'd needed this reassurance as much as she had. He moved in closer and she tilted her hips against his and wished she was the kind of woman who could throw caution to the wind, because her imagination was throwing out some very insistent suggestions as to what could be done with him, her and that great big table right behind her.

When reason reasserted itself and she reluctantly broke the kiss, she rested her head against his chest and breathed in his musky dampness. "Thanks. I needed that."

His lips grazed the top of her head. "Me, too."

"Lousy day?" She swallowed hard. "Second thoughts?"

"The only second thoughts I've had are to wonder whether or not this is right for you."

"It sure feels that way. At least at the moment."

"It does, doesn't it?" He ran one finger lightly down her back, barely touching, yet it was enough contact to push her closer to him again.

"How about you?" he asked against her ear. "Any doubts? You know it's allowed."

She shook her head slowly, reveling in the brush of her cheek against the firmness of his chest. "I'm nervous. Anxious. But like I said, I think I'd regret not doing this a whole lot more than I'll ever regret going through with it."

"Positive?"

"Well, maybe not totally." She tilted her head back to grin up at him. "Kiss me again and I'll let you know for sure."

"Forget it." He stepped away from her, hands behind his back. "I don't know how to tell you this, Lyddie, but you have an amazing mouth. I'm not going near it again until we have a whole lot more time and freedom, and you have the reassurance you want." He bent, scooped up the briefcase she'd knocked to the floor when she attacked him and withdrew a green-and-white pharmacy bag. "Shall we?"

The knowledge that he thought her mouth was amazing gave her the courage to nod. "Okay. Let's do the blood one first and get it over with. Where are the directions?"

"I've done this before." He opened the box and handed her the instruction sheet. "It's not as intimidating as it looks, trust me."

Trust him? She could do that. Resisting him was the hard part. It was a damned good thing they only had two weeks together. The way J.T. slipped an arm around her waist and pulled her against his side as they scanned the directions told her this man could definitely become her addiction.

"Okay," she said at last. "I'm ready if you are."

He extended his palm. "Go for it, doc."

Holding his finger steady with one hand, she

shook out the antiseptic swab and used it to slowly, methodically wipe his finger.

"You, uh, you do that well."

She had the feeling he wasn't talking about her cleaning ability.

"Now we have to let it dry." She set the wipe back on the napkin she'd spread out as her work area, but didn't let go of his finger. He was her anchor. As long as she had hold of him, she'd be fine.

"I ran into your mother-in-law on my way here."

She clenched his finger hard enough to make him wince. At least now she understood the desperation in his face when he first appeared at the door.

"Sorry. I take it she talked to you?"

"Talked *at* me is more like it."

She forced out a long and slow breath. "How bad was it?"

"Not all bad. She had some valid points." He touched her cheek. "She's worried about you."

"She's mostly worried that I'll run off and take the kids away from her. Or do something to disgrace Glenn's memory."

"I think she really does care what happens."

"Yeah, I know. That's what makes it so hard." She shook her head and checked her watch. "Okay. That's long enough. Ready?"

He looked like he had another question, but he gave a swift nod. "Go for it, Dracula."

She tightened her grip on his finger, blew out a chestful of tension and positioned the lancet.

"Sorry about this." With a quick and decisive thrust, she pushed the point through the skin. He barely flinched. But she couldn't help noticing the way his free hand balled into a quick, white-knuckled fist.

When he spoke, he sounded as casual as ever. "Are you always this good with blood?"

"I'm a mom, remember? Boo-boos are my specialty."

She applied pressure and collected the berry-red drops as instructed. He was right—it hadn't been as complicated as it seemed. Still, she felt the stiffness drain from her shoulders as she pressed the cotton swab to the wound, then applied a bandage.

"Dang." She scanned the directions in mock dismay.

"What?"

"They forgot the most important part."

Quickly, she pressed her lips to the bandage, letting them linger far longer than was probably wise. But even through the sterile covering, he felt too warm, too enticing, for her to maintain her facade of brisk efficiency.

"You know, Lyddie, you make it damned hard for a man to stick to his honorable intentions."

She raised her head and took him in: the fullness of his mouth, the heat in his eyes, the way he leaned closer as though he couldn't stay away. It had been a long time since she'd felt this power. Damn, but she'd missed it.

"Good," she said softly. "Because I think there are times when honor is highly overrated."

Some indiscernible emotion—pain? confusion?—flitted across his face. Then he reached for her cheek with one finger, gently turning her back toward the instruction sheet.

"Better seal it up."

Right. Thank heaven he knew this drill. She was so giddy with lust and nerves that she needed all the help she could get.

She put the test in the preprinted envelope, removed the sticker with the tracking number and stuck it in the notebook she'd pulled from her purse.

"Okay." She handed him another test set from the kit. "My turn."

"You?"

"Of course. Why do you think I told you to get two tests?"

"I thought you were worried about messing one up. Lyddie, you told me your history. You don't need to do this."

"Yes, I do. For all you know, I could have jumped every tourist with a Y chromosome. All you have is my word that there's been nobody else." She offered her hand. "You deserve certainty as much as I do."

With those words, J.T. knew that his fate was

sealed. Who was he kidding to think he could spend two weeks making love to Lydia and then walk away? She wasn't the kind of woman a man left willingly. She was the kind that made men rearrange plans and rethink everything they'd ever believed about themselves.

A smart man would walk away now while he could still get away unscathed.

But even though he knew he was letting himself in for a hell of an ordeal down the road, he wasn't strong enough to turn away from the promise in Lyddie's touch. Nor could he slap her down after she'd pulled together the guts to get this started.

He almost rolled his eyes at his own delusions. Like the only reason he was doing this was to make her happy. One glance at the way her polo shirt dipped into the hollow between her breasts and he was reminded of exactly why he was willing to take this chance.

He took the hand she continued to hold out to him. "I promise to be gentle."

"That's okay." Once again she looked him straight in the eye. "Gentleness is also vastly overrated."

Nope. No way he could walk away now, even if he wanted to. And he most certainly did not.

He swabbed her finger. As when she was cleaning him, he could feel her texture through the wipe, the softness of the finger pad, the slight callus at one side. He stroked the roughened spot again.

"This part gets used a lot?" His voice sounded huskier than usual, even to him. Not that he could be one hundred percent certain, what with the blood roaring in his ears and all.

"Writing orders. Pushing the handle on the coffee machines. Signing homework."

All the bits of her regular life. The life, as Ruth had reminded him, that she would have to resume when he tore himself away and went back to Tucson.

"Time to dry." He tossed the wipe on the paper towel, tugged her finger upright and blew a soft, steady stream of air across the moist surface. The momentary widening of her eyes was all the encouragement he needed.

"By the way," she said, far too casually for him to believe, "Jillian was in today. Taking great delight in telling me my paperwork had gone missing and the planning board wouldn't be able to review the sale this month."

"Surprised?" He blew again, short puffs, and felt the shiver radiate from her finger and up her arm.

"Not in the least."

"Pissed off?"

"A little." Her laugh was breathy enough to make him consider messing up his own paperwork, just so he would have to stick around past mid-August. "Then I think, Lyddie, you hypocrite. You can't complain about people putting you on a pedestal and then get mad when someone treats you… Um…okay, that's probably dry by now."

"One more second." He blew a long, slow breath across her finger, then up her palm, lowering his head until he was but a whisper above her skin as he hovered over her wrist and moved toward the crook of her elbow. He might have to resist her lips for a couple more days, but he would take his pleasure where he could. And filling himself with Lyddie's warm vanilla scent was most certainly a pleasure.

Especially when he glanced up to see her with her eyes closed and a look of pure rapture on her face.

I did that.

The rest of her world could make her look worried or happy or concerned or angry, but he was the only one giving her this bliss, this fulfillment. And damn, it felt good.

Unable to stop himself, he leaned forward and brushed a light kiss against her mouth. It wasn't what he wanted. But from the sheer delight in her eyes when they flew open, he knew it was exactly what she had needed.

He grinned down at her. "Ready?"

She nodded. He'd lay money that her agreement had nothing to do with the test.

He allowed himself one more moment surrounded by her, then backed off and steadied himself. Time to focus.

"Hang on." He picked up the lancet, pulled it from

the protective wrapper and poised it above her finger. She inhaled sharply. He glanced up, surprised, and saw her grimace.

"You okay?"

"I hate finger sticks. Had three kids without drugs, but these… Ugh."

Hated them, but insisted on going through with it.

"I wish you'd told me earlier."

"Why?"

"I wouldn't have bothered pretending to be brave when you stuck me."

She laughed, and he moved into position once again. He tightened his grip, positioned the lancet. He hadn't been lying: he'd done this before, more than once. But he could never remember being quite so apprehensive.

"On the count of three," he said, hoping to steady himself. His lunch danced in his stomach. He blinked to clear the haze clouding his vision.

"One…"

What the hell was wrong with him? He was a scientist, for God's sake. Why was he suddenly getting squeamish about a simple finger stick?

"Two…" she whispered. Her voice sounded tight. The moment he glanced up at her, he knew he'd made a mistake. Her eyes were screwed shut. Her face was turned away from him. Worst of all, her free hand was clamped over her mouth, no doubt to muffle the squeal of pain she was obviously anticipating. Pain she didn't need to go through but was willing to endure…for him.

And in that moment, he knew he couldn't do it. It would take a gun to his head—no, to *hers*—to make him willingly inflict pain on her. There was no way in hell he could stab Lydia Brewster, hurt her or make her suffer.

Because somewhere in the past weeks, he'd fallen in love with her.

CHAPTER TWELVE

HE HAD NO idea how long he sat there, gripping Lyddie's finger as if it were the only thing keeping him from hitting the floor. The part of his brain that could still function realized that it was pretty ironic—being saved by the woman who made him fall in the first place.

She shifted on the stool, tilted her head toward him.

"J.T.?"

He croaked out an odd strangled sort of sound. Her eyes widened with something that resembled horror. She dropped his hand and lunged across the table to grab a huge stainless steel bowl that she shoved into his arms.

He blinked as if coming out of a drug-induced stupor. "What's this?"

"A bowl. You know, to catch—unless you think you can make it to the bathroom. It's just over—"

"No." He shook his head, set the bowl on the table. It wobbled in perfect time with his stomach. "No, I'm fine, I don't—I'm fine."

"You're sure? You looked pretty green for a minute there."

He laughed, a short, decidedly unmerry bark, and swept his face with his hand. "Yeah, I imagine I did."

"What's wrong?" She wrinkled her nose as if trying to sort things through. "Oh, my God, are you afraid of blood? Is that it?"

"I… No…uh, I mean, yeah." He wasn't above grabbing for whatever help she could give him. Anything was better than the truth. "It doesn't bother me most of the time, but I, uh, did some work in the garden after lunch. With the heat and all, I guess it's getting to me." He gave her a rather desperate grin. "I know the shop is closed, but could I get some water?"

"Sure, of course."

As she pushed herself off the stool and bustled about behind him, he stared blankly out the window, searching for guidance in the river running just beyond the door.

How had this happened? He barely knew her. But even as he thought that, he realized it wasn't true. He knew the important parts. She was brave and caring and concerned for others, and she'd been willing to give him a chance when no one else had.

Maybe that was it. Maybe this wasn't love. Maybe it was gratitude mixed with a healthy dose of lust.

Then she sat down across from him again, bringing cheese and juice and a light hand to his arm, and all his swirling confusion calmed. This was the truth.

He was a goner.

"Thanks." He nibbled the wedge of sharp cheddar, buying time.

"How are you doing?" She placed a cool palm against his forehead and frowned. "You do feel a bit warm."

"That's your fault," he said, delighting in the faint blush that rose in her cheeks, the way she looked down, unable to meet his eyes for the briefest second.

When she lifted her head again, though, he saw nothing but determination. "Uh—you might want to look away." And before he could swallow enough to lodge a protest, she took one sharp breath and poked her own finger.

"Lyddie," he breathed when he finished swallowing. "Damn, honey, you didn't have to do that."

She scrunched her nose as she squeezed blood onto the test circle. "Not a problem. We need to save your strength, you know." Again, pink rose in her cheeks.

"I'm not usually such a wuss." *Only when I figure out I'm in love with a woman I'll have to leave in a few—*

Damn. It was all he could do to keep from choking yet again.

A month. Five weeks if he were lucky. Barring a miracle, that was all he had with her. Five weeks to fill himself with this woman who'd crept into his heart when he wasn't looking.

It wasn't enough. He could never have enough of her.

He watched her from behind, drinking her in as she packed up the test: the way her ponytail dipped straight to her nape, the curve of her neck above her shoulder, the planes of her shoulder blade beneath her shirt. Knowing that in just a few days she would be his was enough to make him dizzy—for real, this time.

"There. All set." She turned to face him, smiling in a way that lifted his heart even as it broke within him. And in that moment, he knew what he had to do.

He had five weeks to make Lyddie fall in love with him. Five short weeks to convince her that he was as necessary to her life as she was to his.

But he had a feeling that making her fall in love would be easy compared to convincing her to leave Comeback Cove.

THREE NIGHTS LATER, Lyddie sat down with her children and Ruth, served up spaghetti and wondered what kind of mother spent her last meal with her family wondering how she could slip away to call for the results of her potential lover's HIV test.

The answer, obviously, was a very lustful one.

Ruth spooned dressing over her salad and said,

"Tish, I ran into Miss Lockhart from school today. She said she'll have first grade again next year, so it looks like she'll be your teacher."

Tish's fork clattered dully against the polished oak table. "May I be excused? I lost my attepipe."

Ben snorted. "It's 'appetite,' drama queen."

"Ben, leave your sister alone." Lyddie shared a worried glance with Ruth—the first time the woman had looked her in the eye since the night of J.T.—then reached for Tish's hand. "What is it, sweets? Miss Lockhart is supposed to be very good."

"She makes me feel funny."

Lyddie remembered Tish saying something about that before, then blowing it off. "How?"

Tish stuck out her bottom lip, crossed her arms over her chest and stared at her spaghetti. Lyddie sighed. So much for sneaking away.

"Patricia Grace," Ruth said in the tone that always made Lyddie want to shake her, "you know there's only one section of each grade in school. It's not like you can switch to another teacher. Whatever is bothering you, you have to get over it."

Lyddie counted to three in her head—the highest she could manage before the need to speak spilled over. "Tish, come on. If there's a real problem we'll find a way to work around it—" she stared pointedly at Ruth for a moment "—but we can't help you if you don't talk to us. So fess up. What's the problem?"

Two fat tears plopped into Tish's spaghetti.

"Ah, geez." Ben tossed his fork onto his plate. "Tell the truth, DQ. It's because of Dad, right?"

"What?" Lyddie was sure she hadn't heard correctly. Ruth opened her mouth to say something, then bit her lip and watched the children.

Tish's braids bobbed up and down as she slowly nodded agreement.

Lyddie turned to Ben. "What's the trouble?"

"Well, whenever I see Miss Lockhart, she always talks about Dad, about what a great guy he was. That kind of thing." His casual shrug was offset by the pinkness beneath his freckles. "I think she liked him, you know?"

Lyddie sagged against the carved wooden chair and tried to make sense of what she'd just heard. "Ben, buddy, I know this is uncomfortable, but could you be more specific?"

Ruth stood up. "Lydia, could you help me with dessert, please?"

Oh, geez. This was going to be interesting.

Ben rolled his eyes. Lyddie gave Tish a quick hug before following Ruth.

She found Ruth frowning viciously at the pan of Rice Krispie squares she was slicing. Lyddie gave an involuntary shudder. She was mighty glad she wasn't on the receiving end of that glare.

On the other hand, she was getting pretty tired of being treated like a pariah in her own home. It might be worth a few minutes of discomfort if it meant she and Ruth could get past this.

"So, Anna Lockhart." She decided to deal with Tish's dilemma first and proceed accordingly. "What's the story?"

"I didn't want the children to think poorly of their teacher. But Anna was always sweet on Glenn, back in school. He was a couple of years ahead of her and she used to worship the ground he walked on. I know she always hoped he would come back to her someday."

"Well, that's all fine and good, but it was twenty-some years ago. Don't you think she should be over it by now?"

Ruth stabbed the squares. Lyddie gave her a second, then drew a deep breath and went on.

"Ruth. If a grown woman is still mooning over her high school love—enough that it causes discomfort to his children—don't you think that's a problem?"

Another direct hit to the pan.

"You know, Glenn never mentioned Anna to me. Was this a reciprocal thing, or all in her mind? Because if he was never even interested in her, but she's created something, I'm really worried about my child—"

"They went out a few times."

Well, at least it was an answer.

"It couldn't have been very serious if nobody ever mentioned it to me before."

"There are some who think it's more admirable to stay quiet about certain things. Not flaunt their affairs in front of others."

That did it. Lyddie marched to the counter and grabbed the pan, noting that Ruth had carved the squares into pieces so tiny that they were practically individual crisps. "Look, could we cut the crap and get down to the real issue? You don't care about Anna and what might or might not have happened with her and Glenn. This is about me and J.T."

Twin spots of dull red appeared on Ruth's cheeks as she stared out the window.

"I'm sorry you don't like him," Lyddie continued. "I'm sorry you don't approve. But this is my life. I still love Glenn and I'll miss him until I die, but I'm not going to spend the rest of my life as some kind of martyr."

Ruth took a deep breath and clasped her hands in front of her. "Why him?" she said, very quietly.

There were half a dozen easy answers, but only one that mattered. "Because he makes me feel alive again."

Ruth stifled a sob. "He's no good. He's dangerous, Lydia, he'll hurt you like he's hurt everyone else in this town. He'll lie to you and leave you and—"

"Yes, he'll leave me." And God, how she already

dreaded that final farewell. "But he's not any of those other things. Maybe he was, back when he was a kid. But people change. They grow. You might not have noticed, but he's bent over backward to make this sale possible. If not for him offering to hold the mortgage, I would have to move River Joe's, pack up and leave the building where you first met Buddy. Would you want that?"

"No. No, of course not. But that doesn't mean you have to get involved with him, or pay him with your body like a…"

"Like a common tramp?" The words came out low and hard, but since Ruth was suggesting nothing more than what Lyddie herself had said to Zoë, she couldn't cast stones. "I was faithful to Glenn the whole time we were together. I never even fantasized about another man, except maybe George Clooney once in a while. But I've been alone for four years."

"You don't have to tell me how long it's been."

"I know, Ruth. And I know you lost even more than I did, and I don't know how you managed to keep going. But we did, both of us." She touched the faded blue cardigan Ruth wore around the house, no matter what the season. "We kept going, but I feel like somewhere along the line, I stalled out. I'm frozen in some place I don't want to be. You, the town, everybody has this picture of who and what I should be, and I just… I'm afraid that if I don't do something now, while I have the chance, that it will be too late."

"Would that be so bad? Your life here isn't that terrible."

"No, it's not. I have the kids, and you, and a business I enjoy in a place that I really do love." She wrapped her arms around herself and moved away from the window. "But I don't like what I see happening. To me, to Glenn's memory. People keep forgetting that he was human. Think. Do you believe it's normal for an old-maid school teacher to obsess this way?"

"Anna isn't obsessed."

"Maybe not, but if she's making my kid uncomfortable, I don't think she's exactly normal."

"There's nothing abnormal about remembering someone. About respecting what they did."

"If that was all it was, it would be fine. But damn, Ruth, it's going too far. Glenn was a good man. So was Buddy. But we're in danger of forgetting how real they were, of turning them into cartoon heroes. Is that what you want for them?"

When Ruth merely tightened her lips, Lyddie plowed ahead, uncertain if she was making things better or worse. "I don't want that. I want my kids to know everything about their father, the good and the bad, all the things that made me love him, from the way he sang them to sleep to the way he could never remember to put the bread back in the fridge after he made a sandwich. I want to give them that, and let them know how much he meant to me, and make sure they never ever forget him." With a long breath, she added, "But I'm still here. I want a life, too. Nothing will be helped if I act like I died when he did."

At last Ruth turned to her, anguish clear on her face. "I can't lose those children. You and the children are all I have."

It would do no good to point out that this was J.T.'s other major attraction: that there was no time to build emotional ties, no worries about falling in love and upsetting everyone's lives. All she could do was simply say, "I know. And I have no intention of taking them away from you. I'm doing everything I can to keep things the same, to make sure—"

But Ruth shook her head, her mouth working as she strove to hold back tears. "Don't you see, Lydia? It's not up to you. It's him. That Delaney boy could make the angels themselves turn away from the light. If he makes up his mind that he wants you, then you'll have no say. You'll be gone before you even know what he's done." Her face crumpled as the tears finally fell. "And I'll be left with nothing."

With that, she fled into the hall, no doubt headed for her bedroom. Lyddie stood alone in the kitchen, surrounded at last by the solitude she'd yearned for earlier.

Solitude. But no peace.

IF THERE HAD ever been a slower day in the history of humanity than Tuesday, July 16, J.T. didn't want to know it.

It would have been easier if he could have forgotten what lay ahead. But every action, every sentence, seemed to take him back to Lyddie. From the first sip of his morning coffee to the moment he hustled through the dairy aisle at the supermarket, aiming for some half-and-half but coming to a dead standstill in front of the pudding display, she surrounded him.

And drove him crazy.

He hadn't been this nervous in years. He wasn't blasé about sex, but other than the usual will-we-or-won't-we deliberations that came with new relationships, he hadn't really worried about it since he was a teen.

But he'd never been anyone's first time after heartbreak. Never been anyone's way back to life. Never been so scared-out-of-his-brain in love that he could barely breathe when he thought of leaving her.

And that was what left his hands shaking as he paced the length of the cabin dock in the dimming light.

Would she show?

He'd meant what he said. If she'd changed her mind, well, he'd live with it, taking consolation in the fact that he'd been deemed worthy of even the thought. But God, how he hoped…

His footsteps echoed in the lonely night, a slow counterpoint to the rapid drumming of his heart. He'd spent a good chunk of the day at the cabin, stocking the fridge, sweeping out corners, making up the bed with fresh linens. Everything was in place.

Everything except his partner.

He reached one end of the dock. Paused. Checked his watch.

8:37 p.m.

Not late. Not yet.

Maybe he should call. Tell her that if she didn't want to go through with it, it would be okay. That way she could stay home and watch a movie and they would still be able to look at each other in the morning.

Or maybe—

Gravel crunched beneath car tires. His heart dropped, rebounded and bounced ridiculously in his chest cavity—all of which he knew was physically impossible, but damn, it sure felt like it.

A car door closed. A soft voice called, "J.T.?"

One giant load of worries slid off his shoulders, making it easier for him to fill his lungs as he headed toward her.

It was time.

She stood uncertainly beside her car, clutching her purse tightly to her side.

"You're here."

Her smile was small but the tilt of her chin was determined. "I'm here."

He followed the direction of her gaze. What was she thinking?

"It's lovely," she said at last.

He glanced at the small cabin, covered with cedar shakes and trimmed in deep hunter green. "It's a nice little place. If it was a rainy week you'd go stir-crazy, but it works."

"I tried to get Ben to describe it to me, but all I got from him was that it felt a lot bigger than it looked." She took a cautious step forward. "It's good that you got to it before it fell apart. It's sad to see something so pretty go untouched."

He lifted a gentle hand to her cheek. "Yes. It is."

She closed her eyes briefly at the contact. For a moment he worried she would bolt. She leaned deeper into the caress and rubbed against his palm.

"Let's go inside."

He'd never heard sweeter words in his life.

He held tight to her hand as he guided her up the steps. "Careful. That second stair is a bit soft. I still need to replace it."

"Okay," she said, but didn't tug her hand away, even when they reached the small porch. She glanced around, a small smile softening her lips. "Love the glider."

It had been an impulse buy that afternoon, spurred by the memory of the chairs on her porch on the night when he first knew he wanted to kiss her. Putting it together had taken three frustrating hours and left him with a gash on his thumb, but with that smile, he knew it had been worth it.

He followed her into the one-room interior and tried to look at it through her eyes. To the right, a small kitchenette. Green-dotted curtains danced at the open window above the sink. Past that, a tiny wooden table, on which rested a place mat, two wineglasses and a corkscrew. She smiled when she saw the glasses. Over on the left, a cushy tan love seat and a side table gave the illusion of a living room. And tucked into the far left corner—

He saw the slight hunch of her shoulders, the momentary cessation of movement, and knew she'd noticed the bed. He'd lay dollars to doughnuts that her reaction hadn't been prompted by the fluffy new tan-and-hunter comforter he'd picked up on his shopping expedition.

"Lyddie?"

"Uh-huh?"

"You want some wine? I have champagne, or there's red if you prefer."

She glanced at the wineglasses almost longingly, then shook her head. "Not now. Maybe later."

Later...

"If you want to, you know, sit out on the porch and talk, that's okay. We don't have to—"

"Yes. We do." She looked directly at him for the

first time that night. "I won't kid you, J.T. I'm more nervous than I've been in years. Maybe decades. But I'm not going to spend the rest of my life thinking shoulda-woulda-coulda."

He remembered what she'd said to him the day she offered her proposition. *I want to feel alive again.* She looked it now, with her lips slightly parted and a combination of desire and determination sparking in her eyes.

"Okay." He tossed his keys toward the love seat. The jingle was swallowed up by the deep cushions.

A slight smile tugged at the corner of her lips. "That's more like it."

He debated yanking his polo shirt over his head and sending it in the direction of the keys, but decided against it. Instead, he took her by the hand and pulled her farther into the cabin.

"Come on," he said softly. She tossed her purse beside the keys. He dropped into the love seat, patting his lap with his free hand.

"Come here."

The look she slanted toward him was equal parts amusement and disbelief. "No way."

"Way."

"I'm too old for monkeying around like that. I don't bend that way anymore. I'll break your legs."

"I'll take that chance." He tugged her hand. "Shoulda-woulda-coulda."

Her laughter was full-bodied and utterly contagious. "No fair."

"I know."

"All right." She moved in closer, aiming for his
lap. "But remember, you can call a halt at any time.
I'll be okay."

He grinned at having his words parroted back
to him, but when she hesitated, he decided she was
taking entirely too long. She was the one in charge
but he had a few needs of his own. And right now,
he needed her in his arms.

So he pulled. Not hard. Just enough to disrupt her
careful descent and send her tumbling onto his lap.

She shrieked. He laughed. His arms went around
her, steadying her against him. Just as he'd imagined,
her head nestled directly below his in a gratifying fit.

"That was uncalled for." The words were indig-
nant but the tone was anything but.

"Had to show you my knees were up to the challenge."

She rubbed her cheek along his jawline and
peeked up at him. He saw mischief and wonder and
awareness, all in eyes the clear blue of the river on
a sunny day. It was enough to make him tighten his
grip just a little, slide his hand just a smidgen farther around her waist.

"How about the rest of you?"

"What do you mean?"

"Well, you said your *knees* are up to the challenge. How about the rest of you?"

She was warm and soft, she fit him perfectly and she made him laugh. If he hadn't fallen for her already, that combination alone would have pushed him over the edge.

"Why don't we put it to the test?" He tipped her chin up and lowered his mouth to hers.

WITH THE FIRST brush of his lips, Lyddie knew she'd made the right choice. Yes, she was nervous. Yes, she still couldn't believe she was actually going to climb into that gorgeous bed with this gorgeous man. But with that first taste she knew it would be okay.

She leaned into him, reveling in the feel of his hard chest pressing against her. His lips teased hers and she arched up higher, sliding her hand across the stubble on his chin. He was rough and firm and hot, totally and completely male, everything she'd been missing in her life for too, too long.

Long-forgotten hunger flared within her. She pressed closer, deepening the kiss, her lips and hands demanding that he keep pace. For a second he matched her, nipping at her lower lip, sliding his palm higher up her rib cage until it rested one agonizing fraction of an inch below her breast. Then he abruptly broke away, his heart slamming against her.

"Lyddie? Are you—"

She cradled his face with both hands. "J.T., listen.

You've been really patient and considerate and all that jazz. But the time for that is over."

Way past over.

"Don't hold back now. Don't worry about me. I want this and I want it strong and fast and soon." She took a deep breath and let her hand slide down his stomach, aiming for the hem of his shirt. "Real soon," she whispered as she made a beeline for that mouth.

His lips closed over hers, meeting her heat and kicking it up a notch with his own. He finally, *finally* cradled her breast, satisfying one hunger while starting a new one. She pushed against his palm and moaned into his mouth and gave deep and abundant thanks that she had found the one man in a million who could follow directions.

She tugged at his shirt, needing to feel skin against skin. But instead of helping he pulled her in closer, stymieing her efforts but—oh, yes!—sliding his own hand beneath her loose cotton blouse. She knew she'd chosen the right clothes the moment his palm glided across her back and curled around, teasing the side of her breast. The damned bra was still in the way but she thought she could handle it a few more seconds…until his finger slipped beneath the lace and she jolted against him.

But she still couldn't get his shirt untucked.

She tore her mouth from his. "This is not working."

"What?"

"Wait." She pushed herself off his lap, stood, then reseated herself, straddling him this time. She'd planned to say something light and funny but it was lost to the sudden exquisite pressure exactly where she needed it most.

Damn, but she had missed this.

She gripped his shoulders and bowed her head into his chest and breathed deeply, knowing she was close to falling off the edge, desperate to make this last. She'd waited this long. She could hold on a bit longer.

At least she hoped so.

"Permission to speak?"

Laughter welled up and overflowed. She drew in another breath, deeper, steadier, and drew back just enough to see the smile playing on his lips.

"Surely I'm not that bad."

"*Bad* isn't the word I'd use to describe you right now."

"Oh?" Feeling a bit more in control, she dared to inch forward, finally able to tug at the shirt. "Never wear this again. The color is good on you, but it's too frustrating. What word would you use right now?"

Her fingers finally hit flesh. His stomach was smooth and firm to her touch. She tilted closer once more, resting her forehead against his heart.

"I think the word I'd choose is *wanton*. Or maybe *irresistible*." His hands began an exploration of their own, gliding up her ribs toward the hooks of her bra.

Her hunger jumped up another notch. Or twelve.

She reached higher, searching, not even knowing what she needed until she brushed crisp chest hairs. The feel of them curling around her fingertips made her suck in a deep breath, filling her with his musky-woodsy scent.

Male.

He was undeniably, overwhelmingly male, made to fit her, to fill her. He was everything she'd needed for so long, the biggest chance she'd ever take. And in the morning the only thing she would regret was the hours she would have to pass until she could fill herself again.

She sought his lips, opening her mouth in a desperate need to drink him in. She needed more. Everything he could give her, beginning with the feel of his skin against hers.

She pulled back, whispering words between the butterfly kisses she dropped on the corners of his mouth.

"Want to play a game?"

He unhooked her bra. "Oh, yeah."

"Okay. Here's the rules." She grabbed his shirt and yanked it over his head. Not that he was fighting. "First one to get the other naked wins."

"You always play dirty?" He sounded a little choked. Lyddie wasn't sure if it was because his lips were in her hair or because she was nuzzling his neck, but when his hands slipped under the loose bra and surrounded her breasts, she realized she didn't care.

"Tell me this isn't a new blouse."

She had an idea where this was going. "Ancient," she lied.

"Any sentimental value?"

"Only if you rip it off me."

"You didn't tell me you were psychic."

He tugged. She raised her arms. He pushed the fabric toward her elbows. She gave a moment's thanks that the setting sun had reduced the light to mere shadows, then his lips closed over her breast. She rolled her head back in the cocoon of blouse still surrounding her, arms trapped upright, whimpering at the rough scrape of tongue across aching, puckered flesh.

"J.T.!"

"Mmm?"

"Get this off me!"

"Sorry." He moved to the other side, swirling his tongue in a slow spiral from chest to nipple. "I'm busy."

So was she. Busy holding on to the edge he seemed determined to push her over, busy trying to tug at the blouse with arms she could no longer move, busy falling deeper and deeper into the need and the heat and the delight that was J.T.

"Argh!" She gripped fabric and wriggled, desperate to both free herself and wrap herself around him.

But her brain had been fogged by the mouth nibbling at her nipple. She forgot that wriggling would only increase the contact in other places. Lower places. Places that demanded immediate attention as she worked to get herself unclothed and unfettered.

"J.T., please…"

"What's wrong?"

"You win."

"What's that?" He arched upright, torturing her, daring her to hold on. She couldn't see anything but the deep peach of her blouse but knew that he was smiling.

"You win. I played dirty, you played dirtier and I don't care. I need you now before I—"

The words were smothered by her blouse as he yanked it over her head. She gasped for breath, then gasped again as he stood, sliding her against him as her feet slipped to the floor, guiding her backward to the bed. They tumbled down, reaching, searching, shoving at waistbands and zippers and elastic.

"Thank God this place is small," she murmured against his neck as she pushed at his shorts.

"Now you know why we called it the honeymoon cottage." He stood again, and in an instant was naked before her. She wanted to take a moment to peer through the deepening shadows and look at him, really look, but then his hands were at her waist and he was fighting with the button on her stupid, *stupid* skirt. She reached to help him. His lips locked over hers. Fingers collided, meshed, flew in separate directions—his to weave through her hair, hers to fumble with the button until it popped free. She tugged at the zipper and his mouth slid lower, breathing a heated line from her neck to the valley between her breasts, then lower still until he rested over her navel and blew a shot of pure desire that erupted out through her extremities.

"The skirt's ready," she said, struggling for breath.

"Me, too."

He gripped. Pulled. This time, mercifully, there were no games. He yanked the fabric down past her feet before returning for her panties. His erection brushed her thigh and she had to breathe, *breathe,* willing herself to wait, begging him to hurry.

"Just one more thing," he whispered, reaching toward the nightstand. She heard the rip of foil and gave frantic thanks that she wasn't going to have to wait much longer.

He kneeled on the bed and braced himself over her, one hand on either side of her head, dipping down for one kiss, two, while she pushed her legs against the thighs straddling her, hungering for him to take the hint before she had to beg.

"Lydia." Her name echoed hoarsely beside her ear. "Lyddie, open your eyes and look at me."

When had she closed them? She opened, searching the darkness to see him gazing down at her. No smiles. No joking. Just a mirror of her hunger and desire mixed with a desperate search for control.

"Last chance. You're sure?"

Something like wonder fluttered in her heart.

"Positive."

His eyes closed and a tiny sigh escaped his lips. "Thank God."

At last he shifted, lifting first one knee, then the other, to settle between hers. Her hips rose to meet him. He brushed against her, searching, then thrusting, filling and stretching her, pushing away the doubt and the fear and leaving only him. Only J.T.

And he was so much more than enough.

CHAPTER THIRTEEN

J.T. LET HIS head drop against Lyddie's shoulder and hoped to hell he could remember how to breathe.

It wasn't exertion that had knocked the wind out of him—hell, no. It was the fist to the gut that hit him when he realized that right now, with Lyddie lying beneath him and the sound of her final gasp still echoing within him, with her hair on his arms and her softness beneath him and her vanilla perfume surrounding him, he was the most complete he'd been in a long, long time. Maybe forever.

If he weren't so utterly content, he would have been scared silly.

"J.T.?" Her voice had a breathy quality that went straight through him. Still too blown away to put words together, he settled for licking her neck.

She giggled and squirmed, sending dozens of energizing aftershocks through his body. It wasn't much but it gave him the strength to untangle himself and slide onto the bed beside her.

"Too heavy, right?"

"No. I was just going to say thanks."

He closed his eyes, let the wonder of her words

sink in, opened them and searched for her face in the darkness. "I think I'm the one who should be thanking you."

Silence.

He ached to hold her, to pull her close and pillow her head on his chest, but something made him hesitate. He didn't know why. He'd never had a problem being tender after sex. True, he wasn't much on pillow talk, but he liked the way it felt to hold the woman who'd just held him deep inside her.

But this, this was different. This was Lyddie. She was the one setting the pace here. And if he felt like he'd just been sucked into something ten times stronger than he'd expected, he could only guess what she was feeling.

He hadn't given a moment's thought to Glenn until this moment, and he was willing to bet she hadn't, either. But now, in the quiet moments after, he was willing to bet she was thinking. And probably missing.

This might not be the best time to remind her she was in bed with someone new.

On the other hand, if she were having second thoughts, she could probably use a friend. They might have crossed that line, but there was no law that said he couldn't hop back and forth as needed.

He raised up on one elbow and realized they hadn't bothered pulling back the comforter. Who was he kidding? They were lucky they'd made it to the bed.

The night was growing darker by the minute, but he didn't need light to guide his hand to her face. He pushed back soft strands of her hair, surreptitiously checking for tears. So far, so good.

"You know, this is the first time I've seen you with your hair loose."

She turned toward his touch. Her lips brushed his palm. "I've always been on duty."

"This is pretty unusual for you, isn't it?"

"I told you, there hasn't been—"

He pressed a finger to her lips. "Shh. I said that wrong. I meant, being off duty is unusual for you." He traced her mouth in the gloom, letting his fingers memorize her shape, her feel. "You're always working or with the kids. There's not much time for Lyddie, is there?"

"I... Well, no."

"And when you did get some time, you chose to spend it with me."

"That wasn't exactly a hardship."

The slightly jealous male in him preened.

"It wasn't the worst favor I've ever done for a friend, either." He shifted closer, daring to ease his way back to her.

"Is that what we are now? The whole friends-with-benefits thing?"

"Let me think. We make each other laugh. That's important in friends."

"We can talk to each other." She turned toward him, pillowing her head on her hands.

"We've been honest with each other. We trust each other."

"We do, don't we? I never thought of it that way."

He ran one hand slowly down her side, shoulder to ribs to hip, learning the silky curves that hunger had forced him to skim past the first time around. She was softer than he'd expected. A shiver ran through her. He thought about yanking the blanket over them, but then she shifted in his direction and he realized it wasn't the temperature making her react.

"So I guess we're friends." His hand rested on the rise of her hip but he kept a steady distance as he leaned forward to brush her lips with his own. Hands and mouth were the only points of contact, yet still he was as aware as if they'd been pressed flush against each other.

She sighed. The muscles beneath his hand tensed, as if she were stretching, then settled back into softness. He stroked her with his thumb, slow and light, giving her time to breathe, to decide what should happen next.

"J.T.?"

"What?"

"Does your definition of friendship always include licking?"

He kissed her forehead—still light, though he had to admit that with the aroma of raw sex still scenting his every breath, "keeping it light" was getting harder by the moment.

And that wasn't the only thing.

"Licking is a new one. But it beats the hell out of tossing the old pigskin around."

One hand crept from beneath her head to follow the dip of his lips, just as he had done to her. His breath caught somewhere in the middle of his chest.

"Lyddie."

"Hmm?"

"Two things."

"I'm all ears."

All ears? More like, all he ever wanted, needed or would wish for. For the rest of his ever-loving life.

"First one. Remember how I said that you could change your mind at any point? That still goes. If you want to do something else with your nights, or take a break, whatever, just say the word. You're still calling the shots."

"Okay. Next time, I want music."

"What?" His ability to think was temporarily derailed by the combination of her closeness, her request and the fact that she'd said right away there would be a next time.

God, he should have come home years ago.

"Music, huh? Anything special?"

"Donna Summer. Disco." She ran a finger down

his cheek, returning to play her thumb back and forth across his lips. "I kind of liked that sofa thing. It brought out my inner lap dancer. But dancers need music."

First thing in the morning, he was downloading every Donna Summer and Bee Gees song he could find.

She inched closer. "What was the second thing?"

"The second thing—uh, right…" It was something important, he knew that, but Lyddie was rubbing her cheek against his chin, like a cat against a door, and his center of concentration was rapidly moving south.

"Why do you do that?"

"What?"

"Rub against my jaw."

"Oh." She stopped abruptly. "I'm sorry. Does it bother you?"

"God, no. Just wondering."

"It— I—" A tiny sigh echoed between them. "It's so masculine. The roughness, I mean. I missed it."

His hands slid around her waist. "That reminds me of the second thing I need to know."

"What is it?"

"Are you okay?"

"Oh." She giggled just a bit. "I'm sorry, I've never been a screamer, but you don't need to—"

"No, not that. I mean here." He tapped her chest, drawing on every bit of strength he'd ever had to refrain from letting his hand slide back to the swell of her breast. "Any regrets?"

Again there was silence. She stayed quiet for so long that he worried he'd pushed too far, but she never even flinched within his embrace, so he held his breath and stroked her hair—the only touch he would allow himself—and waited.

"I will always miss Glenn." Her voice was small but steady in the darkness. "I'll never understand why he chose to face off against that guy. There are a million regrets around him, and a million things I'll never understand, and I will always, always wish we hadn't lost him."

"I didn't mean—"

"No, I know that's not what you were asking. But I want you to know. I loved him. I still do. It's different now, but it's still there. Always will be."

In that moment, he knew that he could never tell her about Glenn and the fire. No matter what happened or didn't happen between them, he would stay silent.

"But as for this—this wild version of friendship we've found—believe me, I have no regrets whatsoever."

A piece he hadn't known he was missing fell into place. "You're sure?"

"Positive." She slipped closer, sliding against him in a way that ignited both body and heart. "The only regret I could have had about this is if I hadn't had the guts to ask you for it."

"I'm damned glad you're a gutsy woman."

She smiled against him in the darkness, her lips teasing the corner of his mouth while her hands moved up and down his back.

"And I'm damned glad that you were gutsy enough to accept the challenge." She hooked a knee over his leg, bringing them closer still, making it absolutely clear that she had no intention of backing out now.

"You up for another challenge?" he asked as he buried his face in her neck.

"You're on."

He smiled. "How do you feel about gliders in the moonlight?"

A COUPLE OF afternoons later, J.T. punched a button on his cell phone, ending the call that should have been welcome but instead left him feeling unsettled and suspicious. He left the shade of the grape arbor to rejoin Iris in the middle of her row of pole beans. She glanced up when he approached and looked at him with open curiosity.

"Well? Who was that?"

"The Realtor. We have an offer on the boathouse."

"Oh." Surprise and disappointment warred in Iris's eyes, a perfect match for his own conflicting emotions.

"I know." He reached through the long green

leaves and snapped off a couple of beans. "I hate to see them go, too, Ma, but even with you spending summers up here, you won't need this many places. One cottage, maybe another to run that brothel you've always wanted, but—"

"Oh, you." She threw a bean at him, grinning the way she used to when his dad was around, and for a moment all was well. But her smile faded as she looked around the yard. J.T. watched her drink in the sights he knew she would ache for, watched her eyes absorb the hundred shades of green in her garden, saw them linger on cherry tomatoes and pink snapdragons and then lift to watch the river in the distance.

"It's so brown out there," she said at last. "I'm going to miss the colors."

"It's only for the winter months." He reached through the mass of vines, found her fingers and squeezed. "We'll fill your place with plants. And you can paint the walls pink or purple or even bright red if you want."

She smiled, but her heart wasn't in it. "I know I've asked before, but I have to do it one last time. Are you sure there's nothing that would keep you here?"

"I'm sure. So you can stop leaving those ads for physics teachers on the table."

"Children need to learn those things here just as much as down in Arizona."

"I know they do, but I'm not—"

"What about the person who's been keeping you out until all hours of the night?"

For a moment it was as if Lyddie was in the garden with them—that was how real she was to him, even when they were apart. The leaves brushing his hand were her hair, the robin's trill was her laughter, the sapphire-blue river in the distance was her eyes. He needed her and wanted her and wished to God he was in the cabin, holding her. But still—

"No," he said softly. "Not even for her."

He stood still while Iris watched him, her hand shading her eyes against the sun as she studied him. At last she spoke.

"You're in love with her, aren't you?"

"Yes."

"Does she know?"

"Not yet."

Sadness shadowed her face. "Will she go with you?"

He couldn't answer. Saying no would make it too real. Saying yes would tempt fate.

"She's rebuilt her life once already," Iris said. "I see why she wouldn't want to do it again."

"How did you know it's—"

"Justin Tanner Delaney, I may be old, but I'm not blind. I can still put things together." She peeked through the vines, shook her head and moved on to the next pole. "Besides, she's the only woman you've mentioned since you came back."

That sounded reasonable. Still—

"There's no talk in town about her, is there?"

"None that I've heard. Of course, they don't discuss you around me, but I think I would have noticed something like that."

"Good." He nudged a bit of dirt with his foot. "I don't want things to be awkward for her when I'm gone."

"Is that why you can't stay? To make things easier for her?"

Where was she going with this? "Mom, this isn't about me."

"Don't you dare say it's all because of me. There's more to it than that, and you know it." When he opened his mouth to protest, she rushed in. "Wait. Be honest. If things were different—with me, I mean—would you ever consider moving back? Maybe not here, in Comeback Cove, but somewhere around here. Upriver, or even in, say, Ottawa?"

The automatic denial was halfway to his lips when he stopped.

Would he?

Two months ago he would have laughed at the idea. Even two hours ago, if Iris had posed her question right after he got the latest phone call from Jillian accusing him of tearing the town apart. But now? Seriously?

He'd thought that twenty-five years away would have loosened the hold this place held on his heart, but once he came back…back to the river, the hills, the hint of cold weather that tinged the night air even in summer…

They were a part of him and always would be. They were bred into him. Tucson was home now, yes, but despite all that had happened, Comeback Cove would always be the place he came from. The place that a part of him would always want to return to.

"I've missed a lot of it. More than I realized." It was all he dared say, walking the fine line between the honesty she'd asked for and the guilt he knew she would quickly embrace if he said more than that.

"I thought so. You have that look about you."

"What look?"

"Settled. Content. Not when you're in town, or on the phone, but when you're here. When you don't think I'm watching, and you sit out on the deck and look at the river. I can see you soaking it in."

Okay. He'd give her that.

"You know," she said as she plucked a ladybug from the trellis, "last winter was very bad for me, but until then, I always managed. Your father knew what I needed. He made sure I took care of myself."

"Uh, did I miss a step in this conversation?"

She sighed and rapped a fist on his forehead. "J.T., the biggest danger for me isn't the lack of sun. It's the lack of support. What I need most of all is to be with family, with people who won't judge me for being…ill…and make sure I get to the doctor and do my light therapy and take my medication."

"That's why you're coming to Tucson. So I can help you with all of that."

"But I don't need to be in Tucson. Not if I have you."

"Mom—"

"Stop. Just stop and listen. I've lived with this since you were a child. I admit, I wasn't always good about taking care of myself, mostly because I hated admitting there was anything wrong. But I had dozens of years of managing. As long as I had your father pushing me to do what needed to be done, I could manage. Even here."

Fear squeezed his gut. "I'm not Dad. I don't know you the way he did, Ma, I don't… He knew how to help you. I don't."

"You could learn." She pinched a leaf from the plant. "You have a PhD, Justin. Learning is something you excel at."

"There's a big difference between studying astronomy and learning how to help you manage this. Nothing bad will happen if I screw up an equation."

"You won't mess up."

"In Tucson, I wouldn't have to worry about it. I would know you're fine."

"I would be fine. But I wouldn't be happy. I understand you can't move to Comeback Cove. But Cornwall, Brockville, Ottawa… They all need teachers.

They're all close enough that I could make a home there, by you, and still stay part of everything I love here. And, my dear, so could you." She lightly tapped his chest. "Think about it, J.T."

She turned away from the beans and headed for the snap peas, but he stayed where he was, frozen in place as surely as if January had just reached out a hand and grabbed him. Because if he moved, as scared as he was, he just might shatter the fragile wand of hope his mother had just handed him.

ON THE SATURDAY night of their second weekend together, Lyddie was the first to arrive at the cottage. She balanced a bag of groceries on her hip while letting herself in with the key J.T. had given her. This, she thought as she unpacked milk and eggs, would be a special night. She didn't have to go to work in the morning. They were staying all night and all tomorrow and the night after that. Hours and glorious hours together.

She had it all planned: make a little food, make a lot of love, fall asleep in each other's arms. Repeat. Intersperse with laughter and stories. Enjoy. Lock each moment away in her heart to give her something to hold when they had to say—

No. No, she was going to live in the moment and revel in the togetherness and not worry about what would happen later.

She pulled a loaf of cinnamon bread from the bag, then a box of lemon pudding mix.

"Oh, the things I have planned for you," she murmured as she ripped the box open.

She had the pudding heating on the two-burner stove when her phone rang. A quick glance at the display had her smiling.

"Sara!" She gave the pot a stir, lowered the heat and headed to the love seat. "What's up, chickie?"

"Oh, Mom, you won't believe it! Ms. Rasmussen—you know, the clarinet teacher—we had the best lesson today. And she said she wishes I was staying here, because she would tell me to try out for the Youth Symphony. She said I would be a shoo-in, Mom."

"That's wonderful, babe. What a great thing for her to say." Lyddie hoped her voice conveyed nothing of the dread she felt each time Sara mentioned the words she'd come to hate—*if I stayed.*

"But that's not all." Sara's voice dropped the way it always did when she was about to reveal something so special, she barely dared say it aloud. "There was this guy at the lesson today. I thought he was just there visiting, you know, like, her boyfriend or something? But when we were done, she said he was from the university, and she told him he should hear me, and he said I have a ton of potential and I really need to be studying with someone who knows what they're doing, you know?" Her excitement was palpable even in her hastily drawn breath. "And he said he's gonna call you in a couple of days to talk about my future. My future, Mom, can you believe it? He thinks I have a future!"

Lyddie closed her eyes against the weight bearing down on her chest. She knew why the teacher was planning to call. He was going to ask for Sara to stay.

"Wow," she managed to say. "That's so…incredible."

"Incredible? It's the best thing ever! Oh, Mom, I'm so glad you let me come here! I'm having so much fun with the boys, and little Emily is so cute—wait till you see her. Yesterday I got to give her her very first bottle. But Mom, the music here." She sighed in sheer bliss. "I can't believe everything they have. It's so awesome, you know?"

Yes. She knew. She could feel it in every muscle, in every tendon that had carried this child through nine and a half long months. Sara was hers, damn it, one of the only things she had to hold on to. They couldn't have her. Not yet.

She stuffed her hand in her mouth and bit down, welcoming the pain because it pulled her back from the edge. Sara prattled on about her cousins and the friends she was making—"It's so great, Mom. Nobody knows me. It's not like I have to worry about what people will think"—and all the while, Lyddie bit harder on her hand and stared out the window with eyes too blurred to register anything.

Something touched her shoulder. Something warm and solid, something strong and sure. In another second J.T. was kneeling in front of her, brushing tears from her face, tugging her hand from her mouth and wincing at the bite marks.

Seeing him, feeling him, brought her back. She managed to breathe—how long had she been holding it in?—and said, in a reasonably steady voice, "Well, doll, you've had a remarkable day. I can't wait to hear from this teacher."

"Okay, Mom. And make sure you ask him— Oh, I have to go. Emmy's awake. Aunt Zoë left me alone with her while she took the boys to the playground. She said she wouldn't trust her with anyone else this early, but I'm the exception."

"That you are, sweetie. Okay. Go get the baby and I'll talk to you in a couple of days."

"Bye Mom. Love you."

"Love you, too, sweets." But Sara had hung up as soon as she finished speaking, leaving Lyddie talking to dead air. She clung to the phone for a minute longer before slowly lowering it.

J.T. was there immediately, reaching for the phone, reaching for her. She went into his arms gratefully. A long, shuddering sob broke free. She burrowed her face in his shoulder and held on, so very glad that he was there, that for this moment, she didn't have to face it alone.

His hands were warm on her back as he drew her closer. "Bad news?"

"Only for me," she whispered, and told him everything. When she got to the part about the impending call she started to cry again while he rubbed her back, slow circles that centered her, steadied her, strengthened her.

"She'll want to stay, won't she?" he said when Lyddie finally stopped talking.

"Probably. I keep telling myself maybe she won't, that it's one thing to plan on the summer and another to think about a real move, but I know it won't make any difference. She'll want to stay."

"And?"

She lifted her head from his shoulder. "And what?"

"What will you do?"

"She's only fourteen. I can't let her go yet. She'll have to go someday, I know, but not yet."

"She'll hate you for it."

Lyddie sank back in weariness. "I know."

"The good news is, she probably won't hate you forever."

"Just a decade or two, right?"

"Lyddie…" He kissed her softly, pure comfort, before saying, "This is none of my business, and I'm not a parent. But if she's as good as they say she is, you might want to speed up your plans a bit."

"You mean let her go? Now?" She shook her head. "No. Not yet."

"People do it. I had a student, a figure skater. She went as far as she could at home, but she ended up moving to Colorado when she was about Sara's age."

Lyddie shuddered. "How could they do that? How did her parents let her go?"

"It wasn't easy. But I think they felt that if they said no—" he hesitated "—I think they figured if they kept her from following her dream, they would end up losing her, anyway."

"You think I should let her *go?*"

He slipped his fingers through her hair. "I think you are one of the strongest women I've ever known."

"Why do I have a feeling that's not such a good thing right now?"

"You've survived worse. And if you decide this is what's best for her, you'll be fine."

"Ah, God, this is so hard." She leaned back into him, rubbing against the rough bristle of his cheek. "I don't have to decide right now, do I?"

"No. You have time."

She did. Not much, but some. Just like what she had with J.T.

"You know," he said slowly, "you might have more options than you realize."

"What do you mean?"

"Well…Ottawa has an orchestra. Maybe even one for kids."

"I… You know, I think they do. There was one in Peterborough." At his raised eyebrows, she realized she had never spoken much about her old life. "That's where we used to live."

"Ever think about going back?"

"Um, have you forgotten that I'm buying a building from you?"

"Right. Sure. Of course." He hooked his pinky around hers. "Just wondered."

"Afraid I'm going to back out on you after you've had to face the wrath of Jillian?" She kept the words as light as she could, but now that she wasn't quite so miserable, she could see the tension in his shoulders. As if there were more to his questions than he wanted to let on.

Was he afraid she would change her mind? He'd gone through a hell of a lot for her.

"I do think about it, of course," she said. "Not moving back, but, you know. The way it used to be. The house and the neighborhood. It was a good place. But this is home now."

He nodded, but the movements seemed mechanical, as if she hadn't reassured him at all.

"It's a good option for Sara. I'll have to check it out, and I'm so glad you thought of it." She wound her arms around his neck, pressing a kiss in the curve of his shoulder. "Thank you for being here. I've kind of forgotten how nice it is to have someone to share these things with."

"No place I'd rather be, babe." He gave a shake, almost as if he were trying to push away a bad memory, then gave an exaggerated sniff. "Um, is something burning?"

"Oh, crap. The pudding!" She bolted from the love seat to turn off the heat, but it was too late.

"Scorched," she said, letting the spoon drop into the pot. "And I had such great plans for it."

His arms crept around her waist and she relaxed back against him, closing her eyes as he kissed the side of her neck.

"There's always tomorrow night," he whispered, and she smiled.

He was right. For a little bit longer, they still had tomorrow.

CHAPTER FOURTEEN

J.T. WOKE TO darkness and a rumbling in his stomach. Oh, yeah. They'd forgotten dinner.

Again.

He grinned as he eased himself from the bed. No point in waking Lyddie if he didn't—

"Hey, sleepyhead."

Her voice surrounded him but he didn't see her. "Lyd?"

"I'm outside," she called. He pulled on sleep pants and followed the sound of her voice out to the porch where she sat on the glider, wrapped in a fleece throw. She made room for him, snuggling against his side when he sat. He pulled her close and breathed her in for a long moment.

"Been awake long?"

One shoulder bumped against his ribs as she shrugged. "Maybe fifteen minutes."

"Thinking about Sara?"

"Actually, no. I was thinking about you."

"Good stuff, I hope."

"Mmm, very good." Her hand crept along his chest. "You're half-naked. Are you cold?"

"If I am, can I share your blanket?"

"Nope. I'm a selfish wench. Besides, I'm *all* naked, and if you get under here I'll get distracted. And I really should take a break and get something to eat."

"Excellent idea." But of course, neither of them moved.

"J.T.?"

"Yeah?"

"Did you expect anything like this?"

Hope flared within him. Could she be realizing there was more than just awesome sex building between them?

"No. If someone had told me that I would end up having the time of my life during a summer I was sure would kill me…huh. I would have laughed in their face."

"Me, too."

He didn't dare intrude on her thoughts, not when they seemed to be heading in his direction. He was content to hold her and hope she could figure out that some people went their whole lives without feeling what they shared.

Most of all, he hoped she figured it out soon.

"J.T.?"

"Mmm?"

"Can I ask you something?"

"Anything, babe."

She took a breath and pulled the blanket closer

around her. "What happened that night? I mean…
You don't have to tell me, but…" She gave her head
a little shake, a barely perceptible movement in the
darkness. "The fire. Glenn never talked about it."

No surprise there.

His first instinct, just as it had been all those years
ago, was flight. But this time was different. This
time he had Lyddie to hold.

"Okay. First thing you have to know is, probably
everything you've heard about me back then is true.
I stole. I lied. I wasn't a bully, I never set out to hurt
anyone, but most other stuff was fair game."

"No virgin sacrifices?"

He nuzzled her hair. "Only my own, babe. Anyway, there was this tradition that after graduation,
the kids would do something wild. Kind of a se-
nior prank. One year they TP'd the school. Another
time they stole all the forks from the cafeteria and
used them to spell out Comeback Cove on the school
lawn. That kind of thing."

She made a little sound of encouragement. He
tucked her tighter against him and stole a corner of
the blanket.

"When it was our year, everyone expected me to
come up with the plan. I decided we would have a
sleepover in the Old Village. I knew a way to sneak
in from when I worked there the summer before. So
once they cut the cake and finished the speeches, a

bunch of us grabbed our sleeping bags and got ourselves inside."

"It was all authentic buildings, right?"

"Yep. All houses and stores from a couple of hundred years ago, moved here from miles around." And God, that still hurt, thinking of what he had helped destroy. "When I screw up, I don't hold back."

Her hand was warm where it cupped his cheek. "I'm sorry."

"Yeah. Me, too." He turned her hand, kissed the palm. "Anyway, we were all there having a good time. A couple of the guys had brothers old enough to buy us a few bottles, and we sure as hell took advantage of them that night." That, at least, was a good part of the memory. Just him and the guys, hanging together, getting totally wasted in a way that was totally irresponsible, but made for some damned good times.

"That was about it. A bunch of guys, drinking, smoking, shooting the—the breeze. Then I left them for a while."

"Out for a breath of fresh air?"

He hesitated, not certain how much further to go. There was only one person in the world who knew the rest of that story, and she sure as hell wouldn't want this part known.

But this was Lyddie. Lyddie, who he wanted for the rest of his life. If ever there were a person he could tell, it would be her.

He was omitting Glenn's name. He could leave this one out, too. Lyddie would never know.

"No fresh air," he said at last. "I was meeting someone. We'd set it up earlier that night."

Her voice was warm and indulgent. "Let me guess. A girl."

"Right in one."

"No surprise there. So some lucky gal decided to have her own forbidden celebration, huh?"

Actually, the girl in question had been acting more out of spite, spurred by a fight with her jealous boyfriend. He'd known it even then. But a kid at his sexual peak wasn't up to thinking too clearly when offered the chance of a lifetime.

"She met me in the building next to where my buddies were. She brought wine. Not that I needed it by that point, but I think she thought that was what you were supposed to do. So, we had a glass. Real fast. And then we got down to business, so to speak."

For the second time that night, she smacked his arm.

"You know, if you hit me again it's gonna leave a bruise."

"Then I'll kiss it and make it better. So what happened then? That wasn't your first time, was it?"

"No. It would have been, but we didn't get that far. Came damned close, though."

"If she changed her mind, she was a fool."

He kissed the top of her head. "Thank you. No,

she probably would have followed through, but we were interrupted."

"The buddies came looking for you?"

"Nope. The buddies ran screaming out of the building next door, two steps ahead of the fire."

"Wait a minute." She pulled away from him, astonishment clear even in the dim light. "How did the fire start?"

"Matches, a few joints, an old building and a bunch of kids too plastered to stay safe."

"No, I mean—you weren't even in the building when it started?"

"Nope."

"So you had nothing to do with it?"

"I had the idea to go there. I got everyone inside. I knew what they were doing. I'm not innocent, Lyddie."

"Okay, no, but you weren't— How did you end up taking the blame?"

"I stayed back a minute. Made sure all my buddies were out. And I had to wait for my, uh, companion to get her clothes on."

"You were that close?"

He pulled her warmth back against him. "Close enough that for years, I had to check for smoke before I could put on a condom."

She snickered. "I'm sorry. I shouldn't laugh."

"S'okay. I hate to think what it did to her."

"You never saw her again?"

"No," he lied. Telling that particular truth wouldn't benefit anyone. "Anyway, we got out and were almost off the grounds when she remembered her ID bracelet. She'd left it in our building."

"Don't tell me you did the hero thing and went back for it."

"I had to. The fire was spreading, but in the other direction. I wasn't in any danger. But when I got back to the spot in the fence, all the others were gone already. Running home as fast as their drunken legs would take them. The only person I saw was Harley Prestwick, running toward the flames."

"Oh, my God. So you were the only one they could pin at the scene."

At least he hadn't had to spell that part out for her. "I knew I was dead meat. I was the one with the reputation. The other guys might have tried to protect me but they couldn't deny I'd been there. They had no idea what I was doing when I wasn't with them."

"And the girl?"

He snorted. "They could have put her on the rack and she would never have admitted to being there with me."

"So you ran. And no one ever stood up for you? None of them stepped forward?"

"People do stupid things when they're afraid."

"But—"

"Lyddie, we were seventeen, eighteen years old and dumber than dirt, but we knew when to keep our mouths shut. Some of them had to stick around for grade thirteen. The others were getting ready to leave for college." Like her future husband. "I was gone before morning. There wasn't enough evidence to press charges. From their point of view, letting me take the heat was the best course possible. I would have done the same thing."

"No, you wouldn't. I might not know all the details of your life, but I know that you're decent and brave and far too honest to ever do that to someone else."

Was that what she saw when she looked at him? If so, then it had been worth the risk of telling her.

"Thanks," he said softly. "But I wasn't always such a paragon."

"Bull. Those traits don't come from nowhere, J.T. They were in here all along." And she rested her hand over his rapidly beating heart.

He kissed the top of her head, filling himself with her. Then he tipped his face to the stars and sent the most heartfelt wish of his life to each and every one of them.

LYDDIE SPENT MONDAY eyeing every local man who seemed to be about the right age, trying to decide who else might have been at the fire. If any of J.T.'s so-called friends were still in town, she wanted to know who they were. Not that she planned to do anything with the information. J.T. was right: the past was the past, and she could certainly understand why a scared adolescent would keep quiet. Still, she wasn't sure if she could find any sympathy for a grown man who continued to let someone else take the heat.

It wasn't until closing time that she realized she didn't need to keep giving all the men the once-over. She had Nadine. Nadine, who had worked in the school cafeteria all those years and lived here her whole life. If anyone could guide Lyddie in the right direction, it would be her. But no sooner had she locked up than Nadine was in her face.

"Lydia Brewster, what the hell is going on around here?"

Okay. So Lyddie wasn't the only one who'd been waiting for a moment alone together.

"What is this, Nadine, *Jeopardy!*? Because if so, the answer is, 'What is the problem?'"

"Here's the problem. Something's going on in this town and I don't know what's behind it. And that bugs the hell out of me."

Lyddie grabbed a half-empty coffeepot from the counter and shouldered her way through the swinging door to the kitchen. "Geez, Nadine. You have control issues, you know that?"

"This isn't about me." Nadine was right behind her with a tray of mugs. "But something isn't sitting right. Have you noticed that Jillian hasn't been in lately?"

Huh. Come to think of it, it had been a few days

since either of the Royal Couple had made an appearance in the shop. "It's summer. They might be on vacation." But even as she said it, anxiety curled in her stomach.

"They're not. They're just avoiding this place. Avoiding me, too, when I pass them on the street."

"And you're complaining?" Maybe if she made a joke about it, she could convince herself that there was nothing to worry about.

"Hell, no. That part I can live with. But here's the thing, Lyddie. A whole lot of other people have been making a point of talking to me. Seems they all want me to know that J.T. has supposedly been spotted paying close attention to a string of tourists, if you know what I mean."

Thank God for the steam rising from the coffee Lyddie was dumping into the sink. Not only did it hide her face, but it also gave her an excuse for the coughing fit that struck from nowhere.

J.T. and tourists? *Oh, hell.* She didn't believe it. Not for a second. Not only had he spent all his recent nights with her, but she was pretty sure there was no way he would have the energy to leave her as limp as he did while doing someone else in the daytime.

But if people were telling Nadine about these supposed dalliances...

"At first I thought folks were just sharing the usual gossip and slander, but then I thought, y'know, I don't usually hear the same story from so many folks so close together. So I said to myself, 'self, people are telling me this for a reason.' And there was only one thing that came to my mind." Her hand settled on Lyddie's shoulder. "Honey. You and J.T.? Really?"

Lyddie froze.

"Ah, hell." Nadine took the pot from Lyddie's fingers, clunked it on the counter and reached to turn the water off. "How did I miss this? I must be getting old. Maybe I should retire. Can you get someone to take my shift tomorrow?"

"For heaven's sake, Nadine, get a grip. You're going to outlive all of us."

"I don't know. I'm losing my touch."

"What if you're not losing anything? What if you're just plain wrong?"

"Wrong?" Nadine snorted and leaned against the butcher-block island. "Okay, Lyddie. Look me in the eye and tell me you aren't rolling in the hay with J.T."

Lyddie tried. She stared at Nadine and tried to stay sober, tried to think of boring things like shopping and washing dishes and interminable sermons. But shopping made her remember J.T. buying the test. And dishes made her remember the way he'd dabbed soap suds on her neck the other night, then slowly toweled them off. And sermons made her remember exactly what she'd been doing last Sunday when she would normally have been in church. And before she knew it, Nadine was sitting back with an annoyingly satisfied smirk on her face.

"Sit down and tell me everything."

"There's nothing to tell." Lyddie sat anyway, if only because her feet hurt. "But I have some questions of my own."

"Uh-uh. Not until you give up some answers."

"Nadine—"

"Nope. It's tit for tat, or nothing at all."

"I should dock your pay for this."

"Go ahead. You know I'm independently wealthy and only do this to keep me entertained."

Lyddie sighed and sank down in the chair, pulling her left foot up to rest on her right knee. "Fine. Two questions. That's it."

"Two questions, huh? Fair enough. Is he as good as he looks?"

"Nadine!"

"Okay, okay. None of my business. How about this one—what the hell are you thinking, getting involved with a man who's gonna break your heart?"

"Why does everyone in this town act like he's the devil incarnate?"

"Did I say anything about that?"

No, come to think of it. Nadine hadn't said anything against J.T. except that he was going to leave.

"Sorry. His reputation is kind of a sore subject for me these days."

Nadine gave a shrewd look. "I just bet it is. So

tell me. What possessed you to fall in with someone who's going to pack up and leave in less than—"

"I know exactly how long it will be until he leaves. And believe it or not, that was one of the chief attractions. We'll have a little fun while it's convenient, and then he'll go. No messy complications, no worries about whether the kids like him or—or anything else. It's perfect."

"That is such a load of bull. I haven't seen you this happy in all the time I've known you. You really think you can just let him go? You?"

"That's at least your third question. Maybe fourth, if we count the totally inappropriate one. But I'll answer it anyway, and then you'd better start talking."

Nadine grunted.

"Okay, you're right. Letting go is going to suck. He's a great guy, no matter what everyone says, and we've had some very…um, very special times together. But come on. I've known him less than two months. It's not like I'm in love or anything like that."

Nadine stared at her again, long enough to make Lyddie's gut twist. She braced herself for another onslaught. But to her surprise, Nadine merely tipped her head and gave a little nod before saying, "So what did you want to ask me?"

Well, that switch was fast enough to make a girl dizzy. "I want to know who used to hang out with him when he was in school. Especially near the night of graduation." She drew a deep breath and added, "And if it's the same people who are trying to convince you that he's been playing doctor with the tourists."

Nadine's careless slouch fled as she jerked upright. "Don't go there, Lyddie. You don't want to open that can of worms."

"There's no worms involved. I just want some answers."

"No."

"Hello? I answered all of yours."

"No, you didn't. And it doesn't matter. I wouldn't tell you, anyway."

"Why not?"

"Lyddie…" For one of the few times ever, Lyddie saw hesitancy in Nadine's eyes.

"What is it?"

"People are…anxious. Some of 'em are pissed because they want that Randy Cripps guy in here, and no, it's not just Her Worship and company. Some are royally ticked that anyone would try to push you out. They're talking about petitions and letters to the editor and storming the next planning board meeting. And some folks just shake their heads and say everything will be fine as soon as J.T. leaves town."

Lyddie's stomach threatened to jump into her throat. "I don't understand."

Nadine sighed. "Sweetie, people will cut you a lot

of slack because of Glenn and just because they like you. But J.T.—he's dividing the place."

"It sounds like Jillian is the one pushing people into different camps."

"Say what you will about Her Worship, but I have to give her this. She really believes it's the right move. That's not going to win her any popularity contests. Like I said, people think a lot of you."

"Really? Even if they think I'm sleeping with the enemy? Because if they're busy telling you lies about him, they obviously want those stories to come back to me, and the only reason they would want me to hear it would be to make me end it with him."

"Because if you end it with him, there's no chance of him, say, falling for you and deciding to stay here, no matter what anyone says about him."

"And who on earth would be so caught up in the past that they—*oh*." The answer was so obvious that she couldn't stay seated. She jumped from her chair and started shoving mugs into the dishwasher.

"It's the other people who were there, isn't it? The ones who were at the fire. They're afraid J.T. will rat them out if he stays."

"Who says there was anyone else there that night?"

"Nadine. Do you honestly believe he was there all by himself?"

Nadine shook her head, arms crossed. "No. Never did think that."

"Then why—"

"No one talked. No one even gave up a hint, and, Lyddie, if you had been here when it happened, you would know why. It was… Well, I'm not proud of how a lot of folks acted in those days. I sure as hell can't blame those kids for letting J.T. take the heat, either. Not when he was up and gone and they were still here, listening to all that anger and hurt."

"I don't blame them, either. Not for what they did then. But now? Why should they get off scot-free while he has to walk around with it all on him? Is that right?"

"No, but it's the way it is."

"And that's why you won't tell me who he hung out with in school, isn't it?"

Instead of answering the question, Nadine took a mug from her fingers, set it on the rack and curled her hand around Lyddie's. "Be careful, honey."

"Be careful? Damn it, Nadine. All I wanted was to feel alive again. Remind myself that there's more to me than what other people think. Have some fun."

A ghost of Nadine's usual smile twisted her lips. "From the way you turned red when I asked if he was as good as he looked, I'd say you have the fun part covered."

Lyddie squeezed Nadine's hand before turning back to the dishwasher. "You're really not going to tell me who he hung out with in school, are you?"

"No."

"And it's for my own good."

"That's about it."

Okay. Fine. She could respect that.

But if Nadine thought that silence would make Lyddie drop this, then Nadine was sadly mistaken.

J.T. KNEW SOMETHING was up with Lyddie the moment she walked into the cottage that night. It was pretty obvious. If he hadn't guessed there was a problem from the tension in her shoulders or the lack of laughter in her greeting, he would have known from the way she launched herself at him, barely giving him a moment to catch his breath before she had him on his back straddling him and kissing him with a desperation he'd never felt from her before.

Not that he was complaining, especially since he was still trying to shake off the memory of walking into the hardware store to find Jillian and Steve deep in a conversation that ended with them springing apart when they noticed him. Their guilty expressions had haunted him through the rest of the day. So he was more than ready to oblige Lyddie. There was a new urgency, a hunger that made him think her need for him was becoming as strong as his for her.

But she had to need him for more than release. If he had any chance of ever getting her out of Comeback Cove, he had to make her see that there was more between them than great sex.

So he let her ride out her demons. He held her while she clutched at him, filled her and loved her and let her use him to block out the world for a few moments. But when she was done, when she picked herself up from where she'd collapsed on his chest and slithered down to the bed beside him, he pulled her close and pushed the hair back from her face and said, "So not that I'm complaining, but what was that all about?"

"You don't believe I just thought about you all day and couldn't wait another minute?"

"Nice try. Makes me feel good." He tweaked her nose. "But I think there was more than that."

She sighed. "You know me too well."

God, how he hoped to make that true. "Come on. Out with it. Did Sara's teacher call?"

"Not yet."

"Ben? He's having a problem with camp?"

"No, I talked to him today and he's in geek heaven. And it's not Tish, and not even Ruth, though she still hasn't forgiven me. But that might be because Tish made her go on the Small World ride six times in a row."

"So if it isn't any of them..."

She nuzzled his chest, sending hope flaring within him. "It's you."

"Oh, yeah?"

She ran a finger lightly down his chest. "Someone told me today that people are spreading rumors about you. Did you know you've been doing every tourist in town?"

Ah, hell. "I take it you know better than to believe that."

"Good Lord, of course. You're an amazing man, J.T., but even you need time to recover."

"Glad to hear you have faith in me."

"Don't ever doubt that."

He squeezed her shoulders, pulled the blanket a little higher. "On the other hand, if worrying about rumors is going to get me that kind of reaction, I might start a few of my own."

She laughed, but he heard the worry beneath it.

"I think some people are worried you might decide to stick around."

Ah, crap. He wasn't sure there was enough blood in his brain yet to navigate this minefield.

"That's really nothing new."

"It's so…so ridiculous. I know I complain about folks here, but really, most of them are totally kind and caring and way too reasonable for this nonsense."

"Fear will make people do crazy things."

"Really? I was pretty damned scared when I heard that little nugget today, but I didn't run around spreading lies or trying to interfere in other people's lives."

"I think we can both agree that you handled your emotions in a far better way."

She giggled before burying her face in his chest.

"I can't help it. I don't want bad things to happen to people I…people I care about."

She had to feel the way everything in him tensed in preparation of jumping for joy, but he was willing to risk it. "You care what happens to me, Lyddie love?"

The endearment just slipped out, but he was running out of time. He had to start taking chances.

"Of course I care," she said softly. "I know we said no strings, but that doesn't mean no emotions whatsoever."

"Me, too. You're pretty special."

"And you," she said with a soft kiss to his neck, "are the best chance I ever took."

Was it time for him to take an equally big gamble? Should he lay everything out—tell her he loved her, tell her he was considering moving close by so he could have more time with her?

No. Not yet. There was still one step he had to take. He had to get her out of Comeback Cove, with him. Had to make her see how it would feel to be a real couple, out in public, with no need for secrecy.

"You ready to take another chance?"

"Maybe." She rose up on one elbow, gave him a smile that sent him stirring.

"Wanna go away for a night together?"

"I thought we spent the last two weeks doing that."

"I mean *away* away. Somewhere else."

Curiosity chased resistance across her face. "I don't know… When could we do it? Ruth and Tish come home the night after tomorrow."

At least it wasn't an outright refusal.

"Here's what I'm thinking. Don't you have to go to Toronto Saturday to get Ben? That's a four-hour drive each way, and you've had a hell of a week. You should probably drive part of the way the night before. Like, to Brockville."

"Okay." Her words came slowly, as if she were thinking aloud. "That would make sense. Especially if, you know, I want to do some shopping or something before his closing ceremonies."

Yes!

"We would have to take separate cars, though, unless you want to get a bus back Saturday morning."

He tried to hide the twinge of hurt. "Sure. I guess it might freak people to see us driving off into the sunset together."

"It's not that, though Ruth… Well, I don't want to hurt her. But Ben was pretty suspicious anyway, and if we both came to get him, he might…well, he might start thinking things. Get his hopes up."

Ben wasn't the only one. But she was right. J.T. could handle risking his own heart. He wouldn't do that to a kid.

"So you think it would work?"

She leaned over and brushed her lips lightly over

his. "I think it's an excellent idea. Especially if it means extra time with you."

He rolled her over and kissed her slowly, praying that this would do the trick—that this one extra night with Lyddie would be the next step to a lifetime.

CHAPTER FIFTEEN

LYDDIE HAD PREPARED herself to feel sadness on their last night at the cottage, had expected to feel unhappy when it came time to walk away that last morning. Even so, she hadn't been ready for the fist to the gut that hit her when the time came.

She wasn't the only one. As she stood on the porch, fighting back tears she told herself she wouldn't shed, J.T. stepped behind her and slid his arms around her waist, pulling her tight to his chest. She sagged against him. His touch proved to be the key that unlocked her resolve.

"I promised myself I wouldn't do this." She brushed at the tears, forced the words out past the damned lump in her throat. "I said I would go with a smile. But it's not that easy."

Movement against her neck told her he was nodding. She had a feeling that words were playing hide-and-seek with him, too.

She clutched his hands, rubbing the rough skin. "I'm so glad you suggested Friday night."

"Me, too, babe."

She sniffed and tried to laugh. "Nadine's going

to have a field day wondering why I'm showing up with red eyes this morning."

"I think she'll figure it out. Especially when I park myself outside the door and howl like a sick dog."

At that she laughed for real, though it ended on a hitch that bore a very strong resemblance to a sob. "J.T.?"

"Mmm?"

"Thank you."

"God, Lyd. Do you have any idea how much I should be the one thanking you?"

"Well, I'm glad I made it worth your while. But still, I…"

This wasn't right. She needed to face him. She turned in his arms and buried her head in his chest. "If you only knew what you've done for me…."

His hand cupped her head, wove through her hair, pressed her closer. "Same here, babe. If you only knew."

IF YOU ONLY KNEW…
The words followed her through the day. At least she had the joy of Tish's homecoming to help her through the first night alone. He didn't even have that. Alone in her bed that night, staring at the ceiling by the glow of the Sleeping Beauty nightlight Tish had insisted on giving her, she let the tears come. She missed him. She missed curling against him. She missed waking up and rubbing her foot

against his leg to reassure herself that he was there. She missed giggling in his arms, laughing so hard that if they had been standing, she would have fallen to the floor.

If it was this bad after this preliminary farewell, how was she going to get through the real thing?

Maybe she shouldn't go away with him. Maybe she should end it now, clean and easy. What good would be served by another night, another goodbye?

But she had promised him she would go. He'd asked so little of her in their time together. Surely she could do this for him, give him this one last night.

But no more. They would go to Brockville, they would have a final memory and that would be the end of it. Finished. She'd done what she set out to do. The rest of the world might still look at her and see the brave little widow, but she knew who she was. She was a woman who could still take a chance, feel, astound herself. She was still alive.

Ironic, then, that the next night, she found herself quaking in her boots as she told Ruth she'd be leaving Friday night to get Ben instead of Saturday morning, and that she wouldn't be taking Tish along.

"She'd be so bored. After all the driving she did from Florida, I can't ask her to do that again."

Ruth pulled her old blue cardigan tighter, her mouth set in a thin, disapproving line. "Really, now."

"Really." Lyddie dug her thumb into a pea pod she was shelling and split it down the middle. "I know I made it there and back in one day when I took him, but it really wore me out. I think this will be far more sensible."

"Sensible. That's an interesting way to put it."

Oh, damn.

"Tell me, Lydia. Are you at least going to take separate cars, or is the whole town going to see you heading out with him?"

She could do this. She had propositioned J.T., lanced her own finger, walked into that cabin despite the fact that she hadn't been that nervous since her first time in labor. She had done all that. She could sure as hell face down Ruth.

"I'll be leaving around five Friday night, Ruth. In my own car. I will pick up my son the next day, all by myself, and I will be back home with him that night. Anything else that happens or doesn't happen is really only important to me."

"Lydia Brewster, I have to hold my head up in this town. Do you have any idea how I felt today when I walked into the post office and everyone stopped talking?"

Lyddie ran her finger down the row of plump peas, popping them free one by one, sending them into the big yellow crockery bowl. "Well, now you know what Iris Delaney has been living all these years."

Ruth's red cheeks were a clear indicator of anger, but thankfully she kept her voice low as she pushed the bowl to Lyddie.

"And you think it's just a coincidence that the same man is at the root of both of our heartaches?"

"Good Lord, Ruth, you make it sound like he violated me against my will."

"You might think you made your own choices, Lydia, but you didn't. Not really. That J.T., he can talk anyone into anything and make them think it was their own idea all along. He's nothing but bad news and this town can't be rid of him fast enough."

So many thoughts pushed at Lyddie's brain, so many words hovered on her tongue. Maybe she should say them. Maybe she should spell it all out for Ruth.

Or maybe she should try to dam the river single-handedly.

"You're wrong, Ruth. About a whole lot of things. But you know what? I don't care. I know the truth, and that's what matters." She plucked another pod from the basket and stabbed her thumb into it. "Meanwhile, you are Tish's grandmother and you love her and she loves you. Are you able to look after her while I'm gone, or shall I ask if she can have a sleepover at Millie's?"

"You would leave her with someone else?"

"I don't want to. I would much rather she stay here, in her own bed, with you. But if you are planning to spend the entire time I'm gone sighing about what a horrible person I've become, just because I want to move on with my life, well, I can't see how that would be a good thing for my daughter to be hearing nonstop. You know?"

The redness in Ruth's cheeks faded to a dull burgundy. "Is that how it's going to be, Lydia? You threatening to keep me from my own grandchildren, all because of that man?"

"No, Ruth. I'm just spelling out the consequences so we both know exactly where we stand." She rose from the table before she said anything worse. "And for the record, I'm not doing any of this for J.T. I'm doing it for me."

THE NEXT AFTERNOON, Lyddie gave Steve McCoy his order, walked into the kitchen and waited. It didn't take long.

"Lyddie?" Nadine was about five seconds slower than Lyddie would have expected, but then, she'd been in the middle of drawing a coffee when Lyddie had done her disappearing act.

"Lyddie, are my ears playing tricks on me, or did Steve ask you to go sailing with him on Sunday?"

"He did."

"Holy doodle. You think life can't get any more interesting, then bam. Here comes the blindsider."

"Tell me about it." Lyddie peeled off her apron and tossed it in the corner. "So, you would know better than I do. Has someone been spiking the water or something around here? Because I've known Steve since before Glenn and I got married, and he never…

I mean, he was wonderful to me after Glenn died, and he's a great guy, but I… He… For heaven's sake, Nadine, he hasn't looked at anyone since his divorce was final. At least none that I know of."

"Nobody. You can trust me on that one."

"So why me, of all people?"

Nadine turned away, fast, but not before Lyddie caught the glimpse of guilt on her face.

And Lyddie got a clue.

"Oh. Maybe the real question isn't why *me*. Maybe I should be asking why *now*."

"I didn't say anything."

"Of course not. I wouldn't expect you to." Lyddie glanced at the clock. Just a few minutes until three. She had a little over an hour before she had to get Tish from day camp.

"Any chance you could close up, Nadine? I have a hot date with some high school yearbooks."

"Lyddie, don't—"

"If you can't do it, no problem. I'll come in early tomorrow and get things set."

"Lydia—"

She stopped in her flight toward the door. "Nadine. Were Steve and J.T. in the same year in high school?"

"I told you—"

"Yes, you did. You warned me. But I'm a big girl, Nadine, and someone I care about has spent too damned long being this town's scapegoat. I'm not going to rock any boats, but I want to know the truth."

Nadine shook her head. "Lyddie—"

"You know I'm going to figure this out. You can tell me what I want to know, or you can make me go home, drag out the yearbooks, get pissed off when I see the answer and probably be late getting Tish. So why don't you give me a hand and—"

"Steve and J.T. weren't in the same year. Steve was a year ahead."

"Oh." She felt oddly deflated. It had made so much sense…Steve and J.T. partying together after they graduated, the fire, Steve worrying that J.T. would spill his guts to her… Okay. So they didn't graduate together. Then why the big—

And then a hundred bits and pieces fell together.

"If Steve was a year ahead of J.T., then he was in Glenn's year. Which means the fire was the year after they graduated. Except…" Her mouth was suddenly so dry that she could scarcely form the words. "Except Ontario used to have grade thirteen. And J.T. told me he didn't make it that far, that he left after grade twelve. So the graduation was—help me, Nadine. We didn't have this in Winnipeg. Did they do one ceremony, or two?"

"Things changed over the years, but back then, they all walked after grade twelve. If they stayed on for the extra year, they could walk again."

"So even though they were a year apart, Steve and J.T. graduated at the same time."

Nadine nodded. Lyddie reached for the sink to steady herself.

"Which means Glenn did, too."

Nadine's eyes closed. And all Lyddie could hear was outtakes from conversations. Not the words, but the pauses.

J.T. refusing to name anyone who had been in the village with him that night.

The way Glenn had never mentioned the fire, even when she'd asked him about it.

J.T. telling her that most of the people who had been with him either lived in town still or had family there.

Ruth's continued insistence that J.T. could talk anyone into anything and make them think it was their own idea.

Oh, dear God.

"Glenn was there."

Lyddie waited for Nadine to shake her head, to wave away the suggestion, to tell Lyddie she was being a damned fool. But all she did was say, very quietly, "I wasn't there, Lyddie. I don't know."

But Lyddie did. She knew exactly what had happened.

She had opened herself to J.T. Told him everything, about Glenn, about herself. Trusted him with the ugly parts of her that didn't want to be on a pedestal, that didn't want Glenn to be turned into something he wasn't. She had told him all of that—

And he lied to her.

He had listened to her and kept his secret and patted her on the head and said nothing. Nothing. He kept it all from her because Glenn was a hero and she was the brave little widow who had to be shielded from the truth.

He had been no different from the rest of them after all.

J.T. HALF WALKED, half jogged toward River Joe's, his heart slamming, but not from exertion. The words of Lyddie's text pounded through his brain in time with his feet.

I need to talk to you NOW.

His fast reply that he was on his way was met only with a terse Fine.

Something was up. Jillian? She'd been riding his ass all week with calls and emails about how he owed the town the chance to bring in more opportunity. She might have pushed Lyddie to her breaking point, but somehow, he doubted it.

He reached the coffee shop and yanked open the door, thankful that it wasn't locked despite the Closed sign.

"Lyd? Lyd, I'm here. What's wrong?"

"Over here."

Her voice came from the love seat by the fireplace, hidden in shadows that his eyes couldn't pierce immediately on entering from the bright sunshine. Though when he drew closer, the carefully blank expression on her face scared him more than he would have thought possible.

"What is it? Sara? Ben?"

He reached for her hands. She looked up at him but kept her hands tightly knotted on her lap.

Oh, shit.

"The children are fine. Thank you for asking. I'm sorry if I frightened you."

"Okay. Then what the hell—"

"Glenn was at the party that night."

If he'd walked into a fist in a dark alley, he still wouldn't have been as stunned as he was by her words.

"Lyd…babe, listen…"

"No, J.T. You listen." Her voice trembled but she shook her head, pinched her lips together and carried on, low and terrifying. "I trusted you. I told you more about myself than anyone else in this town would ever believe. I laid it all out for you, and in return, you deliberately concealed information from me that I had every right to know."

He wasn't going to deny anything. What was the point? Everything she'd said was true.

But maybe, if he could make her understand why…

He dropped into the chair across from her, careful to sit far enough back that his knees didn't brush hers. "Okay. Yes. Glenn was there."

She inhaled, short and sharp. "Why?" The word was a broken whisper, but she carried on. "After everything I told you, everything you knew I wanted... why didn't you tell me?"

"It's complicated."

"Oh, I just bet it is." She leaned forward, eyes glittering. "Tell me anyway."

"I... God..." His tongue was too thick to form the words. "There were lots of reasons, okay? Different ones at different times. At first, I didn't see any need. He's not here to defend himself, nothing could be changed, so what was the point? And, yes, at that point, I was buying in to the widow thing. Because no matter what happened when we were kids, Glenn did deserve to be remembered. I didn't know you the way I do now, and I thought, hell, you'd lost enough. What would be the point in taking away what little comfort you might have?"

She sat silent for a minute and nodded. "I'll give you that. But after? After I told you how I felt about the way he was being idolized, about the way people treated me? Why didn't you speak up then?"

"Lyddie, there's a hell of a difference between telling stories about church group pranks and telling the truth about something that nearly killed this town."

"You didn't think I could handle it."

"It wasn't—"

"It wasn't like that? Fine. Maybe you weren't being noble and protecting me. Maybe you were only thinking of all those other folks. But damn, J.T. I trusted you with all of me, with my secrets and my body, with my *child,* and you still couldn't trust me with the truth?"

"It had nothing to do with trust."

"Then what was it? What was so damned important that—"

"I fell in love with you, okay?"

The sudden whiteness in her face was his second sucker punch to the gut. She'd had no idea.

She spoke very quietly. "That's not possible."

"The hell it isn't." Damn it, if he was going to lose her anyway, he was going to make sure she knew the truth this time. "I couldn't say anything about Glenn because I didn't want you to think I was trying to—to drag him down, to make him look bad so I would look better. I wanted to do the right thing by him. Because I love you."

"You can't. I don't… No."

For a moment he thought she was trying to disappear into the chair. But no sooner had he thought that than she burst forward, out of his reach.

"No. This wasn't supposed to be about emotions. All I wanted was something for me, something to make me feel… My God, J.T., you're going back to Tucson next week. You can't possibly—"

"I have to go back. Yes. But I— Look, things are complicated that way. I have a contract, and my mother—" Just in time, he stopped himself before blurting out Iris's secret. "We've been talking. Dragging her down to Arizona, away from everyone she loves, that wouldn't be good. We thought, maybe, I could move to Ottawa, get her a place there so she could still be close to here, and then you and I would have more time to— Listen to me, Lyddie. I was going to tell you this tomorrow, when we went to Brockville and I could do it right. God, Lyddie. I never meant to hurt you. I love you."

She flinched. He realized she had done the same thing every time he mentioned love.

"Were you ever going to tell me the truth about Glenn?"

Ah, God. "Not if I could help it. No."

"Because it was more important to make sure I looked good in your eyes than to give me the information that could have made a difference to me."

"What would have changed? You're the one who knew him as he really was. You're the one who was so determined to hold up his warts. Would you have thought any better or worse of him if you knew this?"

"No." Her voice seemed far away. So sad. "It wouldn't have changed what I thought about him. But it would have made a difference in what I'm thinking about you."

"Lyddie, no. Please. You can't let this change things, not when I—"

"Stop!"

It was one of the worst sounds of his life—angry and heartbroken, choking and pleading, all at the same time.

"You are not in love with me. I refuse to believe that."

"You can't tell me what I feel."

"Oh, yes I can!" She swung her arms violently as if trying to push away his words. "You don't love me. You're just grateful because I treated you better than everyone else did. Or, you know, brain-dead from two weeks of sex. But you are not in love with me. You are not moving to Ottawa, not for me. There is no future for us. No seeing what happens. Nothing."

He wanted to tell her she was wrong, so wrong, but his muscles wouldn't work and there was no air in his lungs to push out any sound.

"I told you when I came to you with this—this deal or proposition, or whatever it was. Two weeks, that was it. No strings. You're not changing the rules now."

"Why not? There's no planes to Tucson? No chance you'll ever change your mind about staying here? No way you could even think of falling in—"

"No!"

The single word hung in the air, slicing between them. He stared at her, willing her to take it back.

"I'm not in this for a relationship. I'm not looking for anything emotional. Don't you get it?" She spread her arms wide. "This is all I can give you. This body. That's all I offered and all I wanted. You knew that. You agreed. You promised."

"Lyddie—"

"No! Damn it, J.T., I didn't want anything honorable or important or permanent. Why the hell do you think I chose you?"

Something shifted deep inside him. "What does that mean?"

She turned away from him. From the way she gasped for breath he knew she was either crying or trying to hold it back. He was torn between the deep need to help her and the deeper, gut-twisting need to know exactly what was behind her words.

"Don't do this, Lydia. Don't pretend you didn't say anything. Tell me what you meant."

She pressed her fingers to her forehead. Hard. Like she was trying to push something so far back in her mind she would never have to think of it again.

He grabbed her hands and held them apart so she couldn't push away the truth any longer. Toe-to-toe, face-to-face, he looked into the eyes that he'd thought could see beyond the surface and said, once more, "What did you mean?"

"Exactly what I said."

"You said you chose me because I wasn't permanent. Or important. Or honorable."

He felt every part of her tense. She seemed on the verge of denial, and God, how he needed her to say it. Her lips parted and with every fiber of his being he willed her to say she knew him better than that. He'd laid himself bare to her. She had to understand.

Then the tension faded as suddenly as it had appeared. Just like that, he knew he'd been wrong.

Dead wrong.

Heartbreakingly wrong.

He dropped her hands, let them slap to her sides as he stepped back.

"You know," he said softly, "it's almost funny. You asked me to sleep with you so you wouldn't see yourself the way everyone else does. But you have no idea that you pigeonholed me the exact same way."

The sudden paleness in her face told him that he'd hit the mark.

And he'd never in his life been so sorry to be so right.

CHAPTER SIXTEEN

SHE WASN'T GOING to cry.

Lyddie repeated the command to herself as J.T. slammed the door behind him, even though the crack of the wood made her wince.

She wasn't going to cry. Even though his last words about pigeonholing him had cut right through her and made her long to grab him, to say she hadn't meant it, that she knew he was more than what everyone else saw. She couldn't say it. Couldn't encourage him, couldn't do anything to make him think they had any kind of future. Because that just wasn't possible.

She held back the tears while she locked up the shop, bit on her lip to keep from losing control while she drove to day camp. She gathered up Tish and hugged her tight and even cracked a joke for her and her friend Millie. She loaded Tish into the van and listened to her chatter all the way home and never let so much as a tear escape.

She had done the right thing. Maybe she hadn't needed to be as…forceful as she had been, but she couldn't let him think for a minute that there was a chance of them ever… It hadn't come out right, and she'd been so wrong, but then, so had he. He should never have lied to her. Should never, ever have let himself think he loved her.

She followed Tish into the house and told herself it was better this way. If they had gone away together as planned, that would only have given him false hope. He might have thought that she cared more than she did. Because of course she cared. Of course he meant something to her. But not love. Anything but that.

She walked into the kitchen where Ruth sat calmly slicing tomatoes and was flooded with such a burst of rage that she thought she might pass out.

Ruth knew about Glenn. Lyddie had no doubts about that. Ruth would have known that Glenn went out that night. She would have seen him over the next few days, when he was undoubtedly jumpy and guilty and just as screwed up as any kid had ever been, and she would have heard the rumors. Even if she hadn't known for sure—even if Ruth had been too afraid to come out and ask Glenn if he'd been part of the fire—she would have suspected. And in her heart, she probably knew.

She knew all that, and yet she'd been willing to lay it all on J.T. Even now. Because it was easy. Because it meant that her life as the heroic widow would go on, untarnished.

Lyddie dropped Tish's backpack onto the hard

wooden chair and had a moment of satisfaction when Ruth jumped in her seat.

"Lydia!" Knocked out of her rhythm, Ruth raised a hand to her heart. "Heavens, you startled me. Is everything all right?"

No. No, nothing was right, and J.T. was hurt, and Lyddie shouldn't care about him because he had lied to her, but Ruth had lied, too, and nothing made any sense anymore.

She couldn't say anything. She gripped the back of the chair and tried to take deep breaths, but all she could see was J.T.'s face when she said she'd chosen him because she didn't want anyone honorable. All she could hear was J.T. telling her that he loved her.

He loved her. But he'd lied to her about the one thing he knew would hurt her most. Because he loved her.... But it made no sense.

"Lydia?" Ruth set the knife on the table and hurried forward. "Lydia, child, what's wrong? Are you sick? You look pale. What's happened, Lydia? Talk to me!"

It wasn't the words that got to her. It was the panic beneath them that shook Lyddie out of her anger and confusion. She tightened her hold on the chair and looked at Ruth and opened her mouth—

And stopped.

Ruth stood before her with her hands over her mouth, staring, frozen and frightened. Just the way she had looked at Roy Delaney four years ago when he brought them the news about Glenn and Buddy.

In that moment, Lyddie knew she couldn't say anything. Never. She might be trying to move on but Ruth couldn't. Wouldn't. No matter what Glenn had done in the past, Ruth had lost her only child that day. If seeing him turned into a saint gave her some small comfort, Lyddie might not agree with it, but she damned well wouldn't take that away from her. She, too, would keep silent.

Just like J.T.

"Oh, God," she whispered, and then she was in Ruth's arms, crying on Ruth's shoulder, assuring Ruth that she was fine, the kids were fine, there was no need to be afraid. But she couldn't stop crying.

She had condemned J.T. for keeping silent and then turned around and done the same thing. She had been so wrong. So misguided.

Almost as misguided as he had been to fall in love with her.

J.T. USED TO BELIEVE that he could never despair the way he had the night he left Comeback Cove. But on Monday afternoon as he packed a U-Haul truck with furniture to deliver to the resale store in Brockville, he knew that leaving home had been a walk in the park compared to leaving without Lyddie.

"That's everything?" he asked. Iris nodded and

he slammed the heavy rear doors. "Guess I'd better grab the keys and get on the road."

He walked back into a house that ached. The living room was completely empty. His footsteps sounded all around him as he walked across the hardwood floors to fetch the keys from the mantel. The other rooms, he knew, weren't quite as bleak. Those holding items to be moved were actually crammed full. Others held a few bits and pieces that were to be given away—a hodgepodge of tables and trays and the ornate carved buffet that Iris had deemed too heavy to move, even though she'd inherited it from her grandmother.

But it was the living room, stripped of all but the paint and curtains, that called him. He could empathize with this room. He knew exactly how it felt: like a shell, purged of everything that brought it to life.

He shoved his hands in his pockets and stared out the window. It was an hour each way to the drop-off site. He should get on the road. But somehow, when he stood in this room that mirrored him, he didn't feel quite so alone.

"Did you find the keys?"

Iris's question made him turn to face her. "Yeah. Just, you know, going over the directions in my head once more."

"You take Highway 31 to the 401, you get off at the second Brockville exit and take Route 29 to King

Street. Since when did that become so complex that you have to think about it?"

He shrugged. She sighed and crossed the room to lay a hand on his shoulder.

"Are you going to tell me what happened?"

"Probably not."

"J.T., you're going to be the only person I know in Tucson. I'll have plenty of time to badger you about this. You might as well tell me now."

"You don't hold back, do you, Ma?"

"Not when it comes to you. Now out with it."

He tossed the keys in his hand. "Not much to tell. I gave it my best shot and she said no."

"No, she didn't love you, or no, she wouldn't move?"

"Both."

"Do you believe her?"

"Strange question."

"Humor me."

He thought about it for a moment. "Leaving— yeah, I believe she'd stay here. She thinks the kids need to be here, and she's not going to do anything to hurt them."

"Even if it means losing you?"

"Even if."

"What about her feelings for you?"

His sigh was so filled with frustration that it almost shook the chandelier. "That's the worst of it. I really think she might love me. Or she would with just a little more time. And it kills me that she might not figure it out until it's too late."

"Would it ever be too late for you?"

"No. No, she could pick up the phone three years from now and I would still want her with me. But if I'm not here to help her see what we've got, I think she'll just pretend it never happened. Or that it did, but it meant nothing."

Iris nodded and crossed her arms over her chest. "That sounds like a load of defeatist claptrap to me."

He blinked. "What?"

"Are you really going to let her go that easily?"

"What do you suggest, Ma? Kidnap her while she's sleeping and stick her on the plane with me?"

"Don't be ridiculous. She's not going to uproot those children just for you. She needs to do it for them."

"You never mentioned any of this before."

"I didn't want you to think I was saying it just to get you to move up here for me."

He would have protested. Then he remembered the secret he'd kept from Lyddie, just to avoid any hint of ulterior motives, and he shut up.

"You have a long car ride ahead of you—plenty of time to figure out a way to win her over. Pretend she's one of your students. What do you do with them when they won't listen to reason?"

"Back off, give them what they think they want and let them try it their way."

"Then think. How can you make sure Lyddie gets exactly what she thinks she needs—now, while you're still here to remind her of what she stands to lose?"

On Tuesday night, Lyddie sat on the sofa with Tish cuddled against her, listening to Ben slam basketballs in the driveway, inhaling the aroma of pot roast as only Ruth could cook it, and tried to convince herself that the giant hole in her heart was because Sara wasn't with them.

She was doing a lousy job.

"I liked Magic Kingdom the best, because I liked going down Splash Mountain. But at the other one, Mommy, they had Beauty and the Beast!"

"Did you meet Belle?"

Maybe her melancholy was due to the long-anticipated call from the esteemed music teacher. He had finally made contact earlier that day. Lyddie had had no idea how high up he was until he started listing his credentials.

Sara was going to hate her forever.

"No, not Belle. But I hugged Lilo and Stitch, Mommy, really, I did. Gran took a picture. But they had this show. With Belle and the Beast. And Chip and Mrs. Potts and all the others. And they sang the songs and there were fireworks!"

Fireworks. That's how it felt—like all the fireworks were gone from her life, forever.

It was almost like when she lost Glenn. Except then, she'd been too numb to understand the depth of her loss. This time, she knew.

Which was absolutely ridiculous. She had loved Glenn with all her heart. She couldn't love J.T.

"And then Gaston—you know, the bad guy—he sang the song about kill the beast. And there were bats that glowed in the dark."

The phone rang. Lyddie started to sit up, damned fool hope pulling at her, but Ruth called that she would get it.

Tish continued, snuggling back against Lyddie's side. "Gaston thought it would be easy to kill the beast. But he didn't know about the magic."

Lyddie swallowed, hard. She had thought it would be easy to find excitement with J.T. Simple and uncomplicated. She, too, hadn't counted on the magic.

Ruth appeared in the doorway. The phone was tucked against her shoulder and disapproval was clear in the tight lines of her face.

"Lydia. It's that Delaney man."

"J.T.?" She could barely get the words out past the treacherous bubble of hope rising within her.

"He wants to talk to Ben. Something about taking him fishing tomorrow. But he insisted I check with you first."

Ben. Of course. Ben hadn't thrown J.T.'s heart back in his face.

She was so damned stupid.

"It's fine."

Ruth scowled. "Really, Lydia, do you think that's—"

"Yes, I do. It's absolutely fine with me."

The glare Ruth bestowed on her as she went to call Ben made it obvious that Lyddie was going to hear about this.

Good. She was more than ready to light into someone tonight. Fighting with Ruth would give her a few minutes' respite from thinking she was making the biggest mistake of her life.

"Mommy! Are you listening to me?"

"Sure, honey. Tell me more."

But as Tish told the saga of Beauty and the Beast, Lyddie didn't dare listen. It struck too close to home, especially when Tish got to the part where the whole town chased the Beast— "But Belle knew he wasn't that way, not really."

Lyddie sank a little deeper into the sofa and pulled Tish closer, burying her face in her daughter's soft blond hair in case a stray tear or two leaked out. Holding for dear life to one of the biggest reasons why she had to stay in Comeback Cove.

HE'D GIVEN BEN his word, or so J.T. told himself as he slammed the door to his car and walked up Lyddie's driveway. He had to take the boy fishing.

Of course, there was no law that said he had to set a pickup time so early that he knew Lyddie would still be home. But everyone knew that fish bit better in the morning.

He vaulted the three steps to the porch. The inner door stood open. An invitation?

He knocked softly and let himself in, aiming for the voices he heard in the kitchen. Lyddie rounded the corner into the hall. She stopped short, hand to her mouth, eyes wide and wary. Her hair still tumbled loose around her shoulders, triggering a vivid memory of how she looked when she lay beside him.

He drank in the sight of her. Neat, tidy polo shirt hid the curves he knew rested beneath. To the world, she would look fine.

To him, attuned as he was to her smallest changes, she looked…fragile. Her eyes were too shadowed. The lines around her mouth were too brittle. And the way she took a tiny step back when he moved toward her broke his heart.

"Morning, Lyddie."

She nodded. For a second he thought he saw everything he was feeling reproduced in her face— all the fear, the hope, the desperate need. But then she turned toward the kitchen.

If she called for Ben, his chance would be gone.

"Wait. Please."

She hesitated, glanced his way. It was enough to make him press on.

"Lyddie, I know I came on too strong the other day." He kept his words low, so they wouldn't be overheard and to lure her closer. "I've known how I feel for weeks now. I know you need time to... I don't know. To catch up to me. I'm sorry I didn't give you any warning. I know you can't uproot everyone just like that. I wasn't trying to make things worse."

She palmed away a tear. He took the last step to stand beside her and slowly traced the still-damp track on her cheek. When she didn't push him away he reached for her hand, holding it close to his chest.

"It came out wrong, I know, but I meant all the important parts. I love you, Lyddie. And I think, maybe, you might love me, too."

She shook her head, mouthed a silent "No," but the fact that she was still with him, still holding tight to his hand, made him think she might be trying to convince herself more than him.

"We don't have to decide anything now. All I'm asking you to do is think. Remember those nights in the cottage. The way you needed me when you were scared about Sara. Think about how good we are together, about that night we sat outside and you said I meant something to you."

At last she turned toward him. Her river-blue eyes were liquid now, flowing with pain.

"Lyddie," he whispered. "Lyddie, tell me you don't feel anything. Tell me it meant nothing to you, that you haven't been walking around like the living dead just like I have. Tell me that, and I'll walk away from here and never bother you again."

She closed her eyes and turned away.

"Or," he said hoarsely, "tell me you love me and I'll wait forever."

He'd thought she was frozen in place before, but now she seemed to turn to stone. The seconds ticked past.

At last she opened her eyes. She inhaled, a catching breath that cut straight through him. She stroked his bristly jawline, the way she always did after they made love.

Then she turned away from him.

"Ben," she called, with a hitch in her voice that stabbed him. "Your ride's here."

SHE MADE IT through the rest of the week, forcing herself to sling coffee with a smile, hiding the hurt as Ben gushed over the fishing trip. She silently endured Ruth's pointed comments and judgmental stares. She even slept at night—that is, if dozing off between bouts of staring at the ceiling could be called sleep.

At last, it was Sunday. Lyddie kneeled in front of the remains of the old tree trunk, pouring her emotions into her saw as she sliced through the last hunks of roots. Her movements were jerky, much like her breath. She was too distracted to be doing this safely and she knew it. But she couldn't sit in the house and wrestle with thoughts of Tuesday's planning board meeting, wondering if J.T. would be there. And if he was, could she stay?

No, better to be outside, forcing her attention on the blade cutting through the splintered wood. She could do this. She could rip these roots from the ground and haul them away. She could look at the gaping hole where the tree used to stand and tell herself she would fill it with daisies and petunias and make the yard better.

While she was at it, she could tell herself that the salty liquid burning her eyes was just sweat.

She paused, backhanded her bangs out of her eyes, checked her progress. She'd burnt and hacked her way almost to the end of the job. She could finish it up tonight with just another hour or so.

And forty-eight hours after that, the meeting would be over. She would never need to see J.T. again. On Thursday, he and Iris would drive to Ottawa and get on their plane and all this...insanity would be over. She could get her real life back.

If only she could silence the voice inside her that insisted there weren't enough daisies in the world to fill the hole J.T. would leave in her life.

She adjusted her position, leaned forward, grabbed another hunk of root.

"Mommy!"

Tish ran across the lawn, phone in hand. Lyddie considered straightening, then decided she didn't have the strength and plopped back on the grass, not caring where she landed. She needed a shower, anyway. What difference would a bit more dirt make?

"Who is it, Tish? Aunt Zoë?"

Tish shook her head hard enough to make her pigtails fly across her face. "Nope. It's Sara. She's crying."

Lyddie scrambled to her feet, reaching for the phone. "Sara? Baby, what's wrong?"

"Mom...tell me...say it...isn't true." Sara's voice was so choked by tears that Lyddie could barely make out the words. She frowned in concentration.

"Sara, sweetie, take a breath. I don't know what you're saying. What's the trouble?"

"I...had...my...last lesson...today. Ms. Rasmussen said...she said..."

Lyddie closed her eyes, holding back the words she couldn't say in front of Tish. The nitwit teacher had told Sara everything.

"She said...she said they wanted me for the advanced music school...that I could get in there this year, that I could be good...and you said no!"

The words ended on a wail of such agony that Lyddie had to hold the phone away from her ear. She checked on Tish, motioned her away from the saw and pushed herself upright to pace in tiny circles around the remains of the trunk.

"Sara, honey, take a breath. Breathe, okay? Can you hold it together for a minute and let me explain?"

"No! I don't want to listen to you! You ruined everything! I worked so hard, I practiced and practiced, and I did it, Mom, I got in, and you won't let me go!"

"Sara, that's not true. I told them you could do summers there but not—"

"I hate you, Mom. You're going to make me stay in that stupid, stupid place, and there's nothing there, and no matter how good I am they'll never let me be a musician because Glenn Brewster's daughter *has* to be just like he was, and I can't do that anymore, I can't and I won't and I'm not coming back and you can't make me!"

Lyddie ceased her pacing, stopped by the sheer intensity of Sara's words. She felt like she'd been swallowed by an avalanche and had no idea how— or where—to begin digging her way out.

"Sara. Did you hear what I said? You can go back for the summers. We'll sign you up for the Ottawa youth orchestra. And when you're done with school, if you want to go to college there, you can."

"Oh, stop it! Stop pretending you're going to let me go! You want me to rot there, just like you. Everyone thinks it's such a great place, but I hate it there, Mom! I hate who I am when I'm there and I hate you!"

"Sara—wait—" Damn! Lyddie glanced at the sky, but there were no answers to be found in the deepening shadows. She cursed the miles separating her from her child. "One thing at a time, okay? I know you're upset and don't want to listen to me now, but once you come home we can—"

"No! Don't you get it, Mom? I'm not coming back. I'm not! I won't get on that plane. You'll have to tie me up and kidnap me, and then I'll run away, over and over. And no matter how many times you find me, I'll keep going. Because I can't live there, Mom, I—"

There came the sound of other voices, a brief discussion that left Lyddie pulling at her hair in frustration while shooing Tish back inside. The crying and screaming faded and Zoë's voice came over the line.

"Lyddie? Are you okay?"

She blew past the lump of distress in her throat. "No. This sucks. Where's Sara?"

"Kevin took her out back. She'll be okay, I can see them out the window. She's pacing and crying but it looks like she's calming down."

"I'm going to kill that teacher."

"I'm right behind you in the line. But, Lyd…it's not just the teacher."

Dear God, what else?

"She's been like this almost from the moment she came. All I've heard, all summer, is how much more she likes it here. First I thought she was just being polite. And hey, when you're fourteen, everybody thinks home sucks, right?"

"I guess. Maybe."

"But she made friends, got to know folks around

the neighborhood. And she's always talking about how it's so much easier here. She says things like, she can tell people her name and not get *that look*—whatever that means." Zoë sighed. "I think the music is only the symptom, Lyd. I think there's something bigger bothering her."

Why couldn't life ever be easy? Why did the simplest, most foolproof plans always backfire and get complicated and rip your heart out?

"What's she doing now?"

"Still outside. I think—yep, it looks like he has her smiling a little. She's crying, but she's not hysterical anymore."

"Thank God." Lyddie dropped to the grass. She lay on her back and stared at the sky and wondered how she was supposed to hold things together when they all seemed destined to fall apart.

"I wish I was there with you," Zoë said.

"Me, too," Lyddie replied, even while she kept remembering the way J.T. had held her when she had her last Sara-induced panic attack. What she would give to be able to go to him now....

But she couldn't. Not anymore.

"Zo? Do you think she means it?"

"I don't know. It's been a long time since I was fourteen, but as I recall, most of my emotions changed about as fast as Dad used to flip through the TV channels. For her to be so adamant about this for so long... It makes me wonder."

"Me, too."

"Lyd, I know why you moved there. You needed all the support you could get after Glenn died, and by God, those folks came through for you big-time. But I wonder if, maybe, it's time to let that go."

"But how else am I supposed to keep his memory alive for them?"

"Maybe… Don't freak on me, okay? But maybe you're not. Not anymore. I don't mean you should never talk about him or anything like that," she added quickly. "But, honey, maybe it's time to move on."

Move on?

"Think about it, Lyddie. You said it was getting to you, seeing how people had turned Glenn into the next thing to a saint. You were feeling stifled by it. Maybe the kids are feeling that, too."

"But this is our home. The only one Tish knows. Not to mention Ruth is here, and I promised her I would never—"

"Stop. Just stop. Don't you dare tell me you're staying there because you promised Ruth you wouldn't leave."

Lyddie blinked at the sudden vehemence in Zoë's words. "No. Of course not. But I—"

"You don't go back on your word. I know that. I also know that your duty to your children goes far and above what you owe Ruth."

Hard words. Harsh, even. But Lyddie knew they were true, even if she didn't like to hear them.

"You really think I'm doing the wrong thing, keeping them here?"

Zoë made a sound that could have been a sigh or could have been a laugh. "I don't think you could ever do the wrong thing, because you're there with them, and you will always give them what they need. But I wonder. If you were to go someplace else— someplace where they weren't the kids of a saint— maybe they wouldn't need you quite so much."

Lyddie fell silent, thinking of Tish and her teacher, Ben and the school, Sara's painful outburst. "I know there are things that bother them. I just thought the good outweighed the bad."

"Maybe it does. I don't know. I'm not living there, and heaven knows I might be way off base. But listening to you, and Sara, and all the things you've said about Ben and Tish, I wonder." She paused. "Would you ever go back to—"

"Not Peterborough. No. Not an option." That part of her life belonged to Glenn.

"Someplace else, then, with no memories. A fresh start for all of you."

"Have you forgotten I've just gone through hell and back making it possible to buy my building?"

"Oh. Right. That." Zoë fell silent, and Lyddie could easily imagine her sprawled over her sofa, chewing on her pinky fingernail. "You said there was another buyer. It's not like you would be leaving the seller high and dry."

"No." Lyddie picked the words carefully "No, I think J.T. would survive."

"Wait. J.T.? Hang on. Isn't he the one you were thinking of…"

"He was."

"And did you?"

The sudden excitement in Zoë's voice was enough to make Lyddie smile, if only for a moment. "Um…"

"Lydia Stewart Brewster, you've been sitting on this all this time and you said nothing?"

"I didn't want to talk about it."

"Why the hell not? Damn, girl, I am stuck here in the 'burbs doing the 24/7 dairy-cow thing, and you were having a nooky adventure and didn't tell me?"

"Sorry. I didn't think—"

"Oooh. So good you couldn't think straight, huh?" This time, Zoë's sigh reeked of happiness. "I am so proud of you."

Proud of her? The irony was too much. Before she could stop herself, Lyddie started to cry.

"Lyd? Honey, I thought I was the one with the raging hormones. Why are you crying?"

"Oh, Zoë. If you only knew… There's nothing to be proud of. I…I hurt him. Horribly. I said the most awful things, and told him…he said he loves me, Zo. And I can't…I don't…"

"Holy crap. You made a guy fall in love with you in a month?"

"It was longer than that, and I didn't *make* him do it. I wasn't trying to do anything but, just, you know. Feel like me again." She wiped tears from her cheeks. "And then he did that."

"So you feel nothing for him?"

"Of course I do! He's a wonderful guy. I like him a lot. But I don't—you know."

"Uh-huh."

"What does that mean?"

"Nothing."

"You're not making any sense. Go check on Sara."

"Sara is fine and you are avoiding the issue. Which, I have noticed in my thirty-six years as your little sister, is exactly what you do when you don't want to talk about something."

"You're crazy, Zo."

"Yet you're the one crying because you hurt a guy you claim to not love."

Lyddie pushed upright, all the better to scowl at the phone. "Of course I don't. I've only known him two months. He's funny and sweet and I like spending time with him, but that doesn't mean I love him."

"You do realize you're tap-dancing like hell to avoid saying the actual words."

No. She couldn't be.

"Lyddie?"

It had to be something else. Yes, she had longed

for him to comfort her, but that was just an associa-
tion, because he had helped her the last time. Sure,
she had spent the past few days in misery, but it had
been a horrible ending to a wonderful time. And of
course she felt awful about the things she had said.
No one wanted to hurt someone they—

"Oh, my God."

"Told you so," Zoë said with such satisfaction that
Lyddie knew she was smirking.

"I can't be." Lyddie hit the grass again, not out
of choice, but necessity. Her knees weren't working anymore and she had started shaking something
fierce. "It's too fast. Too complicated. Too…too…"

"Too scary?"

Oh, hell. The black spots dancing in front of Lyddie's eyes told her that her little sister might well be
onto something.

"Zo?"

"Uh-huh?"

"Why am I sitting here on the verge of a panic
attack at the thought that I might be—you know—
with J.T.?"

"Oh, sweetie. Who the hell wouldn't be terrified
after what you went through?"

"They all think I'm so brave," she whispered into
the phone. "But the thought of being in love again…
Damn, Zoë, I'm falling apart here."

"Of course you are. But you're smart enough to
remember that real bravery isn't about never being

afraid. It's about being so scared that you could pretty much die, but doing what has to be done anyway."

"And what exactly am I supposed to do? The things I said…"

"If he's half the guy he must be for you to have fallen for him, he'll understand. As for what you should do next—"

"Hang on. I think I've got that part covered."

And with that, Lyddie threw up all over her mostly uprooted stump.

CHAPTER SEVENTEEN

ABOUT AN HOUR before the planning board was scheduled to meet, J.T. stood on the sidewalk by River
Joe's, the river at his back and Town Hall in front
of him, waiting for a clot of tourists to move so he
could cross the road. Even though he was leaving in
a couple of days, he couldn't bring himself to break
the first rule of the town: in a conflict between a
tourist and a townie, the tourist always comes first.

As soon as the camera-slinging crew was gone
he hitched his backpack higher on his shoulder and
glided swiftly across the road on his blades. From
there he navigated the stone steps leading into the
building, pleased when he slipped only once.

Skates had never been designed for bombing up
and down the halls of buildings. Wearing them in
here, flanked by the police station and the town of-
fices, was like painting a giant target on his back.
But right now he had a job to do. An impression to
make.

A deal to make with the devil.

He rolled down the hall, jauntily saluting the one
poor befuddled soul coming out of the men's room

before stopping in front of the simple oak door that proclaimed he was at the Office of the Mayor. Below the dull brass plaque was a smaller, shinier one that reminded him the current occupant was Jillian McFarlane.

As if he could forget.

He hoped she was alone. He really didn't want to deal with the Ted factor, not that he would let Jillian know that.

He knocked quickly, pulled up a cocky grin and pushed the door open. A brief yip let him know he'd caught her off guard. Good. He needed all the advantages he could get.

He skated in and let his backpack fall to the floor. "Hello, Jillian."

She glared at him, one hand over her chest, the other clutching a ballpoint pen like a weapon. "What the hell do you think you're doing?"

"Do you know how glad I'll be to never hear that question again?" He chose a chair in front of her desk and sprawled across it before glancing around the painfully neat office. "Nice place. You've painted."

"And you are out of line. I have a meeting to prepare for. Leave. Now."

"Sorry," he said with mock cheerfulness. "No can do. I need to talk to you before that meeting."

"There will be time on the agenda for you to make your presentation."

"There will? Great." He sat up, all bright and

eager. "I'm sure there's a lot of folks who would love to hear what I have to say."

She glanced toward the door. Probably checking to make sure no one could overhear them.

He felt a twinge of conscience, but refused to let it stop him. There were two futures on the line—Lyddie's, and hopefully his. As long as Jillian did her part, no one would be the wiser. He couldn't back down now.

"Here's the thing," he said softly. "I've heard the rumors, Jillian. I know you're still trying to block the sale. I think it's time to talk."

She didn't even blink.

"You say you want to do what's best for the town, and you know what? I believe you. The fact that you've been pushing for Mr. Crispy all this time tells me you're sincere. I have to salute you for that."

"There's a hell of a *but* behind those words, isn't there?"

"More of an *and.* You've mentioned a number of times that this issue is dividing the town, that I'm stirring up trouble. You and I both know that there's more to it than that. People are afraid of me and what I know." His lips twitched. "Lucky for you, none of them know that you're in on the secret, too."

Again, not a sound, though she looked a little green around the gills.

"The real problem isn't the store, Jillian. It's the fear. The fear and the guilt. As long as people are afraid that the truth will come out, they're going to keep doing stupid things."

She nodded slowly. "It's a sorry day when I agree with you, but I think you're right."

Thank God. If she could say that, he was halfway there.

"So here's what I want. I'm going to go into that meeting and make a speech that will guarantee everyone in the room will not only want Lyddie to have the building, they'll be volunteering to pay the mortgage for her. All I ask is that you refrain from saying anything that would change their minds."

"I'm only one person. I only have one vote."

"You're the only one with half a brain on the committee," he said bluntly. "They'll do whatever you say and you know it. They trust you." He paused, then added, "Do this, and I will give you exactly what you need to make sure this is the end of the fire problems."

"What, are you going to turn back time?"

"No, I will stand up there and take full, public and sole responsibility for what happened that night."

Her eyes widened.

"And," he continued, "I give you my solemn word that if this goes through, I will never set foot in this town again."

"Your word? Seriously, J.T., if you expect me to put a lot of faith in that—"

She stopped, eyes fixed on the old, slightly tarnished ID bracelet he had pulled from his pocket.

"I promised you I would never tell anyone that you were with me that night." He tossed the bracelet on top of her papers. It landed with the name upright, clear and undeniable. The faint jingle as the clasp slipped onto the wood of the desk hung in the air between them like the echo of a long-ago song.

"If I give you my word, Jillian, you can damned well believe me."

LYDDIE WALKED INTO the planning board meeting without the faintest idea of what she was going to say.

"Place is packed," Nadine remarked from beside her. "You'd think there was going to be a hanging."

Lyddie looked around the overflowing room, searching for the one face she longed to see. She strained to hear through the drone of low conversations, listening for the only voice that could soothe her and settle her and make her believe that things might actually work out.

Try as she might, she couldn't find J.T.

Behind her, Nadine sighed. "I hope this crowd doesn't slow things down."

Lyddie gave a quick, reflexive thought to the kids, but she knew they were fine. Tish was happy at her friend Millie's house, and Ben had become decidedly more responsible since he'd started working with J.T.

Sara, however, still wasn't speaking to her.

"Where is he?" she murmured as they picked their way toward two seats in the front row.

"You know J.T.," Nadine said. "Probably waiting to make a grand entrance. Swing from a chandelier or something like that."

Lyddie gritted her teeth and gave thanks that the only empty chairs weren't together. She loved Nadine but couldn't listen to her now. She needed a few minutes to catch her breath, to think, to put everything out of her mind while she figured out what in God's name she was going to say when it was her turn to address the board.

She sat in the molded plastic chair and pulled a notepad and pen from her purse, tapping them together in the hope it would convince her neighbors that she was deep in thought. Anything to focus her attention instead of constantly looking for—

"Hello, Lyddie."

So much for hiding. She looked up to see a pair of familiar brown eyes gazing down at her. Unfortunately, they were in the wrong face.

"Oh, hi, Iris. I didn't expect to see you here."

"I had to come. Couldn't miss the show, you know."

"What show?"

"You'll see." Iris was obviously enjoying whatever secret she held. She looked more animated than Lyddie had seen her in months.

"Is Ruth here?"

"She's over on the other side of the aisle." Lyddie pointed to where Ruth sat in deep conversation with Harley Prestwick.

"Ah, so she is. I think I'll go remind Harley that a true gentleman always gives his seat to a lady in need."

"Wait." Lyddie gulped and reached for Iris's sleeve. "I don't see... Where is— Is J.T. going to be here?"

"He'll be here." Iris bent closer, lowering her voice. "And he's going to show Comeback Cove a side of him they'll never forget."

Oh, Lord. Lyddie slumped back in her seat and wondered how the hell this night could get any worse.

Then Jillian walked into the room and Lyddie had her answer.

Jillian looked like Lyddie felt—totally lost. She seemed dazed as she sat at the conference table heading the small chamber. She was as impeccably dressed as ever but moved with small jerky movements that caused her to bump her hip on the table, not once, but twice as she sat. Her hands shook as she reached for a pitcher of water. Lyddie winced, anticipating a flood, but luckily one of the other committee members grabbed it and poured for her.

It was probably too much to hope that Jillian's distress had nothing to do with the show Iris had promised.

Jillian gulped her water, spoke briefly to the man who'd rescued her from imminent disaster, then slammed her wooden gavel to the sounding block. The vibrations bounced around inside Lyddie like a final reminder that this was it.

"This meeting is now in session," Jillian announced over the final whispers. "The items on the agenda are as follows…"

She read through the list. One other sale, a couple of zoning variance requests and then—

"Proposed transfer of properties at 321 and 333 River Road, Delaney to Brewster."

Whispers buzzed through the room. Jillian looked ready to pass out. Lyddie prayed for strength.

The first two items were handled quickly. The last variance request led to a brief debate, but soon that, too, was decided. Jillian gave some final instructions to the secretary and gripped the gavel. It looked much like the death grip Lyddie had on her pen.

"Number four, Delaney to Brewster."

Jillian ran through the facts of the sale as she had with all the previous items. As before, once she was finished, she asked for comments from the floor.

A chorus of "here"s sounded behind her. Lyddie turned in her chair to see approximately twenty hands shoot into the air.

Jillian gestured to the front of the room. "All those wishing to speak, please move to—"

"Wait a minute, Jillian."

Lyddie's heart thumped at the sound of that unforgettably deep voice booming through the chatter.

The man making his way to the table bore so little resemblance to the one she knew that for a moment she thought she must be mistaken. She saw no shorts, no tank top, no Rollerblades. He wasn't even in a short-sleeved dress shirt, as he'd been that day at the cemetery. Instead, he was formally clad in a navy pinstripe suit highlighted by a baby blue tie. His hair looked freshly cut. He was clean shaven, with no hint of the five o'clock shadow that had brought her such delight.

He made it to the podium before the table, and turned to catch her eye. There, clear on his face for the world to see, was all the laughter and tenderness and understanding that had led her to fall for him. The buzzing in the room escalated.

For one brief moment, she let herself soak in that gaze. Then she looked away.

But she couldn't block out the memory.

A movement on the other side of the room drew her attention. Ruth stood, staring at J.T. with disbelief. Then a thin arm reached up from beside her and yanked her back into her seat.

Despite herself, Lyddie snickered.

J.T. cleared his throat. "Madam Mayor, members of the committee, members of the audience…"

What the heck was this?

"I know that many of you wish to comment on this sale, but I ask for your indulgence. Let me speak first. I can guarantee that when I'm done, the number of others who feel moved to do so will be greatly reduced."

Lyddie stared in amazement at the man addressing the crowd so easily. He'd always seemed so cocksure and certain, strutting through the town with a devil-may-care grin, but this—this was different. He stood and moved and spoke with a confidence and respect she'd never seen before.

Though, yes. She had. When he listened patiently to her stammered proposition. Whenever they were alone together. When he comforted her as she cried over Sara.

When he told her he loved her.

Behind the table, Jillian nodded warily. She looked ready to keel over at any moment.

"The committee recognizes J.T.—"

"Justin," he said with a hard smile. "Justin Tanner Delaney."

Iris's voice floated above the crowd. "Actually, it's *Dr.* Delaney."

Surprised mutters rose and fell like a cicada's song.

"He has a PhD in physics and astronomy," Iris

continued happily. Up at the podium, J.T. turned slightly pink.

Jillian closed her eyes.

"J.T.," she said softly. "*Dr.* Delaney. You may continue."

"Thank you." He offered a deferential nod to the committee before turning back to the audience.

"Folks, we all know why I'm here. I want to sell my properties to Lydia Brewster. And I know why most of you are here—you either wanted the sale to go through weeks ago, or you want those buildings to go to someone who can bring more jobs to Comeback Cove."

Murmurs of agreement filled the hall.

"Let me say, first thing, that I sympathize with you. The town's economic growth is important. And let's call a spade a spade. I know many of you feel the town wouldn't be quite so eager for more jobs if not for the fallout from actions committed by me—" he paused for the briefest moment "—me, and only me, the night of the Big Burn."

What on earth?

Voices rose once again. A couple of chairs scraped. Lyddie's jaw sagged and she stared at J.T., certain she had heard him wrong, praying he wasn't doing what she had a horrible feeling he had planned. She was probably the only person in the room who could read the assurance in the quick glance he shot at Jillian. She knew she was the only one who noticed the way Jillian bowed her head, as if in agreement. Or acceptance.

Holy— Had Jillian been part of the group that night? *Jillian?*

What had he said about the girl he'd been with? Lyddie replayed the conversation in her mind, fast and frantic, and realized he had very carefully avoided saying anything that would identify her.

Holy crap.

Lyddie looked at Jillian, barely holding on, and realized J.T. had lied when he said he never saw the girl again. He had crossed paths with the one person who could exonerate him, each and every day of this long summer.

And she had a horrible feeling that he had turned around and chosen to dance with the devil to ensure this sale went through.

Lyddie tried to catch his eye, to stop him before he said anything even more damning. But now, of course, he was doing his best to avoid looking in her direction.

"I'm here to ask that you all let go of the issues surrounding the Burn. Yes, Comeback Cove survived some hard times back then, but, people, fixating on it and letting it be the basis of your decisions won't do a bit of good. I hurt this town. No argument there. But letting it continue to split you apart? That's going to do more long-term damage than anything I ever did." He glanced down at his notes before looking to the crowd once again. "Right now, I want you to forget ancient history, and focus on something more recent. Something that happened four years ago."

Lyddie bolted upright. He wouldn't. Not after everything she'd told him. Not after promising that he would never pity her.

"Lydia Brewster is here tonight because her husband put his life on the line for Comeback Cove."

No. He couldn't play the widow card. She wouldn't let him.

"Everything she has done since he died has been for one reason—to help his children remember him. She brought them here. Moved into the house where he grew up. Took over the coffee shop where he—"

"Excuse me, can I say something?" Lyddie jumped to her feet. She didn't dare look at J.T. If she did, she wasn't sure if she would kiss him or kill him.

Instead, she kept her gaze fixed on Jillian, who first brightened, then slumped back.

"Sorry, Lyddie. He has three minutes left."

"But I—"

"No."

"But—"

"Lyddie. Sit down before I have to ask you to leave."

Well, hell. How was she supposed to just sit there and listen while J.T. condemned her to life as the Young Widow Brewster? Because that was exactly what was happening. As he went on, talking about Lyddie's sacrifices, about memorializing Glenn in ways that mattered, she could feel the pity level rising ever higher. It was as if the river had overflowed and crept into the room. But she was the only one who would be lost in this flood.

No. She wouldn't. She was an adult who knew who she was now. But her children didn't have that same certainty. Not yet.

At last, he finished. He ended with a final appeal to the committee to do the right thing, to lay aside whatever feelings they might have about him and instead, focus on her and the kids. "Give Lydia Brewster exactly what she has earned," he said to the quiet room. "Give her the chance to keep herself and her children in the building where her husband's memory still lives."

His footsteps were the only sound as he walked back the way he'd entered and left the room. Without ever once mentioning the rest of the story. Without ever once hinting that there was more to Glenn, more to himself, than most of the people in this room would ever know.

Jillian broke the silence. "Is there anyone else who wishes to speak?"

Lyddie paused in anticipation of the sea of hands she'd counted before. But as she scanned the crowd, one by one the faces reddened and turned away. Not a single person approached the front.

"Lyddie?" Jillian toyed with the gavel as if itching to smash it over someone's head. "It's your turn."

Slowly, Lyddie rose from her chair. She'd never been one to fear public speaking, but this time her legs insisted on wobbling as she walked to the front of the room. Once she made it, she took a deep breath and looked out.

There they all were. Ruth, with tears running down a face twisted in both sorrow and fear. Iris, smiling at her in encouragement. Nadine, frowning, gesturing to her to get on with it. And around them, all the people who had come to mean so much to her, all the residents of Comeback Cove who had no idea what they had done—to J.T., to her kids, to her. All those usually kind hearts that had no idea that their good intentions were choking the life out of her.

"Um…hi. Okay, for the record, my name is Lydia Brewster, and as J.T.—uh, as Dr. Delaney said, I want to…"

She stopped. What did she want? It had been so clear, once. Before J.T. had loved his way into her heart as well as her bed. Before Sara's dreams had slammed against her own wishes, leaving her uncertain what was best for anyone anymore.

Before she saw that there was more to Glenn. To J.T. To herself.

"I'm not sure where to begin, but…"

But what?

Someone in the back row shook a head. Lyddie

squinted. Anna Lockhart, the teacher who never got over Glenn. Anna Lockhart, who made Tish uncomfortable with her constant comments.

"I'm sorry. I thought I knew what to say, but then everything—"

The crowd was growing impatient. Feet shuffled, voices whispered. They wanted her to finish so the meeting could end and they could go home and tell themselves they'd done the right thing. And every time they walked into that shop they would remember what they had done for her. Everything they had given up for her. For her and her children.

For as long as they lived in Comeback Cove, neither she nor the kids would be able to escape. And if she, a grown woman, felt choked by it, then what the hell was it doing to her kids?

"Oh, my God." She blushed when she realized she'd said it aloud. There were a couple of titters, but she barely heard them. She was too busy turning to address Jillian.

"Your Wor— I mean, Mayor McFarlane, and members of the planning board, and all the rest of you. I want to thank you for giving this matter such thorough consideration. If I hadn't had to fight to have this sale approved, I wouldn't have had the chance to learn some truths about myself, and about—about some other people. People and history."

In the fourth row, Steve McCoy turned white. A

couple of other heads ducked. Lyddie could feel the mood shifting from impatience to cold, gripping fear.

What was it J.T. had said?

People do stupid things when they're afraid.

Steve and the others—they'd been acting out of fear. For twenty-five years they'd been walking around with that secret hanging over them. It might not have impacted their every move, but it had eaten at them. It had to. Otherwise, none of them would have reacted the way they did when J.T. came back to town.

"Not to worry." Lyddie shook her head before anyone could panic. "I'm not out to rewrite things that have long been accepted as gospel. A very wise man once told me that the last thing most people want to hear is the truth, and I think—no, I know he was right. About that and a lot of other things."

Ruth closed her eyes and rocked in her seat. Iris beamed through her tears and gave Lyddie a thumbs-up. The rest of the audience erupted in a wave of squeaking chairs and rustling papers and fierce whispers that threatened to drown out anything else Lyddie might have wanted to say. That was fine. She could wait.

But not for much longer.

Jillian leaned forward. "Lyddie, we need to vote. Is there a point to this?"

A point? Oh, yeah. Lyddie scanned the faces in

front of her and admitted that she was no better than Steve and the others. She'd been acting out of fear, too. Fear of falling in love again, of having her heart broken again. That was the real reason she'd picked J.T. for her fling. It wasn't just because of the way he filled out those bike shorts, it was because she thought he'd be gone before he could do any damage to her heart.

Everyone said she was so strong, so brave. It was time she lived up to her reputation.

"Lydia…"

"I'm sorry." Lyddie gathered her papers. "You've all been wonderful. I thank you for everything you've done and I'm sorry for wasting your time. I just realized that I really, really shouldn't be here."

CHAPTER EIGHTEEN

LYDDIE HAD A GOOD head start, and the element of surprise in her favor. So she made it out of Town Hall and inside River Joe's before Nadine and Iris caught up with her.

"Are you all right, Lyddie?" Iris patted her arm. "Do you need anything?"

Nadine, meanwhile, simply rolled her eyes and said, "So you finally got a clue."

Lyddie said nothing. She curled up in the love seat by the fireplace with her eyes closed, listening to the women whisper to each other. She really wished they would go away so she could get on with the more important activities ahead of her, but they would need explanations anyway. She might as well get it over with all at once.

She opened her eyes. "Where's Ruth? Is she okay?"

"I'm here."

Ruth sounded weak and wobbly as she walked through the door, but at least she was here and on her feet, not sobbing in a corner all alone.

"You're going to move." It wasn't a question. Nadine grabbed Iris's hand and dragged her toward the kitchen.

Lyddie guided Ruth down beside her on the love seat, grasping Ruth's cold hands tight between her own. "I know this is hard. I know I promised I would stay. But my first duty has to be to the kids, and this isn't good for them anymore. It was the right thing when we first came, but not now. Now they need to grow up without the pressure of living up to the myth this town has created."

"But what on earth is wrong with having a good example?"

"Ruth, think. Ben got caught defacing a school that bears his father's name. Tish is stuck with an obsessive teacher. And Sara wants to go live someplace where nobody knows who her father was, where she can be who or what she wants to be."

"Sara just wants music lessons."

Interesting, that Ruth had no comeback for the other two. "It's more than the music."

"It's because of him, isn't it?" The bitterness in Ruth's voice made it clear that she wasn't talking about Glenn.

Lyddie placed her hand on Ruth's knee. "You probably won't believe this, not now, but it's not because of J.T. We need to move no matter what happens with him."

The first sob broke through as Ruth crumpled.

Lyddie pulled her close, her own tears slipping down her cheeks.

"We're not going far," she whispered. "That, I can definitely say. Not back to Peterborough, but somewhere new. New and close. Maybe Brockville, or Ottawa. That way, if you choose to stay here, we'll be close enough that visiting is easy." She drew in her breath. "Or, if you choose to come with us, you could still keep up with everyone here."

Ruth raised her head. The cautious hope on her face was enough to break Lyddie's heart.

"You—you would want me to come with you?"

"I want what is best for my kids. That includes their grandmother. And even though you and I have had some…some rough times the past couple of months, I do love you and want you to be happy, too. You belong in our lives. That's not going to change."

"But what about…him?"

"I don't know what's going to happen with J.T. I really don't." Her voice faltered. "I would like to think that we might have a chance, because, Ruth, I think I'm in love with him."

A small yip came from the kitchen. Ruth looked from the door to Lyddie, then hiccupped while Lyddie giggled.

"Gotta love a small town," she whispered to Ruth, who nodded. Lyddie turned toward the kitchen, ready to call to the others to join them, but Ruth raised a hand to stop her first.

"I have to admit, I have a lot of hard feelings about that—about J.T.," she said softly. "But if learning to let go of that is the price I have to pay to be with my grandchildren…if you're still willing to give me a chance…I promise I will try."

"He's a good man. He deserves that."

Ruth's nod was small, but it was still so much more than Lyddie would have believed possible that she couldn't help smiling. She and Ruth would get through this. They would find their way.

Another sound from the kitchen made Ruth shake her head. "Iris Delaney, stop trying to pretend you're not eavesdropping and come on out here. You too, Nadine."

"'Bout time," Nadine said as she sauntered toward them. "I was getting a crick in my neck trying to listen to you two through that door." Her unblinking stare made Lyddie twitch. "So? Am I out of a job?"

"Not yet. But you know, I bet you would do really well in the potato-chip business."

Nadine nodded slowly before breaking into a grin. "You might be onto something, kiddo."

Iris nudged Lyddie aside to hand Ruth a tissue. "Since you know we were listening, there's no point in beating around the bush. It just so happens that J.T. and I are also looking to settle in, oh, Brockville or Ottawa. Maybe you and I could get a place together. It would make the move that much easier for both of us, and Lyddie and J.T. will need some grandmas handy to take the children for the honeymoon."

Ruth's hands clenched but she managed a smile in Iris's direction. That was more than Lyddie could dredge up, what with the way her stomach jumped as she thought, once again, of J.T.'s actions at the meeting.

She needed to see him. Now.

"Ladies?"

Three sets of beloved eyes turned in her direction.

"Please don't be offended, but I need you all to leave. It's been a heck of a night. I need a few minutes alone. And Iris, could you please track down your son and ask him to meet me here?"

"Of course." Iris smiled. "Ruth, let's talk this over. I think it's a wonderful plan."

"So do I," Lyddie said. "But could you do it at our place, so Ben won't be alone much longer? And Ruth, could you pick up Tish on your way home and tell her I don't know how late I'll be, but I'll see her in the morning?"

Ruth stopped in the midst of gathering her purse and looked at Lyddie. "Do I dare ask if you'll be home tonight?"

Lyddie never knew it was possible to be both embarrassed and terrified at the same time, but she seemed to have managed. "I don't—"

"Oh, for God's sake," Nadine said. "The girl has made sure all the kids are fine, and she invited you to move wherever with them, Ruth. As far as I'm concerned, she can do J.T. on the kitchen table if she wants." She grabbed Ruth by the arm and dragged her to the exit, turning back for a final wink before the door closed behind them.

Lyddie grinned despite her butterflies. Nadine had just earned herself a huge end-of-business bonus.

She sat quietly for a moment, preparing herself. J.T. would be there soon. At least she hoped he would.

In the meantime…

"Glenn, honey." She spoke out loud, knowing he could hear her even in silence, and making it more real for her. "I love you. I know that you know that, better even than I do, probably, but I want to say it again. Just for the record and all."

The silence didn't bother her. She knew that if there was any way for Glenn to keep playing a part in her life, he would.

"I'm glad I brought the kids here. It hurt so much before, and it was so hard to talk about you with them, that this was the right place to be. I didn't think I could do it myself. Keep you alive for them, I mean." She swallowed, brushing away the tears that she didn't want to stop. "But now…now, you know, I can handle it. It still hurts, and I'm scared to death to start over again, but I know I can do it. You're still helping. This is right for all of us."

She patted the sofa. "I'm taking this with me. I

don't think I'll ever have the nerve to tell Sara we made her on this, but we'll always know. And your deer head, and your bed for Ben, and—heck, I'm taking your mother along, Glenn. What more can you ask?"

Tap, tap, tap.

She laughed softly, swiped a tear from her cheek.

"And, hon? If you have any superpowers to help me stop throwing up when I think about being in love again, could you send them my way, please?"

J.T. HAD INDULGED in a fair number of sins in his time, but gambling had never been one of them. Too bad. It might have given him a better idea for calculating the odds that he hadn't blown his last chance for winning Lyddie.

He rapped on the door and told himself it was probably a good sign that she had asked to see him. Though it would have been nice if Iris had bothered to give him a clue instead of just telling him to get his behind over here.

His gut lurched at Lyddie's approach. She looked nervous. Better than furious, but who could tell?

She looked him up and down from her side of the screen door, eyes lingering on his shorts. "You changed."

If that wasn't the understatement of the year…

"Yeah. I'm not the *GQ* type by nature."

"I don't know. It looked pretty natural on you in the boardroom."

"Thanks. I'll forget about teaching and go into the modeling business." He decided to go for broke. "They approved the sale."

"I figured they had to after your performance."

For a moment, he debated giving her the light and easy response. But bantering around the bush wasn't going to get him what he wanted, which was to be put out of his misery one way or the other.

"Lyddie, I know you're probably pissed at me for playing it that way, but I—"

"Hang on." She pushed the screen door open. "We'd better do this part in private."

Oh, hell.

He walked in slowly, trying to prolong these last moments when he could believe it would turn out fine.

"In there." She pointed to the kitchen.

He stopped in his tracks. "If you're planning to knife me, just do it here, okay?"

Her lips twitched but she merely kept pointing. He sighed. Who was he kidding? He would never be able to resist her commands.

The kitchen was lit only by the exit sign over the door. He moved cautiously in the darkness, but she grabbed his shoulders and guided him forward.

"Here," she said. He bumped his hip against something that felt like the large worktable, then felt the hard wooden stool against his thighs.

Curiosity nipped at him. Hope followed in its path. She was going to an awful lot of work for someone planning to rake him over the coals.

"There. Are you settled?"

"Think so."

"Good. Close your eyes."

"Lyddie, I already can't—"

"Close them."

He gripped the edge of the stool. "Okay. Closed."

"Good." A refrigerator opened. Something clinked, metal on metal, before the door closed again.

"Can I open them yet?"

"One more minute." A dull thump as something landed on the table, then the scrape of wood against slate. Something warm bumped his knees.

"Okay. Open up."

When he did, he found just enough light to let him see Lyddie perched directly in front of him, knees-to-knees, the way they'd been the day of the test. The day he figured out he was in love with her.

"Okay," she said, sounding a little breathless. "First, it took about half an hour after you walked out of here last week for me to realize what a total idiot I was to get mad at you for not telling me about Glenn. I still wish you had said something, but I understand why you kept quiet. And I am so, so sorry for the things I said. For you to think that the only reason I wanted to be with you was for the shock value, I…"

"It's okay." He longed to cup her face in his hands and thumb away the tears he could hear in her voice, but he didn't dare. Not yet.

"A lot has happened the last few days. With Sara, and Ruth, and…and me. I knew that I had screwed up, and that I needed to make some changes, but I wasn't sure how, or…or anything. When I walked into that meeting tonight, I honestly had no idea how I wanted it to turn out. Though that was probably obvious from the way I stumbled around up there."

Holy— Did she mean she had wanted the sale to be *denied*?

"Then you got up there, and said your piece, and I…I didn't know what to think. Part of me couldn't believe you would do that, that you were almost condemning me to everything I didn't want." Her voice dropped. "Then I stopped watching you and started paying attention to Jillian. And I realized that there was a lot more going on than anyone was meant to see."

Ah, hell. "Lyddie—"

"It's okay. I don't need to know the details. Here's the important parts." She raised his hand, his hopes leaping at her touch and ticked off points on his fingers. "One. No matter what happens with us, I hope

Mr. Potato Chip still wants this place, because our sale is off. The kids and I are moving."

He jerked and almost slid off the stool. "Lyd—"

"Two. I'm pretty sure Ruth knows the truth about Glenn, but it's something that will never be spoken. She deserves that peace of mind. You should know this, because she and your mother are planning to share a place together in Ottawa."

"What the *hell?*"

"Three. This is the biggest, so pay attention." She drew in a deep breath. "Remember when you said that people do stupid things when they're afraid? Well, I was the stupidest of all when I said that you couldn't be in love with me. Because, you see, I'm kind of in love with you, too. And that scared the bejeebers out of me, because, well…when you love someone and you lose them, it—"

Whatever she had planned to say was lost on him. He reached for her in the dark, hands gliding over her face, into the softness of her hair, and then he was kissing her, finally holding her again, finally feeling her in his arms and thanking God with every fiber of his being that for whatever reason, Lyddie loved him.

"I love you," he whispered when he could remember how to speak. "So much."

"I love you, too," she said, and framed his face with her strong hands.

"What?"

"I love you," she repeated. "And I'm sorry for not figuring it out sooner. These days without you have been—"

"I know. When I came to pick up Ben and you turned away—"

She placed a finger over his lips. "No more. I won't turn away again, I promise."

"I have to go back to Tucson to get things straightened out. But then we're coming back."

"That's what your mother said."

"Oh, yeah. Right." His head was spinning. "She and Ruth are really planning to move in together?"

"So far. But listen, J.T. I can't spring all this on the kids at once. I think they're going to be happy to move, but it's still going to be an adjustment. I mean, I don't know where you see this going, but I'll need time to—"

"I see this going all the way to happily ever after, Lyd." He lifted her hand to his lips and kissed the palm. "But it's okay. Like I said before, you set the pace."

She sighed and rubbed her cheek against his jaw. "Gladly."

For a moment he simply held her, taking in the miracle of Lyddie in his arms again. "I still have the keys to the cottage."

"Thank God," she whispered. "I thought I was going to have to jump you right here on the table."

He took her hand, ready to bolt for the door, but

she stopped him with a soft palm to the chest. "Hang on," she said. "There's something I've been dying to do since the first time you walked through my door."

"What's that?"

She pushed him back to the stool, reached past him and pulled forward a large silver bowl. Huh. That explained the *thunk* he'd heard earlier.

"Hold still."

Something hit his mouth. Something cool and wet…and lemon.

"You're kidding," he mumbled as Lyddie's finger gently traced the outline of his lips.

"We had lemon tarts on the menu for tomorrow. But I think this is a far better use."

"God, I love you," he said, just before she lowered her mouth and began to lick.

* * * * *